I0562552

From Ash & Darkness

by

J. L. Sullivan

Copyright Notice
This is a work of fiction. Names, characters, places, and incidents are either the product of the author's imagination or are used fictitiously, and any resemblance to actual persons living or dead, business establishments, events, or locales, is entirely coincidental.

From Ash & Darkness

COPYRIGHT © 2024 by J. L. Sullivan

All rights reserved. No part of this book may be used or reproduced in any manner whatsoever including the purpose of training artificial intelligence technologies in accordance with Article 4(3) of the Digital Single Market Directive 2019/790, The Wild Rose Press expressly reserves this work from the text and data mining exception. Only brief quotations embodied in critical articles or reviews may be allowed. Contact Information: info@thewildrosepress.com

Cover Art by *Diana Carlile*

The Wild Rose Press, Inc.
PO Box 708
Adams Basin, NY 14410-0708
Visit us at www.thewildrosepress.com

Publishing History
First Edition, 2025
Trade Paperback ISBN 978-1-5092-6045-4
Digital ISBN 978-1-5092-6046-1

Published in the United States of America

Dedication

To everyone searching for a way out of the darkness.

Chapter 1

I hated that dank, musty cellar, but if I wanted the nightmares to stop and finally lay Ifrit to rest, we had to return one last time. The fact we were about to break into a forgotten basement to bury an ancient djinn on Halloween night was just super awesome timing.

A gust of frigid fall wind barreled between the tall brick walls on each side of us, whipping through my jacket and sweatshirt. I sucked in a lungful, letting the icy sting distract me. Behind us, under the glow of the streetlights, clusters of trick-or-treaters in scary, funny, and unrecognizable costumes lingered on the streets, the roaming mobs from earlier had thinned. No one noticed us ducking into the shadowy alley, wearing all black.

"You're stalling." Ashley nudged me with the back of her hand.

"Well, it wasn't a party last time we were there. You know, being trapped in a djinn vortex and all."

I stared at the old wooden door on the ground, trying to make it vanish. The sight of the weathered door and rusted padlock sent shivers between my shoulder blades. We had to go down there. I needed Ifrit's box out of my room and buried away, out of the reach of idiots like me who might summon him back into the world.

"Should we review the plan again?" Ashley brushed her thick curls behind her ear as she kept us on task. A year ago—heck, two months ago—if someone had told me I'd be taking direction from Ashley Bryant, I'd have assumed they were delirious with a fever. But without her help, I'd have been the first sophomore to single-handedly destroy the earth with ancient djinn magic.

"No, we've gone over it enough. I'm working up to it." I sighed. "Although, I still think doing this on Halloween isn't necessary."

Jason yanked his black sock hat down, almost covering his eyebrows. "A new moon peaks tonight. I'm not sure that means much, but if the super blue blood moon helped us charge the incantation enough to banish Ifrit back into his box two weeks ago, another lunar event might be helpful."

Thanks to Mr. Buchannan's astronomy class, we knew a new moon happened every month—far from a rare lunar anomaly, but the moon appearing nonexistent seemed like a decent enough astrological event to gamble on if we needed some star power. Besides, we couldn't wait 150 years for the next super blue blood moon.

I dropped my backpack to the ground with a soft thud, our cargo protected by the bath towels wrapped around it, and pulled on my sock hat, shoving my thick, curly hair underneath. "The symbolism of doing this on a night devoted to hauntings and demons seems like we're asking for trouble."

"I swear, you guys"—Ashley glanced back to the street—"this is the perfect time to do it. No one suspects our all-black outfits mean we're *actually* going to break in somewhere. Come on, telling our parents we're dressing up as burglars? We don't even need to hide the flashlights. The irony is the freakin' best."

"I don't think that's what ironic means." Jason

clicked on his flashlight.

"What's irony then, genius?"

"I think it'd be like if you said—"

I waved my hand between them. "Let's get this over with."

The garbage odor ruminated in the alley. Black and white trash bags leaned against the dumpsters and against the brick wall of my building while cardboard boxes peeked out of the top of the green recycle bin. Even with the clear night and streetlights, our burglar attire turned my friends into shadowy silhouettes, though my exposed pasty skin glowed while Jason's made him invisible. I should have worn a ski mask.

Ashley rubbed her hands together as if preparing to enjoy a gourmet meal. "I'm not eager to plunge back into that rat's nest, but I will admit, I'm stoked to see Janni. I've missed the little fur ball!" Her voice rose with excitement, ricocheting off the brick walls around us.

"Keep it down." Jason scowled. "Jesus, girl."

We'd racked our brains trying to figure out how to break into the cellar without Janni's magic but couldn't come up with a solution. So, the three of us agreed to bend our No Djinn Rule one last time.

"The box and the ring have stayed dark, yeah?" Jason asked me that daily, concerned we'd accidentally summon Ifrit back into the world. The knowledge that the box remained hidden in my closet weighed on him—on all of us—but Jason wore his worry like a flashing neon sign. He always had.

"I check them every morning, bro. Okay," I said to both of them, "we head downstairs, bury the artifact where we found it, and then haul ass out of there. Bam. Done in twenty minutes or less. Djinn-verse a distant

3

object in our rearview mirror."

Jason nodded, the wheels in his head still whirled. I could almost hear the grinding gears. "And you've got the incantation? Just in case?" he asked.

"Yeah, but we won't need it." I pulled the ring out of my pocket. The large purple jewel on top of the tarnished gold band caught the beam of Ashley's flashlight and threw speckles of violet against the red brick wall. The ring's dormant energy pulsated in my palm, vibrating, beckoning me to rub its jewel.

I shook my head to clear it. What was wrong with me?

I ran my thumb over the jewel. It ignited with a purple glow, coming to life and illuminating the surrounding area. My body temperature dropped as invisible icy pellets rained on me, colder than the October night. The ice trickled over my head, then skittered over my skin, leaving thousands of frigid trails. The tingling prickled from my head to my toes.

I shuddered.

"Come on out, Janni." Ashley rolled her flashlight beam around the alley, lingering between dumpsters and bags. "Where are you, little djinn?"

I shook off the remaining tingles and scanned the area with Jason and Ashley.

Jason sniffed the air. "I don't smell him."

"I do." The unmistakable burnt hair odor wafted just underneath the garbage scent.

"HOW CAN IT SERVE?" Janni's shriek bounced off the walls. Though jarring, a comforting familiarity in Janni's voice brought a smile to my face. He'd saved my life, after all. Without him, I'd still be a floating rag doll in the djinn vortex, subject to whatever torture Ifrit imagined.

I scooped him up before Ashley could and hugged him tight, not bothered by his wet dog stink. His matted white fur tickled my nose as I buried my face against the top of his smelly head. My over-the-top reaction surprised both of us, and he squirmed under my squeeze. I didn't care. The little guy and I had been through a lot together.

Janni yanked one of his arms free and patted my cheek with his rough pink monkey hand. He batted away his dangling beagle ear from in front of his face. "IS BAXTER ALLEN IN TROUBLE?" His purple eyes reflected the glow of the ring.

"No. No trouble. We're finishing what we should have done two weeks ago."

I set him on the ground. He stretched his long arms over his head and yawned, not quite doubling his twelve inches of height. He had squared humanlike teeth, but his tongue curled mid-yawn like a dog's.

Unable to contain herself any longer, Ashley shoved me aside and snatched Janni up into a hug. "I missed your stink, Janni!"

Ashley always knew how to welcome people—or djinn—in the warmest way.

Janni's purple eyes widened under Ashley's loving but crushing embrace. "GIRL IS TOO MUCH. ALWAYS TOO MUCH."

"You've never said a truer statement." Jason snickered.

"I've missed you, too!" She squeezed him even harder.

"JANNI DID NOT MISS LOUD GIRL." Ashley's thick curls covered Janni's head. He blew out a puff of air to clear his face.

"Enough, Ashley, you're suffocating him." I tapped her arm.

As she set him on the ground, he stumbled to regain his footing, then shook in place, starting from his head, then shoulders, then torso, like a wet animal on two legs.

After a deep sigh to collect himself, he asked again, "HOW CAN IT SERVE?"

I kneeled in front of Janni. "We need you to get the keys to the cellar. Do you remember where they are? In Mr. Reynolds' apartment."

Janni's ears fell back against his head, and his purple eyes glassed over. "WHY? IT DOES NOT LIKE WHAT BAXTER ALLEN IS DOING."

"Don't worry. We're not summoning Ifrit." I patted my backpack. "We're burying his box."

Janni's shoulders lowered. "AH." Without further questions, he vanished, releasing a wave of burnt hair stench as he jumped to my landlord's apartment.

"Not gonna lie. I felt a slight twinge of *uh-oh* when Janni showed up. Leftover trauma, I guess." Jason tugged on his black sweatshirt with Washington University printed across the front in cracked red and white block letters.

"Yeah. I keep thinking I'm moving my backpack too much and brushing something up against the jewel." I forced a chuckle, but Jason and Ashley eyed my backpack with paranoid suspicion.

Janni reappeared less than a minute later, holding a key ring filled with dozens of metal-colored keys in different shapes. The weight almost toppled him over.

"Thanks." I grabbed the ring and flipped through for the key labeled: *CELLAR*. I swallowed. "Here we go."

The padlock clicked open, and the cellar door slipped from my hand, slamming against the ground. All four of us—djinn included—whipped our heads to the alley entrance.

Empty.

After a deep inhale, I stepped down the stairs, soft with moisture and time. They bowed under my weight but held. That'd be just great if they collapsed, trapping us in the basement forever with the rats, roaches, and whatever else crawled out from the shadows.

To avoid stray trick-or-treaters seeing an open door and getting nosey, Jason shut the door above us, submerging us in momentary darkness. We waited for our eyes to adjust, letting our flashlights roam the empty cellar, scattering a few shiny black bugs. The light beams illuminated the disturbed dust particles, but so far, no rats.

I led the way between rows of wooden shelves, empty except for the occasional sealed crate, its contents long forgotten by its owner. My flashlight beam wavered as my hand trembled. With them behind me, I didn't know if Ashley and Jason noticed, but I switched hands to my steadier left.

The darkness extended forever in all directions. In my mind, Ifrit's tail wrapped around my ankle, ready to drag me into the vortex. It slinked up my leg, securing its hold. His scalding breath burnt my face with each exhale. The gray smoke curled from his goat-like muzzle and stained my lungs with thick black soot.

A rat squeaked as it clicked by us, ripping me back to reality and our mission. Ashley gasped, and Jason whispered something to calm her. I had never felt such urgency to get something over with.

"You okay?" Jason poked me in the back. "You're slowing down."

"Sorry. Yeah. Fine."

We arrived at the corner of my building's cellar, the scene of our epic battle with Ifrit. Ahead of us, two shelves leaned against their neighboring shelves. One stood crooked on a shredded leg where Ifrit had clutched it, trying to escape the black tentacles drawing him back into the vortex.

"Still gives me the creeps." Jason checked on Ashley over his shoulder, who scanned the floor with her flashlight, searching for rats sneaking up on us.

Beyond the knocked-over shelves, where the reddish-brown brick of the building met the gray concrete of its foundation, a hole gaped. A pile of crumbled bricks, cement chunks, and rubble gathered below it, evidence of time and erosion that vomited the box from its hiding place to the floor where we'd found it.

"THERE'S THE SPOT."

I squatted and unzipped my backpack. "We'll shove it back into the hole and cover it with those rocks."

Jason dug around in his backpack, then held up a bag of dirt and a spray bottle. "We might need to pack mud around it to hold it in."

"Good thinking." Jason always figured out the details. We'd been best friends since the fifth grade, and he'd always been one step ahead of me.

I withdrew the wad of bath towels I'd kept the beat-up box cushioned in for the past two weeks. Placing the pile on the ground, I unwrapped the dangerous package as if it contained a bomb.

But there was nothing to unwrap.

I stared at the navy blue towels. A cold sweat broke out on my forehead.

"Uh, Bax?" Jason shined his flashlight on the pile of linens.

My heart stopped. I unzipped my backpack all the way and peered inside. Panicked, I shook it upside down. My school ID, house keys, and a few crumbled dollars fell to the cellar floor. Unable to breathe, I punched my backpack inside out but found no ancient wooden box with a large purple jewel on its lid.

"Bax?" Ashley shined her flashlight, along with Jason, on the towels as if I'd missed it.

"I-I packed it this afternoon. Rewrapped it in these."

I fell onto my backside as my legs melted under me. The chilled concrete radiated through my jeans. As the blood drained from my head, the dark expanse of the cellar felt confining and small. "Someone stole Ifrit's artifact."

"Your apartment keys and money are still there. No one robbed you." Ashley's voice rose, and Janni covered his ears. "But the freakin' box is gone! Someone has Ifrit!"

Chapter 2

We shuffled back to the stairs in stunned and defeated silence. Ashley didn't even flinch when a rat scurried across our path. Someone stole Ifrit's box. There was no other way its towel wrappings would have still been in my backpack. The thief unwrapped the box, took it, and then returned the towels, leaving my money and keys.

"How did you lose it?" Jason broke the silence as we walked up the stairs. "Not trying to be accusatory, but I mean, literally, what happened?"

"I don't know!" My loud words echoed in the deserted alley. After Jason emerged, I shut the wooden cellar door and clicked the padlock. "I packed it in my backpack after school, getting ready for tonight. You came over, and we grabbed a coffee before Ashley arrived. I've been so crazy paranoid about someone finding it that I kept my bag by my side. I even checked on the box when we got to West End Coffee to make sure it was there and safe."

"So it disappeared during or after you ordered." Ashley rummaged through my backpack as if I'd overlooked an ancient wooden artifact with an oversized purple jewel on its lid.

"NOT GOOD." Janni shook his head, his limp ears swinging from side to side.

Jason leaned against the brick wall, one sole of his

shoe hiked up back against it. He pulled the drawstrings, tightening his hoodie around his face. "When I bought my coffee, you took a piss. You didn't bring your bag with you, did you?"

"No…"

"You left your bag unattended?" Ashley didn't mask her disapproval. "What about being *crazy paranoid*?"

"Jason was at the counter a few feet away. I left it for maybe five minutes. If that!"

Jason held up his hands. "Let's just focus on finding it."

I slid down, back against the rough brick wall, not caring about the dumpster liquid I'd plopped into.

Ashley paced in a small circle; her tennis shoe crunched as it stuck to something sticky on the pavement. The alley needed a good rain. "It's suspicious someone ignored your money and keys but stole the box. That suggests they knew about the artifact and were waiting for you to leave your bag."

"Yeah, but no one knows about the box but us and Warren, and he's never even seen it. And I doubt he's been following me, waiting for the perfect opportunity to strike."

Ashley tapped her chin with a finger. "He *does* know about the whole djinn thing."

"No way, Ashley. It isn't in the realm of possibilities. I mean, we always talked about djinn as an idea for a story. He sort of suspects it's real, but again, he wouldn't stalk me and steal it. I don't buy it."

"You're probably right."

"I am right." I stood. Whatever liquid I'd sat in chilled my butt. Awesome. "West End Coffee is open until nine. We have fifteen more minutes. Maybe the thief changed their mind and dumped the box there. Could have been a snooping kid who unwrapped the box expecting something valuable, saw it, then ditched it."

Jason clicked his flashlight back on. "That whole scenario has pretty slim odds of being true, but it can't hurt to check."

Ashely shrugged. "Nothing to lose."

We started out of the alley, but I hung back. "Oh, wait. Janni, return the keys to Mr. Reynolds. After that, you can jump back into the ring."

Janni scowled. "IFRIT MUST BE FOUND."

"We're trying." I handed him the key ring.

After a deflated waddle, Janni jumped, leaving his signature odor in his wake.

We hurried down the street, weaving between the remaining clusters of trick-or-treaters, nervous we'd arrive at West End Coffee after they closed. How could I have left the bag unattended? I'd unleashed a nightmare of a djinn into the world who almost ruined my life and the lives of everyone around me, but we'd banished him and ended his unfettered access to my darkest thoughts. Now, because of my carelessness, he could be back, playing in someone else's mind.

The possibilities terrified me. Despite considering myself a decent person, Ifrit fed off the worst thoughts from my subconscious. It freaked me out to think about the horrors an evil person, like a serial killer or terrorist, would unleash upon the world if Ifrit started swimming around in their dreams.

As we turned a corner, light from the inside West End Coffee spilled onto the uneven sidewalk. The neon coffee cup sign bathed the stone flower urns at the entrance in a pink glow. Thankfully, it was still open.

As I tugged open the glass door, a young guy in his thirties pushed past us.

"Sorry. Excuse me," he said. Tall and skinny, his bulky gray sweater hung on him, looking two sizes too big. His brown hair draped over thick caterpillar eyebrows and tiny brown eyes. He seemed familiar but I couldn't place him. Maybe I'd seen him at West End before since most of the customers were regulars.

"You know him?" Jason saw my gaze linger on the man as he rushed across the street, paper cup in hand.

"Nah, I don't think so."

I shook my head and entered West End Coffee. The smell of bleach overpowered the typical rich caffeinated aroma. A mop in a bright yellow bucket sat in the middle of the floor, and a guy who didn't look much older than us counted money behind the counter. When he spotted us, he closed the register and scowled. "We're about to close, guys. Sorry."

"We don't want anything. We were here earlier and are curious if anyone found a, um, old box. Wooden. With a purple jewel on the lid." With my hands shoved into my jacket pockets, I crossed my fingers.

"An old box?" The worker raised his eyebrow as the diamond stud in his nostril glimmered. "Is this some kind of Halloween prank? If it is, I will call the cops, man. It's been a long night."

"No prank. I promise. It's an...an antique. I lost it and thought maybe it fell out of my bag here." I scanned the room, but the staff had already cleared and wiped down the vanilla-colored leather booths.

He sighed. "I'll check with the team. You can look around, but be quick."

"Thank you."

Jason and Ashley scoured the shop with their flashlights even though the ceiling lights provided ample illumination. They searched under tables, behind the large potted plants, and on each level of the wooden display shelving piled with bags of coffee and refillable travel mugs.

"We sat in that booth." I pointed. "You guys look there. I'll search the restroom. Maybe someone dropped it there."

The restroom could only accommodate one person at a time with its single white toilet and sink, not leaving many places for a box to hide. I checked behind the toilet tank and trash can. Nothing.

Crap.

I leaned against the sink, head hung low. My palms rested on the cool porcelain as I stared down the rusted drain. Who could have known my backpack contained Ifrit's box? And who could have known enough about the artifact to want to steal it? The banged-up, splintered artifact didn't scream, *Steal me. I'm worth a bazillion dollars.*

Maybe Jason and Ashley found a clue.

As I raised my head to leave, Ifrit stared me down.

In the mirror, he loomed behind me. Hunched over to fit in the small space, his glowing purple eyes radiated over my reflection's shoulder. His snarl tremored the loose bathroom tiles. A wisp of smoke curled from his moist snout, and behind his razor teeth, a flame flickered in the back of his mouth. His ram horns spiraled in on themselves on the sides of his head.

"Here we are again, Baxter Allen." His animalistic grumble vibrated my core. "Have you missed me? I've missed you."

His muzzle curled into something resembling a smile, and a low chortle reverberated deep in his throat.

No!

I spun around.

Nothing.

Just an empty wall with blond tiling from the floor to chest level. No djinn.

I turned back to the mirror. Nothing but the wide eyes of my reflection staring back.

Get it together, man.

Yanking open the bathroom door, I returned to the front of the coffee shop, rubbing my eyes to erase the traces of Ifrit's image.

Someone in the back room yelled, "Put whipped cream on the list, Kim!"

Behind the register, the kid with the nose stud glared at Jason and Ashley, wanting to clock out for the night. "You guys need to hit the road."

He turned to me. "And sorry, dude. No one's seen your jewelry box. Kim already swept and mopped, too. She's gone over the entire floor."

My shoulders fell as his words destroyed my last shred of a lead.

Now what?

"Thanks for checking." I searched the floor near our table in case Kim, Jason, or Ashley missed something. Of course, they hadn't.

The worker untied his forest-green apron and tossed it onto the matching green counter. "Look, if you want to write down your cell, I'll leave a note in the breakroom. If anyone finds it, we can text you."

"Sure." I grabbed a pen and scribbled my cell on a napkin. The guy took it and shoved it into his pocket.

Who knew if it'd help? But it couldn't hurt. Whoever stole it might come running back to me after they realized the world of destruction they'd unleashed.

Jason, Ashley, and I regrouped outside of West End Coffee empty-handed and defeated for the second time that night. As soon as the door clicked shut, the kid behind the counter locked it and switched off the pink neon sign, plunging us into the dimness of the street.

"I saw him," I muttered, unsure I should tell them, knowing what Jason would say. "Ifrit. In the bathroom."

"Wait, what?" Jason's eyes lit up behind his glasses. "And you didn't yell? Why are you throwing that out as an afterthought? Bax—"

"I saw him in the mirror, but when I turned around, he'd vanished."

My friends paused, unsure how to respond.

"Do you think he really appeared in the bathroom?" Jason asked.

"It felt real. He said he missed me. Like, in an ominous, I'm-gonna-kill-you way."

"Hmm." Jason nodded like a doctor diagnosing me. I'd wanted to avoid that. "How'd you sleep last night?"

I knew he'd go there, and it wasn't fair. "I know what I saw."

"How'd you sleep? What does that mean?" Ashley's gaze jumped between the two of us.

Jason watched me over the top of his glasses, giving me a chance to explain.

"It doesn't mean anything. It's not some dark secret." I rubbed my eyes. "I'm just having trouble sleeping. Jason is making it a way bigger deal than it is. Everyone has nights where they don't sleep. That doesn't mean I'm hallucinating."

"I'm not saying you're delusional, bro, but it's been two weeks since you've slept through the night."

"I'm not up all night either. Just restless."

Ashley held up her hands. "Why aren't you sleeping, Bax?"

Jason answered before I could. "Ever since we banished Ifrit, Bax has been having nightmares. He thinks he's fine, but they aren't going away."

Ashley softened her tone. "I didn't know you'd become an insomniac."

I shook my head. "The nightmares aren't all the time, and I'm not an insomniac. My mind just won't stop replaying the dreams where I watched Ifrit hurt people. I relive how he killed Nick and threw your dad down the stairs and all the other horrible stuff he did over and over like it's happening again."

A convertible rolled by with heavy metal music blaring, vibrating the air around us as it passed. I appreciated the break from their interrogation.

"You need to talk to Mrs. Bronson," Jason said. "I mean, her job is to help with these kinds of things."

"And say that I'm obsessing over incidents that didn't involve me, even though they did? I'd have to tell her why I'm dreaming about those things. Look, we have more important issues to deal with. I'm not delusional. I saw Ifrit in the bathroom." Although I said the last sentence with unflinching confidence, I couldn't have been sure. I imagined people who lost their minds weren't always aware their sanity was slipping away from them.

I exhaled a lungful. "Let's pretend I'm not crazy, and he appeared to me. Why would he show up, taunt me, then vanish? He only crosses over from the vortex to manipulate his master's thoughts. I don't think he'd appear to me with the sole purpose of threatening me like a movie villain."

"Hold on." Jason tapped his forehead with two fingers. "Janni knew where to locate Ifrit's box last time. That's what started this whole thing. He led us to the cellar and showed us where the box had been hidden. So why couldn't Janni find him now?"

"Genius! Come on." We ducked between West End Coffee and the neighboring veterinarian clinic for cover, squeezing together in the small space to form a tight circle.

"We've become serious alley dwellers, guys." Ashley blew into her hands for warmth. "At least we found one without a stench."

I rubbed the ring, closed my eyes, and let the tingling rain over me for the second time on Halloween night. The magic pulsated through me, vibrating in my knees. Within seconds, Janni's scent crawled around us.

"HOW CAN IT SERVE?" His face scrunched as he scratched under his ear. "DID BAXTER FIND IFRIT?"

I shook my head, dismissing his question. "Since you showed us where to locate Ifrit's buried artifact before—"

"YOU COMMANDED IT!" His purple eyes narrowed. "DON'T BLAME IT. IT ALSO TOLD BAX IFRIT—"

I raised my hands to quiet him. "I'm not blaming you. Calm down. Since we lost the box, we're just asking if you can point us in the right direction again."

"AH." Janni stared at the dark sky as if in deep thought. We gave him a minute, but after his brief pause, he said, "NO."

"What do you mean, no? Why not?" Jason blurted.

Janni threw him a sideways glare. "IT CAN SENSE THE ACTIVITY. THE TRACES OF MAGIC." He sniffed. "NOTHING IN THE AIR HERE."

Jason kicked the brick wall. "Because Ifrit projected the illusion of the old man, Janni knew his box was in the cellar. Janni can only follow Ifrit when he's been active."

My stomach dropped. "So that means Ifrit didn't appear to me in the bathroom. Otherwise, you'd sense him."

"OLD MAN HANDED BAXTER THE RING. THAT WAS NOT ILLUSION. THAT WAS MAGIC. IFRIT MAY HAVE APPEARED TO BAXTER AS ILLUSION, WHICH IT CANNOT SENSE." He pointed to his head. "ILLUSIONS ARE IN BAXTER'S MIND."

All the rules were frustrating; however, at least my lack of sleep might not be at fault for seeing Ifrit in the restroom. "Two things. One, glad I may not be hallucinating. Two, if Janni doesn't feel traces of Ifrit's magic, then no one's summoned him yet. Also good news."

Ashley unwrapped a piece of Halloween candy and popped it into her mouth. "So we need a disturbance in The Force for you to follow it, Janni?"

"THE FORCE?"

"Yeah, you know, like in—uh, Bax?" Ashley's mouth fell open, and she nodded to the end of the narrow alley.

Jason, Janni, and I turned to the alley's entrance.

Scarlet Lane, the girl I'd been in love with since the fifth grade—another thing Ifrit ruined—stared at us. She wore a short crimson dress with long fangs poking between her lips. Her straightened red hair whipped in front of her face, and her porcelain skin under the streetlights enhanced her vampire costume.

Her gaze fixed on the tiny djinn. "What is that?"

I swallowed. Jason gulped next to me.

"Janni, go," I commanded. He jumped.

"Baxter? Explain what I just saw and how you made it disappear." Scarlet crinkled her nose as a gust of wind blew toward her. "Did that thing make that stench?"

"Who? What? Nice costume. You guys go to a party?"

Scarlet approached us, the short cape from her costume waving behind. "Answer my question. Where'd the talking animal go?"

Janni would have shot her the evil eye if he'd heard her call him an animal.

"It's a Halloween trick."

"Halloween trick?" Ashley moaned behind me.

"Then make it come back." Scarlet folded her arms. "Do it."

I could, but not without confirming Janni's existence, leading to another set of questions. If I let Scarlet into the Djinn-verse, she'd connect Janni to Ifrit, then Ifrit to me, then me to Nick. And I wasn't ready for her to learn Ifrit killed her boyfriend because I had a crush on her. I'd never be ready for that.

She stepped closer, shrinking the gap between us. Her emerald eyes pierced mine. "Explain."

Casey and Latoya arrived at our already too-crowded gathering, peeking down the alley.

"What are you doing detouring into dark alleys, girl?" Casey tightened her green coat over a cream-colored toga. A Greek goddess?

Scarlet kept her gaze locked on mine.

"For real. It's freezing. Let's get home," Latoya chimed in, dressed like an angel. Though I wasn't sure how many angels had exposed midriffs. "Oh. Hi, guys. Fun Halloween?"

"Just fabulous," Ashley answered for us in the most deadpan monotone ever used.

Scarlet's nostrils flared, and her jawline flexed. She stepped closer so only I could hear her. She'd only been that close to me twice in my life. Once when Ifrit forced her to kiss me and once when she slapped me. "I put up with your nonsense before, thinking I'd lost my mind. Not again, Baxter. You promised me it was over, but I have a feeling somehow, everything from…last time…is related to this. That it's not over."

No, not over at all. In fact, it was rebooting.

I didn't move a muscle and didn't speak, hoping I could disappear like Janni and jump back to the safety of my bedroom.

After a long glare able to rip a soul from its body, Scarlet spun and walked back to her friends, heels clicking on the pavement. "Let's go, girls." She followed Casey and Latoya, flipping me the finger as she rounded the corner.

Every muscle in me wanted to melt. I thought we'd seen the end of our djinn issues. Turned out, they just took a break.

Chapter 3

A car honked a few streets over, followed by someone shouting. I didn't need to hear the words; the tone said it all. Above the noise of cars, a truck beeped as it reversed, and garbage cans clattered. The morning's ambient city noises, a mix of distant car horns and bustling footsteps, usually wrapped around me like a comforting blanket, allowing my thoughts to wander. But not even a long shower followed by a walk to school eased my mind.

I scanned the street ahead for anything out of the ordinary, anything amiss. I examined the eyes of each person I passed, searching for the slightest violet hue. When would he strike? Where? What form would he take to lure me close enough to attack?

A gust of wind scooted a small collection of leaves into my path before scattering them each in their own direction. When I looked up, I found myself outside Warren's Cosmos for the first time since swearing off comic books two weeks ago. I'd gone longer stretches in the past, but never after telling Warren I had given up superhero stories forever. Giving up the actual comic books hadn't been too difficult, but I missed my visits with Warren.

The tiny silver bell chimed as it clinked against the top of the glass door, announcing my entrance. The musty smell of paper rolled over me, and I soaked it in, breathing in the soothing nostalgia with a smile.

This is what I need.

"Bax!" As always, Warren's massive frame balanced on the miniature stool behind the counter. His gravel-tinged baritone greeted me better than any friendly hug could. The brown T-shirt stretched across his chest distorted the two parallel axes of Maximan's symbol.

"Hey, Warren." I weaved through the aisle of heroes, legends, and gods, eager to see him. Posters and comic book covers plastered every available inch of the walls, life-sized cardboard cutouts of characters watched shoppers from every corner, and boxes of inventory towered near the door to the storage room. Stains from customers tracking in rain and street debris dirtied the black-speckled white linoleum, a testament to the neighborhood's shared love of Warren's Cosmos.

As I arrived at the counter, my smile faded. Since the first time I'd visited Warren's store, I always asked him if any customers asked about *Shade Slayer, #276, the Haunting of the Ravine.* That issue was the only thing I had from my dad, and I'd naively hoped he'd return to Warren's to buy a replacement. But thanks to Ifrit, I'd learned my dad—Ben—was a scumbag who mistreated Mom, forcing her and me into hiding. After that, comic books only served as a bitter reminder of the years of hope I'd wasted on him.

Uncomfortable approaching the counter empty-handed, I grabbed a pack of gum from the tabletop candy display and slid it to him.

"Just this, please."

He didn't grab it, in no hurry to rush me out. Instead, his leathery skin cracked into a grin. He dragged a calloused hand over his head, hair buzzed super short, military-style. I didn't know if he'd served. Reality only played a tiny role in our relationship.

"I'm assuming you're here to reclaim the comic books you dropped off. Well, I've kept the box safe and sound in back. No one's touched it. Figured you might change your mind."

"No. I told you, you can resell them. I don't want them anymore."

One of Warren's bushy eyebrows raised, with random hairs going in all directions. "Then to what do I owe the visit? Need help with the comic book you're writing, or did you call it quits on all things comic-related?"

I'd told him I was writing a story about djinn to get his help with my actual evil spirit problem. I never knew if he truly bought the whole I'm-writing-a-story thing. We pretended, but not too hard. "I am struggling with a case of writer's block. I loved your idea about burying the box, but my hero waited too long, and someone stole it."

The silver bell dinged as a pink-haired woman opened the store door, letting in a gust of wintery air.

"Sounds like your fantasy is becoming a mystery." He tapped his chin with a finger. "And from what you've told me about your story so far, a smidge of horror. Did the thief summon the djinn?"

"The world hasn't ended yet, so…"

A young guy in his thirties came out from the back room carrying a cardboard box. Under his thin, wire-rimmed glasses, he had thick caterpillar eyebrows and brown eyes matching Warren's. He looked familiar. An employee? I'd never seen anyone working in the store other than Warren.

"Hey, Dad, where do you want the new X-Heroes series? We're building up a decent-sized inventory. Not selling as well as you predicted."

"We'll sell them, so don't stash 'em too far. We'll be restocking at week's end, mark my words."

"Okay." The guy pivoted to return to the back room.

"Scott." Warren caught him. "This is Bax. The kid those thugs jumped a few weeks back."

My cheeks warmed. Great introduction. He'd told his son how Malcolm Reardon's crew beat the crap out of me, another Ifrit gift.

"Hi, Bax." Scott nodded, causing his glasses to slide down his nose. With his hands full, he ignored it. "Glad you're okay. I'm Warren's son, Scott."

"Hey." Weird. I never thought about Warren's life outside of his store. I never pictured him with a kid. Or a wife, for that matter.

Scott noticed the customer who'd come in after me. "Good morning." With a thud, he dropped the box to the floor next to the counter, then reached to the table behind Warren and drank from his disposable coffee cup with *West End Coffee* printed on it.

That was where I'd seen him! Last night, he was leaving West End when we returned to look for the artifact. How did I not see the resemblance to Warren? Sure, he was tall and thin, unlike Warren, but their eyes matched.

Scott went to greet the customer before I could say anything about seeing him the night before. A glimmer of pride twinkled in Warren's eyes as he watched his son work.

"I didn't know you had a son."

"You never asked." He winked. "He doesn't live in town. Just visiting to help with the store a bit."

"You need help?"

"Don't we all?" Warren scratched the scruff on his cheeks with his right hand, his pointer and middle fingers gone past the knuckles. I wouldn't ask him about *Shade Slayer* anymore, but his missing fingers reminded me of our other tradition.

"Warren, can I ask you something?"

His teeth peeked out from between his lips with his smile. He knew what was coming. "You can ask me anything, Bax."

"How did you lose your fingers?"

Warren leaned back on his tiny stool. It creaked under him. His chest expanded and shrunk as he swallowed a deep breath and exhaled. "Well, it's a gruesome story, if you think you can handle it."

I wasn't sure how any of his previous stories, which all ended with him losing his fingers, were *not* gruesome, but I played along. "I can handle it."

"You ever hear of Marrakech?"

"Is it a country?"

"It's a city. Home to one of the most preeminent poker tournaments in the world. In Morocco. You know where Morocco is?"

"Africa."

"You do pay attention in school." He grinned and then cleared his throat. "Well, quite a few years back, as a much younger man, I'd earned a card shark's reputation. I traveled all over the world playing poker. And Marrakech, well, to win in Marrakech is to be a global champion. It's the prize of all prizes." He gazed over my head, savoring the made-up glory of his card-playing youth.

"Seems unusual to lose your fingers playing cards."

"Poker is not *just* playing cards, Bax. Poker in Morrocco culminates in a three-day tournament. I was the youngest player remaining. We were down to five. Myself, three others, and Ridouan Taghi. Of course, you've heard of him."

Warren acted like he would continue but paused long enough for me to interject, "I don't think I have."

"That's incredible." He mocked confusion. "You've never heard of the most dangerous crime boss in Morocco? His nefarious reputation is feared around the world."

I shrugged.

"'Course, Ridouan was still makin' a name for himself back then, so I didn't know about him either. On day three of the tourney, with five players remaining, I went all in on a straight. A straight in poker beats almost everything. And going all in means I put all my winnings on the table, so he'd need to match my money while showing a better hand than me. Impossible, I thought! He'd fold and leave with his remaining cash."

"Did you beat him?"

"He didn't fold. He put all of his money in the pot. When we showed our hands, he had two pairs. Twos and sixes. I won the tournament. Earned me $900,000."

"Holy crap! That must be how you bought Warren's Cosmos." Warren didn't dress or live a millionaire's life, so the story wasn't over. Plus, he still had his fingers.

He snorted. "Nah. When I checked out of the hotel the next night, Ridouan and his goons cornered me. Beat me senseless. Not unlike what happened to you."

I cringed.

"Ridouan didn't play Marrakech often, but no one told me that when he did, he didn't lose, especially to a twenty-something American punk. Bax, that night, with his thugs beating the tar out of me, I figured I'd played my last tournament. Heck, I thought I'd seen my final day on this earth. As I readied myself to meet my maker, they stopped. Ridouan knelt next to me. His breath reeked of cigars and whiskey. He whispered into my ear, 'You pay me nine hundred thousand dollars, and you live. And you will never play in Morocco again.'"

"Not fair!"

"Yep. Ridouan earned and deserved his nefarious reputation. With no other choice, I agreed."

"Wow." I paused. "Wait. That doesn't explain what happened to your fingers."

He held up his right hand. "After I paid them, his men grabbed me. I figured he'd changed his mind and would kill me anyway. They had their money, after all. Instead, in a deserted street near the Hotel Oriso, two men held me while one cut off my fingers with garden sheers."

"Holy crap!" I blurted out. "But you paid them!"

Warren leaned forward on his stool. "He called it the *Mark of Ridouan*. If I ever tried to play cards again in Morocco, other players would see he marked me, and they'd refuse to play me or suffer the same consequences."

I let out a relieved laugh, the kind that bursts out after watching an intense movie scene. "Sorry. I don't mean to laugh, but such a cool story. Bad for you, but you know what I mean."

Warren smiled as he folded his arms across his chest. "Ridouan ended my poker-playing career in

Morocco and everywhere else. I never played again."

I smacked the counter with the palm of my hand. "Excellent story, Warren."

Scott leaned against a shelf, listening in. His smile mirrored Warren's. I couldn't imagine growing up with Warren as a dad. Scott must've listened to hundreds of fantastic stories.

My phone vibrated. "I need to get to school." I handed him a few crumpled bills to cover the cost of the gum. Even though I didn't chew gum, I felt obligated to buy something.

Warren slid my money back to me. "On the house as long as you come back soon."

"Deal." I snagged the gum and left Warren's Cosmos.

****

"So?" Jason plopped into the desk next to me. "No signs yet, I'm assuming."

"Nothing."

He rolled up the cuff of his shirt sleeve. "Hopefully, some kid stole the box, got it home, realized it was junk, and tossed it. Now it's resting in the bottom of a landfill, buried underground as it should be."

"I so want to believe that." I flipped open my cracked and yellowed copy of *The Scarlet Letter* and booted up my laptop. American Literature and Astronomy were the only advanced classes I'd enrolled in. I didn't think reading novels would be so grueling. Overall, I didn't mind the story, but the author would write one sentence scrolling on for three pages with a hundred commas. Thank God Mrs. Macklind didn't make us diagram sentences.

Tired students filed into the classroom, sliding into

their desks. The day after Halloween should be a school holiday. A school night coinciding with a holiday centered on nighttime festivities should be against the law.

Scarlet entered the room surrounded by her chatty, orbiting girlfriends. Her glare cut through them, landed on me for a moment, then softened before refocusing on Casey. As Scarlet's friends claimed their seats in the back of the room, she avoided looking in my direction a second time.

"Ouch," Jason mumbled.

I'd get to discuss *The Scarlet Letter* while Scarlet Lane shot me dirty looks.

The bell rang, and the students quieted. Mrs. Macklind closed the door. "Okay, everyone. I'm sure you are all still crashing from your candy high, but let's jump back into things. Today, we continue our conversation about Hester Prynne."

Mrs. Macklind strolled to the front of the room, standing by her white desk. She strolled everywhere. Around six feet tall and all legs, Mrs. Macklind carried herself with graceful confidence. Her bright amber eyes glowed against her skin, and she wore one of those super-short haircuts, a buzz cut few women could pull off. And, man, she pulled it off. Ashley found pictures online of Mrs. Macklind walking a runway in Spain twenty years ago, and no one doubted the validity for one second. A former runway model taught us American Literature.

"Since you all should have finished Hawthorne's classic novel," she said, "let's dive into the themes. This story is dense with vital thematic elements."

I skimmed my notes. *The Scarlet Letter* was a dark

book for a school assignment. A woman named Hester gave birth to a daughter, Pearl, while Native Americans held her husband captive. So the town knew she cheated on him, and they forced her to wear a big red *A* as a punishment for her sinful affair. But despite her public branding, she refused to reveal the baby's dad. Then, her husband—Chillingsworth—returned to town but made Hester swear not to tell anyone he was back because it embarrassed him that his wife cheated. If that wasn't enough, Chillingsworth befriended an old minister, Dimmesdale, and discovered Dimmesdale was Pearl's dad, so he tortured the poor guy.

Hester confronted Chillingsworth, begging him to leave the minister alone, who was all sad and depressed with guilt. Chillingsworth wouldn't stop, so Hester developed a plan to run off with Dimmesdale and live happily ever after. But before they could escape, Dimmesdale died in Hester's arms in the middle of the town square.

Pretty dark. Or, as Mrs. Macklind would say, *dense with vital thematic elements.*

"Jason, why don't you kick us off? What theme did you pick up on?"

Jason grinned as most guys in class did when Mrs. Macklind called on them as if her finger-pointing anointed them worthy of her sultry gaze. He cleared his throat and pushed his glasses higher on the bridge of his nose. "It's about true love. Hester loves the minister so much that she keeps the secret he's Pearl's dad to protect his reputation. Meanwhile, she wears the scarlet letter and subjects herself to the town's judgment. She's so in love with him, she bears the fallout for them both."

Mrs. Macklind pointed again at Jason as she nodded.

"Very good. Scarlet?"

I flinched at the mention of her name.

Scarlet tapped her finger on her desk. "I think it's more about strength. Hester refuses to play by the town's stupid rules. She does what she wants and almost takes pride in wearing the letter. Her daughter comes first, she safeguards her lover's identity, and she defends her asshole husband for whatever reason. She doesn't bow to the town's rules on what and who she should be. Sorry about the curse word."

Mrs. Macklind held back a smile. "He kind of is, isn't he? *Manipulative* might be a more accurate adjective. But yes, Hester is a strong female character who refuses to let her society's rules define or defeat her."

I straightened, preparing myself to speak up in class. I hated speaking in front of people, but my counselor, Mrs. Bronson, said the more I talked in class, the more comfortable I'd get doing it, so I forced my hand into the air.

"Bax?"

I spat out the words before I forgot them. "One thing I don't get is how even though the town treats her like she's subhuman, she refuses to move. She's not trapped there. Why not take Pearl and relocate?"

Mrs. Macklind tapped her bottom lip with a long fingernail. "Perhaps because Salem is her home, and she doesn't believe the town can force her to leave, like Scarlet said. And don't forget, she loves Dimmesdale, who's the town's reverend."

"Gross," Casey grunted from the back of the classroom. "She's living in constant humiliation for an old reverend. No thanks."

The class chuckled.

"Love is blind, as they say." Mrs. Macklind strolled down the aisle. "The reverend wasn't always feeble. The guilt from the affair crushed him. Their secret killed him from the inside."

She glided across the room, pausing near the windows. "So, all said, a lot is going on with Hester's story. Which brings us to your presentations."

I straightened as if she'd electrified my chair.

Presentation?

The word sent chills racing over me, more spine-tingling than the ones summoning Janni created. Public speaking was not my thing. It was my anti-thing. My mortal enemy. If I had to square off against public speaking or Ifrit, I can't say I wouldn't be rubbing every purple jewel I could get my hands on.

"You'll each give a brief presentation on a theme of *The Scarlet Letter* that resonated with you. We've hit on love, guilt, conformity, and betrayal. There are also strong overtones of evil, sin, repentance, and the challenges of being a woman in a male-dominated society."

Mrs. Macklind wrote *three to five minutes* on the whiteboard in front of the room. "What I want is a theme that spoke to you and why. This is a personal presentation, meaning there's no wrong answer. However, your grade will be based on how you support your opinion, so you must prepare."

Mrs. Macklind set the black dry-erase marker on the whiteboard ledge and leaned against her desk. "You'll research your position by next Tuesday." She shook a sheet of paper in her hand. "The order of presentations will be random to ensure fairness. You may present next

Tuesday or in a future class until everyone has finished. So be prepared and ready next week."

No way. Not only was she forcing me to present in front of people, but I wouldn't know my presentation date until I walked into the classroom that day. Academic ambush.

Sweat dampened my forehead, and orange spots swirled in my peripheral vision. The mere idea of an impending presentation with no due date sent my mind racing, my heart thudding, and my muscles turning to mush. If we started next week with a few people each day, it would drag out until senior year.

I couldn't live my life under that pressure!

I clutched the sides of my desk and slowed my breathing.

Get it together, Bax. You'll cause an episode before you even do the stupid presentation.

"You okay?" Jason whispered.

I turned to him. "Huh? Yeah. Fine."

But I wasn't.

Chapter 4

Ms. Hamilton's typing jackhammered in the empty administration office. Usually, student council members rummaged through supplies behind the desk while kids waited in the orange cushioned chairs to see Principal Clark, who multitasked by clicking through emails as he talked on the phone. On normal days, the office area buzzed with activity right after the final period. But Mr. Clark's office sat dark, and Ms. Hamilton worked in solitude.

She glanced up from her monitor. "Well, hello, Baxter." She stopped typing to greet me at the counter.

"Hey." I let my backpack fall off my shoulder. "Empty in here today."

Ms. Hamilton placed her notebook down and grabbed a pen from the yellow ceramic pen holder with a dark blue Truman High Lancer logo stamp. She waited as if ready to take my order at a restaurant. "Mr. Clark left early, and you're Mrs. Bronson's only appointment this afternoon...oh my."

She set her pen on the notebook and poured the remaining water from her drinking glass into the pot of a drooping plant on a wire plant stand. Watering her plants with her glass was such a Ms. Hamilton thing. Her plants forever lived in varying degrees of wilt and it always surprised her.

She grunted, frowned at the plant, and picked it up.

As she brought it closer to the window, she said over her shoulder, "Let me ring Mrs. Bronson for you."

"Cool." I checked my phone, scrolling through my texts for nothing in particular.

Ms. Hamilton dialed with a fake fingernail that was way too long and way too red. She patted the side of her head, fixing her blonde hair. She embodied every clichéd secretary in every high school movie ever created, portly with short hair and thick reading glasses on a chain around her neck. She even had the trademark pleasant demeanor that must've been in the job description.

"Hi, Mrs. Bronson. Baxter's here." She hung up. "Go on in, sir."

"Thanks."

I snagged my backpack and shoved open her office door. Like the rest of the school, Mrs. Bronson's office had sterile gray floors and off-white walls. The window let in the full afternoon sun, which baked the two fake leather chairs in front of it. I plopped into my usual seat.

"Hello, Baxter." Mrs. Bronson joined me, coming around her desk to the chair across from me with her session equipment: the yellow notepad, a purple pen tucked behind her right ear, and folded glasses that stayed forever in her shirt pocket. Her shiny red hair mirrored the sunlight.

She sighed, as if clearing her mind to focus. "So, how are things going?" Her question opened all our sessions.

"Fine." My typical opening response.

"You look much better than the last time we talked."

"Yeah. The stitches came out a few days ago, and my hair's growing back where they shaved it." I ran a finger over the short hairs filling in the former bald spot over my ear. It still looked short compared to the thick curls on top of my head, but no one noticed anymore. I waited for her to comment on the gray speckles in my hair that appeared after escaping the vortex, but she didn't. No one noticed except Mom, who said her dad turned gray in his late teens, so she didn't see a need for concern.

"Are you walking home from school again?"

"I never stopped." She wanted to ensure no trauma lingered over random thugs lurking in the shadows and attacking me. She didn't know the thugs were Malcolm Reardon and his friends. No one did. And she sure as hell didn't know they assaulted me while high and drunk because they thought I was trying to hook up with their dead friend's girlfriend.

Once again, thanks, Ifrit.

"Are you comfortable talking about what happened?"

Mrs. Bronson didn't pressure me to discuss my attack during our last session. But she'd keep asking if I didn't address it at some point.

"I stopped by a comic book store, and a group of kids jumped me. No one I knew. Very random, so it's not like they'll do it again or anything." I'd told the story so often between Mom, the doctors, and the police, I had it memorized word for word.

Mrs. Bronson scribbled into her notebook. "A random attack can be more stressful because there is an element of surprise, of helplessness. You don't feel any trepidation walking home?"

I tapped the leather arm of the chair. Scarlet asked Malcolm to lay off me, and so far, he'd listened. I still avoided him at school, just in case, but that was how I'd spent high school before he jumped me, so nothing different there.

"I don't live in the greatest neighborhood. Or at least I walk to school through a few not-so-safe neighborhoods. Being careful is how I roll. I've always had to be aware of my surroundings and stuff."

Mrs. Bronson folded her hands on her yellow notebook. "Fair enough. I won't belabor it. How about the vasovagal syncope? Any new episodes of VS?"

Since I changed middle schools in fifth grade, I'd been cursed with *episodes,* as I referred to them. My heart would race while my circulatory system would tighten, cutting off the blood to my brain, which caused me to pass out. Doctors diagnosed it as psychological, which meant each episode could be my last or they'd plague my entire life. No one knew.

I shook my head. "Not since the assembly."

Total lie. Normally, public speaking triggered my VS, but my last episode happened in the djinn vortex. Convinced I would die there, an episode started swirling, but for the first time, I beat it and never passed out, using the methods Mrs. Bronson taught me. But that could have just been luck.

"Mrs. Macklind is making us present to the class."

Mrs. Bronson kept her face stoic. "You've never presented in front of classmates before, have you?"

"Never. Somehow, I've avoided all presentations in my high school career. And to make it worse, Mrs. Macklind's not telling us when we present until class starts." My chest tightened at the thought.

"Dread mixed with anticipation. A deadly combination for VS."

I scowled. "Aren't you supposed to be helping me

feel better about life?"

She smiled, which was unusual during our sessions. It must be a therapist thing. "Sometimes you need to call things what they are. Don't sugarcoat it."

"Well, it sucks. I'll never know if it's my turn until it's time. It's so unfair." My voice elevated.

"Take a deep breath." She leaned forward in her chair. "Baxter, this could be a phenomenal opportunity. Your episodes sneak up on you. While you don't know your date, you know your presentation is coming. In other words, Mrs. Macklind gifted you the luxury of time to prepare and practice. At the assembly, the trivia question caught you off guard. This time, no surprises."

"You're acting like this assignment is the prize of the century."

She shrugged. "It is what you make of it. She's giving you time to prepare."

"That's one way to look at it."

I listened to the clock on the wall tick for a few seconds. Mrs. Bronson let me absorb her words. Talking in front of people on the fly activated my VS. I'd never had an advanced warning.

"So let's discuss some tips you can practice over the next hour." She glanced at the clock. "First, though, how are things at home?"

"Fine. Mom started dating."

"How do you feel about that?"

"He's coming over for dinner tonight. Zia's Candles is where Mom works, and he picked her up during her shift." I smiled but then wiped it from my face before Mrs. Bronson could pounce on my reaction.

Too slow.

"What's funny?" she asked.

"Just thinking. Was the guy like, *Hey, baby, have any candles that smell as nice as you?* It's weird to think about some rando picking up my mom while she's working."

"Weird how?"

Mrs. Bronson always wanted us to uncover hidden drama or angst. "Not *bad* weird. Funny weird. I mean, it's Mom."

She stared, unblinking. "You've never talked about her dating."

"She hasn't. Not that I'm aware of, anyway."

Mrs. Bronson wanted me to be nervous or worried, but I didn't feel uncomfortable. Mom worked two jobs, didn't have any friends, and our only family lived in Chicago. I loved the idea she'd have something to focus on besides stressing out over money or worrying about me.

"I'm glad Mom's dating. They already met for coffee or drinks a few times, so he's coming over for dinner tonight to meet me. I haven't seen her this happy in a while."

"So this isn't brand new, then."

"She's been seeing him for two weeks, I think. She hasn't dated since my dad, but she should enjoy herself now that I'm older and don't need a babysitter."

"Well, Bax, that's a very mature perspective. I'm glad you're supportive."

I shot her a sideways grin. "Unless he's an asshole. Ask me about this at our next session."

"Count on it. All right, let's talk about those tools and tricks you can use before your English presentation."

****

Similar to the administration office, Truman High

felt deserted after my session with Mrs. Bronson. Shut lockers lined the sides of long, empty hallways. An overturned paper cup absorbed a small puddle of coffee next to a trash can. Though impossible, a breeze blew past me.

A click.

I spun around, expecting Ifrit to be standing at full height, smoke rolling at his hooves, and eyes glowing.

The door to the art room shut behind a student.

Paranoid much?

I turned the combination, and my locker squealed open. I grabbed my math book, not wanting to forget it, and shoved it into my backpack. Fun night of algebra ahead of me.

Outside, the football team hollered while cheerleaders chanted their routines, easing my paranoia. Everyone must be on the field. So why did the skin on the back of my neck keep tingling?

I slammed my locker door. Time to head home and meet Mom's new dude.

Thanks to Ifrit, I knew what my dad, Ben, looked like. Thin build but tough, with calloused hands from years as an electrician, permanent scruff on his jaw, and stained clothes. Not a guy you'd mistake for a celebrity. Was Ben Mom's type, or would her new man be a clean-cut office type? She hadn't told me much. Said she wanted me to meet him first.

As I rounded the corner, I froze. My muscles turned to granite. My eyes had to be deceiving me.

Down the length of the empty hallway, an old man blocked the exit. Not any old man, but Ifrit's conjuration. The same old man who'd first tricked me into accepting Janni's ring.

Hunched over, his long, red-brick-colored coat hung on him, too big for his feeble frame. His bald head and thin wisps of white hair glistened under the school's fluorescent lights. Even from my distance, I could see his overgrown curled fingernails twisting from beneath the ends of his sleeves like loose threads.

As I stared, stunned in disbelief, his cracked lips twisted into a smile, exposing his yellow, rotting teeth. His purple eyes glowed on his wrinkled face as he raised his hand. With one finger, he beckoned me to approach.

"Baaaaaaxter." His deep breathiness resonated in my ears, even though he whispered from the other end of the hallway.

"Oh, hell no." I looked around for help. Someone to verify I hadn't gone insane. My lack of sleep, coupled with my guilt-fueled nightmares, blended with my fear of Ifrit's release, were all manifesting into a real-life hallucination. Or was it real?

I spun and jogged in the opposite direction, not wanting to risk it. The old man guarded Truman High's main entrance, but the school had other ways out. My sneakers squeaked on the floor, echoing in the empty halls. I skidded around a corner. I needed other people to validate my sanity and scare him away. He wouldn't stay visible to a group of people; he preferred to torture individuals in private.

The old man suddenly appeared in front of me, blocking the door to the cafeteria. I stumbled to an abrupt stop.

Baaaaaaaaaaxter, he called to me without opening his mouth, letting the word stab me in my brain.

I wasn't crazy. It was happening. How could the entire freaking school be on the football field?

The locker room. I'd detour through there. Maybe I'd get lucky and run into football players leaving practice early.

Never thought I'd be hoping for that.

I tore off again. My jog became a sprint. Down one hallway, I turned right. I shoved my way through the door under the *BOYS LOCKER* sign.

Inside, I caught my breath, doubling over. I sucked in the humid air, tainted with the smell of sweat and socks. No sounds of iron banging in the weight room or guys talking. Seriously? No one?

I hurried past rows of grated lockers to the middle of the locker room, gambling Coach Simmons would be in his office if the team was scrimmaging.

After a sharp left, I stopped in my tracks again.

Ifrit blocked the door to Coach Simmons's office, abandoning his old man disguise and taking on his beast-like form. His thick spiral horns curled inward, and his dark fur stood at attention on his powerful shoulders. His massive chest heaved, and his arms bent at ninety degrees. Gray smoke slinked out of his snout while his nostrils flexed with every inhale. His muzzle morphed into a snarl, drool dripping to the floor, where it landed with a steamy hiss.

"Who unleashed you?" I hollered, praying someone would hear me. "Tell me!"

His baritone chortle erupted from his throat. His eyes burned a deep violet, filling my mind with the nightmares that kept my nights sleepless since we'd banished him. My ears rang with Scarlet crying as Ifrit threw her dog across the room. My gut wretched as stairs slammed against Mr. Bryant's midsection as he rolled down the endless stairwell. My legs buckled as the car around Nick flipped, and metal crushed him. My teeth clattered as Malcolm punched and kicked me against the cement curb.

I balled my hands into fists as if I stood a chance in a physical battle with him. "Who let you out of the vortex?"

Ifrit's mouth didn't open, and he cocked his head to the side as a boy's voice answered me. "Vortex?"

I recognized the voice but couldn't place it.

"What's happening?" I muttered.

The boy's voice came again. "You're losing your shit, man."

I shook my head. Ifrit wouldn't call me *man*.

When I rubbed my eyes, Ifrit vanished. In his place, Malcolm Reardon examined me with a puzzled expression, not sure what to make of my outbursts. He clutched his shirt, in the middle of changing, as I demanded to know who let him out of the vortex.

"What is wrong with you, whack job?"

"Malcolm."

Even though Ifrit had disappeared, my heart continued to pound. Since Malcolm attacked me, I'd seen him at school but worked my ass off to avoid him. I even stalled going into Mr. Prescot's history class—the only class we shared—until a safe number of other students filled the room. Scarlet told Malcolm to leave me alone, which he did, but I had no desire to tempt him.

Malcolm stepped toward me, his hair dripping with sweat from practice, his dark, beady eyes narrow. My eyeline hit him square in the chest, even though he wore no shoes. If anyone saw him on the street, they'd never believe those thick arms and shoulders belonged to a high school junior.

Ifrit delivered me right to Malcolm in an empty locker room.

He tossed his shirt to the floor, upping the intimidation. "Look, Allen, I'm—"

With each of his steps forward, I matched it with a step back. No way he'd jump me on school grounds. Although he did beat me unconscious on a public street. Malcolm acted first and thought later. I sniffed. No traces of alcohol or pot.

"Back off." I fought to keep my voice unwavering.

He held up his hands. Not to throw a punch but in a defensive, palms out I-come-in-peace gesture. "Listen, you could have ratted me out to the cops a few weeks ago but didn't."

My brain raced to keep up with the change in direction. Did he want to talk?

He stopped approaching me. "Thank you for that, I guess."

Thank you?

He sighed as he scratched his stomach. "An assault charge wouldn't have gone over well at home. My record isn't exactly spotless."

No apology for fracturing my ribs, splitting my head, and pissing in my face, but a thank-you for not telling the cops. "I, um—"

"I don't know what happened between you and Scarlet, but she says it's over, so I promised her I'd back off. I even told the guys to stop calling you Flower."

"It *is* over between us." Not sure what he wanted me to say. It never really started between us, but I doubted his brain could handle that explanation.

A few locker rows over, a football player shouted, "You're an idiot. You didn't see her last weekend. She's hot, dude."

"I'm telling you, she's not," someone hollered back.

Malcolm glanced over his shoulder toward the voices. He stepped closer, but I held my ground, braver with other people nearby. "I'm not saying we're bros or anything. Just saying we're cool. Yeah?"

So we agreed I wouldn't report him, and he wouldn't torture me. I didn't need an apology. I could live with that deal.

"Cool."

Malcolm turned and disappeared behind the lockers. He shouted, "You fuckers need to be out there practicing! No wonder you suck so bad."

Several shouts and obscenities responded as water blasted in the showers and locker doors slammed.

Football practice had ended. Time for me to leave.

Chapter 5

The scent of simmering tomato sauce, rich with basil and oregano, welcomed me as I opened the door to my apartment. My mouth watered. I flipped my backpack into my room and followed the savory aroma to the kitchen. Mom rarely had time to cook elaborate meals. She hit the obligatory ones—Thanksgiving and Christmas—but not random Mondays in November.

She had set our small, four-person kitchen table with the starched red napkins typically reserved for Christmas and two thin white candles, even though the late afternoon sun still poured in from the windows. We didn't have special occasion dishes like some families, but Mom set out dinner plates with smaller salad plates on top of them—our version of fancy.

True to Mom's cooking tradition, the tiny portable speaker vibrated on the desk against the far wall. I had no idea where she stashed the pile of bills, papers, and magazines that lived on the desk. Soft jazz danced through the room, and Mom hummed along, absorbed in dicing red onions. She was way into this guy.

No thinking about the old man or Ifrit. I'd figure things out tomorrow. Mom needed me to be present, so I vowed to have a djinn-free evening.

She looked up from the wooden cutting board with a start. "Baxter!"

"Tonight's the night!" I grabbed a glass from the

cabinet and filled it with milk as Mom lowered the music's volume a few notches.

The kitchen chair creaked under me. "What time's he coming over?"

"Any minute. Thought we'd talk and enjoy some apps before dinner."

I whistled. "Salad plates *and* appetizers? Dang, Mom, we should slow it down."

She set her knife on the counter, focusing on me. "Wait, Bax, you said you were ready to meet Max."

"Huh? Oh my God. I'm teasing."

Mom's shoulders softened. "I'm nervous, I guess."

"He should be nervous, not you. He needs to impress *me*. You've seen the movies about a mom who goes on her first date after years of raising a kid. The kid makes the new guy's life hell. That's how these things work. I can make or break this thing. Along those lines, he can buy my approval. I'm relatively cheap."

She threw a dish towel at me that landed on my head. "Go put on a cleaner shirt. I can smell you from over here."

As I headed to my room, Mom resumed prancing around the kitchen, stirring, chopping, and wiping. Her chestnut hair bounced on her shoulders, and her lipstick matched her silky pink blouse. I struggled to remember the last time I'd seen her so giddy.

I yanked the towel off my head as I shut my bedroom door. Once I changed into a green-collared shirt, I tugged my dark brown comforter tight and fluffed my pillows. I kicked a pile of dirty clothes under my bed and dragged my arm across my desk, scooping the scraps of paper, paper clips, pens, pencils, and sticky notes into the open desk drawer and slid it shut. The guy wouldn't be in my room, but it'd make Mom happy to see my effort.

I returned to the kitchen where the setting sun cast shadows from the building across the street into our apartment, making the candles on our kitchen table glow. I flipped on the light over the table.

"You even broke out the special apron, I see."

Mom spun around, wiping her hands on the apron, then pointed to it with a smile. The words embroidered across the front of her apron read: *Proud Mom of a Labrador*. We didn't own a Labrador. As far as I knew, Mom had never owned a Labrador. As a kid—eight or nine—I bought the apron for her, convinced that after months of begging for a dog, it would force her to live up to its proclamation. My plan failed. We never brought home a dog. But she got an apron she loved breaking out when we had guests over to tell them about my diabolical child plotting. It'd become the gift that kept on giving.

"I love it when you show the Labrador apron to guests."

"I know you do." She pinched my cheek.

Our door buzzer squawked.

Mom and I surveyed the gray speaker next to the door as if we'd never noticed it hanging there.

"I'll get it." I took a slow, dramatic step toward our front door.

"No, no, no. Let me." She breezed past me and pressed the button. "Hello?"

"Sara?"

"Come on up!" She unlocked the building's front door with the other button and bit her lip.

"Mom. I'll like him. I'm sure."

She sighed, patting my cheek with her hand.

"You're such a good kid, Bax."

A good kid who almost destroyed the world and was on track to do it again. No one was perfect.

Mom ended up taking off her apron and tossing it under the sink just as a knock sounded. She waited a few feet from the door, watching it, not wanting him to think she was too anxious. After a pause she deemed adequate, she opened the door.

"Max! Hello! Come in!"

Max landed a quick peck on Mom's cheek and handed her an enormous bouquet of white and yellow flowers wrapped in green tissue paper.

She breathed them in. "They're gorgeous."

Not sure what I expected, but not the guy who stood in our doorway. If Ben's opposite existed, Max would be it. He topped six feet tall with olive skin and dark, wavy hair streaked with gray. His broad shoulders filled the crisp button-down shirt, and he carried himself with charismatic confidence without the cockiness. He could have played the leading man in any of the rom-coms Mom loved to watch.

He flashed me a dimpled smile with perfect white teeth. "You must be Bax."

I shook his sweaty, outstretched hand.

"I'm Max. Max and Bax, too funny." He laughed a little too much, erasing some coolness.

I forced a polite smile. He seemed as nervous as Mom, which I liked. Jerks didn't get nervous in new situations.

"All right, boys, why don't you take a seat. Appetizers are ready."

I showed Max to the living room, though he didn't need a guide on the ten-second journey. We sat on opposite couches.

He folded his hands in his lap. "So, Bax. You play any sports?"

"No, not my thing."

"I never did either." He chuckled as he drummed his thigh with the palm of his hand. "I always enjoyed working out and running but never had the skills to throw or catch a ball. Too clumsy."

I nodded, unsure how to respond to that. Should I agree he was too clumsy? Should I say I was, too? After only a second of what started devolving into awkward silence, I asked, "What do you do? For your job?"

He ran a hand through his dark hair, which fell back into place like magic. "I'm a corporate tax accountant. I do company taxes."

That title must come with a fat salary. Point for the new boyfriend.

"Are you from St. Louis?"

"I am. My parents are deceased, and my sister and her family live in Chesterfield. I have a house in Webster Groves."

He had a house and family in town, so he wouldn't be eager to relocate. Another point.

"Any kids?" I'd keep serving up questions as long as he kept hitting them back. Before he could answer that one, though, Mom handed me a glass of iced tea with a lemon wedge floating in it. A lemon wedge? Fancy.

She handed Max a glass of red wine. "Thanks, Sara."

Mom sat next to him. Like, right next to him, with no daylight between the two.

He didn't take the interruption as an opportunity to ignore my question. "No kids. My first marriage ended about six years ago, and we never had children."

No kids. Third point. I'd become accustomed to my only child status and had no desire to change that.

"Okay. My turn, Bax." He took a swig of his wine as he wound up his own questions. "How about you? You're not a sports guy, so what do you do for fun? Any hobbies or extracurriculars?"

Mom rested her hand on his thigh, just above his knee.

Jesus, Mom, relax.

I leaned back on the couch. Extracurriculars? The VS and lack of athletic prowess created a deadly combination of comfortable seclusion from traditional high school activities. But as Mrs. Bronson reminded me at least once a month, *no sports plus no clubs equals no college scholarships.*

"I hang out with my friends, I guess."

"He loves video games," Mom chimed in.

I grunted. While true, a parent speaking on a kid's behalf was always annoying. I could share what I wanted to share when I wanted to.

"What do you play?"

"Right now, I'm into *Archer Annihilation.* It's a game on—"

"Love that game."

I eyed him, expecting a *just kidding* that didn't come. The game had sold more copies than any other in history, but would a hundred-year-old man be familiar with it?

He must've seen the subtle wrinkle in my brow. "I'll admit, it took me way too long to destroy the demigod in level 15 before I figured out I had to use my green arrow to hit the—"

"Secret button to drop the floor."

Wow.

Only a legit player would know that. Game point. Max won my glowing endorsement.

"Oh, that's perfect." Mom flung her hands up as she returned to the kitchen. "Look at what I've invited into my home."

Max leaned forward, his elbows on his knees. "I'm stuck on level 33. It's a killer."

"I hated that level. *AA2* comes out in a month."

"I didn't even realize a sequel was coming. I'd better finish the first one soon. Let's fire it up after dinner. You can give me a couple of pointers." Max flashed me a huge smile. He knew he'd won me over.

"You're on." Mom had grounded me from the game after she caught me sneaking around behind her back. Of course, she didn't know I'd been saving the world from Ifrit. However, after issuing the original punishment of one month, she only enforced two weeks. Who was I to remind her?

Mom placed a colorful tray of cheese, crackers, olives, and salami on the table, then joined Max on the couch with her glass of wine. "Sorry, guys, we're not spending the evening staring at the television. Another time."

"Yes, ma'am." Max gave her a crooked grin, and she eyed him with fake scorn. As soon as dinner ended, I'd be excusing myself. I didn't need to witness all the flirting.

Dinner with Max flew by. Mom laughed way too much at every story he told. But they *were* funny. The two of them poked fun at Zia's Candles' manager, who Max knew from college. They discussed our neighborhood and a biography Mom finished last week about three first ladies in the White House. They tried to include me, but I contributed little to the conversation, which was fine. Max and Mom clicked.

Later that evening, I shook Max's hand—no longer sweaty—and he left after giving Mom a modest kiss.

She sniffed the flowers he brought and rearranged a few in the vase. "I'd say that earned an A-plus for a first meeting." She started stacking dishes and filled the sink with sudsy water.

"He's cool." I cleared the appetizer plates and glasses from the living room.

"I'll wash if you dry." Mom flipped the garbage disposal on.

"Sure."

Mom scrubbed each dish with a smile no one in the history of dishwashing ever wore. She handed me a dripping plate. "So you think he's okay?"

The plate clanked on top of the others in the cabinet as I put it away. "Yeah. I do. Very okay. The guy seems amazing."

She dropped the sponge into the soapy water, and a few random bubbles floated into the air. "He does, doesn't he?"

"That's awesome how he gets to travel to Germany for work. Maybe Zia's will send you to Europe when they expand there."

She laughed as she scrubbed a pot with the square sponge. "Let's not hold our breaths. I can't see jumping into international expansion. A second store in Chicago or Kansas City might make more sense first."

Our door buzzer rang.

"Who's coming by this late?" Mom flung the water

from her hands and checked her phone. "It's eight thirty. Did Max forget something?"

"I'll get it." I tossed the towel to the counter, but it slid off and piled on the floor.

I pressed the answer button. "Hello?"

"Bax?"

Mom's pasta sauce erupted from my stomach and into my throat. Scarlet. Static contaminated her voice. She'd never, in my entire lifetime, dropped by to visit me, announced or unannounced.

"Bax," she repeated, her tone changed from a question to a command.

"Um, yeah, hi."

"We need to talk. In person."

Only one thing could have prompted Scarlet Lane to visit me unannounced at eight thirty on a Monday night to *talk*.

So much for my djinn-free evening.

Chapter 6

Instead of inviting Scarlet upstairs and risking a million questions from Mom, I told her I'd be right down to let her in. Still flying on an emotional high, Mom barely paid attention when I said a friend stopped by, just telling me to be back by nine. The upside of only having two friends was that Mom never asked *who* when I said *friend*, assuming I meant Jason or Ashley.

Scarlet's red hair blew in front of her face before she tucked it behind her ear. The green scarf around her neck flapped across her jean jacket. She tore into me with the door half open. "I want answers, Bax."

I'd wanted to keep her out of the Djinn-verse, but in some ways, Ifrit had already wrapped her up in it. She just didn't know that, and it wasn't fair to leave her in the dark. With Ifrit back, she might be on his radar again.

Her emerald eyes glistened, shimmering with a mix of emotion and the biting cold. Her determined lips pressed together. I'd put her through enough.

"Let's talk on the roof. I'll tell you everything."

I held the door open for her, then escorted her to the elevator and pressed the button for ten. The doors squeaked closed with a tired BING, and the elevator rumbled upward. Her stare fixated on the dents in the elevator doors, sending a clear signal she wouldn't be into pleasantries, so we rode in silence.

The elevator creaked and squealed, and the chime at

each floor hit an original note, not by design, which was why I usually used the stairs. Not that I spent a ton of time on the roof. Our building's modest amenity was too hot or too cold for most of the year.

When the elevator lurched around the sixth floor, Scarlet shot me wide eyes. I responded with an awkward smile accompanied by a shrug. After the doors slid open on the tenth floor, she followed me down the hallway to the red door marked *EXIT*. I led her up the last set of stairs to the roof.

After the rickety confines of our elevator ride, I welcomed the chilly openness of the night. A few stars shone through the city lights above us, and the November breeze jumped the plexiglass walls, then swept across the rooftop, masking the street sounds below.

As I planned how and where to begin, her impatience beat me to it. "What is going on? I want to know, Bax, and you'll tell me. I'm done with your lies. A monster threatened me in my bedroom, and then I saw you talking to a different monster on Halloween *after* you said it was over."

I spoke to the asphalt under my tennis shoes. "He's not a monster. Well, not Janni, at least."

She crossed her arms and widened her stance. "Janni?"

After a deep breath, I unloaded everything. I told her about the old man and the ring and about Janni. I explained how we found Ifrit and how he read my mind and acted on my dark impulses, using his attack on Ashley's dad as an example. I described how we banished him after he'd sucked me into the vortex. After a solid ten minutes of rambling, I stopped.

The whipping wind and a few random pigeons

cooing nearby drowned out the other sounds on the roof. Scarlet stared at me, speechless and confused, while a strange relief washed over me. Confiding in her might have consequences, but I'd deal with the repercussions. No more secrets.

Scarlet opened her mouth a few times to speak, then closed it to rethink her response. She didn't doubt my insane story since she'd seen Ifrit and Janni, but when would she connect it to Nick? It turned out, moments later.

"And Nick? Ifrit…did that?"

The Moment of Truth. To explain Nick meant I'd have to say out loud what I'd never admitted to her: that I'd been crushing on her since middle school. She knew. She had to. Although maybe when you looked like Scarlet, guys harboring secret crushes were part of a typical day.

My mouth refused to open, locked shut with embarrassment.

Come on, Bax. Cross the finish line. Tell her.

I squared my shoulders and forced the words out, using every muscle in my body. "Ifrit knew my feelings for you from reading my thoughts. He knew I've liked you since we met in the fifth grade when you assured me that my first day at a new school would be fine. We walked to school every day that year when you still lived in my building. It felt like we'd always known each other and that I'd always attended Sparker Middle School. Since then, I've gotten to know you and…"

I shivered as if the wind ripped my clothes off, and I stood on the roof with Scarlet Lane staring at me in all my naked glory. I wanted her to say something, but she didn't. She didn't even blink. I fought the urge to run away, but I needed to finish.

"That's why Ifrit forced you to say you wanted to go out with me. To him, Nick represented an obstacle between us he wanted to eliminate. I never told Ifrit to do what he did. I never fantasized about Nick in a car accident or any other accident. Ifrit takes one subtle feeling lurking around in your brain, and *he* decides how to make it a reality."

Even though the winter wind bit, my cheeks warmed. My hands trembled in my coat pockets. The guilt and shame of acknowledging what I'd done caused the nightmares of the past few weeks to scream for attention in my memory. My stomach dropped as the car flipped. As the dashboard rammed downward, crushing Nick's legs. As the shards of glass shredded the skin of his face.

Why wasn't she saying anything?

Scarlet turned and walked to the other end of the roof. The pigeons remaining nearby flew off. Her silence killed me. She must've been deciding between laughing at my admission and crying about Nick, but each second without a response punched me in the gut.

I gave her space, using the time to get myself together. After a million-second minute, she returned. A line of wetness that streaked her cheek glimmered in the moonlight. "I wish you'd told me the truth from the beginning."

"That would have put you in danger. If Ifrit saw you as a threat, who knows what he'd have done?"

Scarlet rubbed her eyes as she shook her head. "I was already in danger. A scary demon appeared in my room and threatened to kill my family, Bax. By not telling me, you weren't saving me from anything. In fact, keeping me in the dark convinced me I'd lost my mind. Why not tell me about him after you banished him?"

I talked to my shoes. "I wish I could give you a better answer than being ashamed I summoned Ifrit into the world and embarrassed that when you figured out the connection, it would force me to admit…"

I couldn't repeat it. Once was all I could handle.

Scarlet sat, leaning back against a tall metal air vent. She sighed as she stared at the downtown skyscrapers in the distance. I wanted her to acknowledge my feelings about her, to say something like she'd suspected it or found it cute or creepy or something.

News about her boyfriend's death far outweighed my stupid crush, but she could at least address it. Give me closure so I didn't continue holding on to the tiny shred of hope she'd say she loved me, forgave me for Nick, and we'd spend the rest of our lives together.

But she ignored it.

"Then why did I see Janni if it's all over?"

I sat next to her. The warm metal against my back put me at ease. "Someone stole Ifrit's box."

Her head whipped around. "Someone has the evil djinn?"

"Someone stole it from my backpack yesterday. I had hoped Janni could help find it, but he couldn't."

"What are you gonna do?"

"Wait for weird stuff to happen, figure out who has it, and then try to steal it back."

"Flimsy plan."

I chuckled and rested my head back against the vent. "I'm open to ideas."

So that was it. My proclaimed love would go unaddressed. Although, not addressing it could be my answer to how she felt about me. She didn't need to say out loud she preferred her men to be a little more *football player* and a little less *video gamer*.

We sat in silence as the vent vibrated and the blower deep in my building rumbled to life.

"Scarlet?" I spoke with my eyes closed. "I am sorry about Nick and involving you in my mess. Ifrit hurt a lot of people because of me."

She didn't respond at first. Maybe she'd ignore it like she ignored my admission of being in love with her for my entire life.

"I believe you." The wind whisked away her muted words. "You couldn't control Ifrit. But I'm angry you didn't tell me, Bax. I felt so alone and scared."

When Jason and Ashley told me to stop contacting them, scared of what Ifrit might do to them the first time we tried to banish him, it created an intense loneliness and desperation in the pit of my stomach. I hadn't thought of how that isolation would feel to her.

Her soft hand landed on mine, sending chills up my arm. "At least now, I don't think I'm crazy. I'm not angry anymore. I'm tired of being angry."

Not the heartwarming forgiveness I'd hoped for, but I'd take it. "Well, if it's any—"

"Can I see Janni?" She removed her hand from mine.

"Huh?"

Her mood shifted. "I want to see him. I need to see him now that I know the entire story."

If that was all she needed, it was the least I could do. I dug the ring out of my pocket and held it out. She didn't touch it but examined it in my palm.

"So djinn live in Halloween costume jewelry and

busted-up boxes. I expected fancy, bejeweled lamps."

Our laughter lifted the emotional heaviness from the roof.

"Right? Okay, you ready?"

She smiled for the first time since arriving at my building, her anxiety dissolved. I loved her smile.

"Does he show up in a cloud of smoke?"

"Not exactly." I rubbed the ring. The jewel radiated, making Scarlet's fair skin appear purple. Even though the night wind blew its chill, the jewel's magic froze me with its tingling ice. I closed my eyes.

"Does it feel weird?" Scarlet noticed me shudder.

"For a second."

She stood. "Where is he?"

I joined her. "He never appears right in front of me."

"HOW CAN IT SERVE?" The breezy roof muffled Janni's shriek, but only a little.

Scarlet spotted him before I did. He waddled up to us.

"Wow." She squatted to his height. "What is he, a foot tall? He looked taller the other night."

Janni folded his arms and puffed out his chest, his purple eyes narrowed.

"Oh, I'm sorry." Scarlet giggled. "I didn't mean to offend you. Hi, Janni, I'm Scarlet."

Janni lowered his arms to his side and cocked his head. "THIS GIRL IS QUIETER THAN OTHER GIRL."

"Other girl?"

"Ashley Bryant freaks him out."

Scarlet giggled again. "Yeah. She can be a lot to handle." She reached out, her hand shaking a bit, and Janni extended his hand to meet hers, letting her stroke the white fur of his arm. As she petted him, he purred and closed his eyes.

Yeah, Janni, she has that effect on me, too.

"What kind of magic does he do?" She patted his head, scratching behind his ear like a dog. Janni groaned with satisfaction.

"He can turn invisible and record conversations. He teleports around. We call it jumping. I had him do dishes for me once, but it didn't end well. Oh, and he can show me things in my mind that he's seen."

"Record conversations? Have you used him to spy on people?"

I never spied on Scarlet but had come dangerously close. "We used him to get the answers to our history quiz but never read them. We wanted to test him out."

"So he could sneak a peek at the schedule for our *Scarlet Letter* presentations if you wanted him to." She didn't take her eyes off him.

Holy crap.

That'd be cheating, though. Wouldn't it?

Stop, Bax. No.

"In theory, yeah. I guess he could."

"Not saying we should. Just curious. Those types of things must be tempting when Janni's magic is at your fingertips."

If only she knew.

"SHALL IT GET *THE SCARLET LETTER* SCHEDULE?" Janni glanced at the sky and inhaled the night as if charting his course to Mrs. Macklind's classroom.

I paused longer than I should have. "No, Janni."

"I have so many questions." Scarlet stood. "What's in the ring? Is the space in the ring the same as the vortex? What were Nick's last thoughts...?" The mention of Nick's name doused her demeanor.

I could tell her his exact thoughts since I dreamed about it almost every night, but she didn't want to know. Not now. Maybe later. Or never. Sometimes, things should remain unknown.

"I appreciate your honesty, Bax. Finally. But I think I need a night to think."

"Sure."

I started following her to the stairwell door, but she stopped. "I can find my way out."

"Oh. Okay."

She smiled at me, but not her usual smile that sent warm vibes racing through me. I could only imagine everything she was processing.

The metal door clicked shut, and she was gone.

Jason and Ashley wouldn't have approved of telling Scarlet, but I had no choice. The truth gave her some peace.

My phone read nine o'clock. I needed to get back downstairs before Mom's love high wore off, and she realized I'd missed curfew.

Janni sat on the cold asphalt roof with his legs straight out in front of him, the soles of his feet facing me, and his hands folded in his lap. He didn't appear the least bit cold under his thick coat of fur.

"I think we're done, Janni."

"NO *SCARLET LETTER* SCHEDULE?"

As if taunting me, Janni triggered Scarlet's question to replay in my ears: *So he could sneak a peek at the schedule for our* Scarlet Letter *presentations if you wanted him to.*

I stared at him, unable to answer. No one would find

out. Besides, cheating meant getting the answers to a test. Finding out my date wasn't cheating. I still had to do the work. Plus, I had VS and might pass out in front of the class. Knowing the date would make it way less stressful, allowing me to focus my energy on the presentation instead of fighting off anxiety over thirty gazes glued to me, analyzing me.

My heart skipped. This wasn't like the history quiz Jason and I asked Janni to steal when we'd first met him—totally different.

"Go to Mrs. Macklind's classroom at Truman High and get the schedule." The commanding tone of my words startled me.

Janni scowled before he jumped.

It wasn't cheating. I repeated that phrase over and over to convince myself. It would help me deal with my VS. I had a medical condition and needed help. It was that simple.

My skin crawled. A medical condition? I'd never thought of my VS as a medical condition. A tiny voice in my head questioned my logic. My VS didn't interfere with my life other than the infrequent humiliating moment. Other people dealt with severe conditions that prevented them from—I shut it down. This wasn't cheating.

Janni reappeared with a piece of paper flapping in the wind. The exact form Mrs. Macklind waved in front of us in class.

The schedule.

He held it out to me in his pink hand.

I grabbed the list, not thinking anymore about it. While not perfect, I'd never stolen anything in my life. This wasn't stealing. Borrowing. Seeking help for my

VS. Even though my hand shook and the tiny voice in my head screamed for me to stop, I read it.

Baxter Allen—November 16th.

I folded the paper, not wanting to see where Scarlet or Jason landed on the list. *That* would be cheating. They didn't suffer from VS. They didn't need the help.

I threw the list back at Janni as if it'd caught fire. Luckily, he grabbed it before the wind whisked it away. "Put it back where you got it."

Janni scowled at my command, snagged the paper, and jumped.

Queasiness mulled in my gut. The tiny voice in my head fell silent.

Because I'd killed it.

Seeing the date of my presentation sure didn't feel like *help*.

Chapter 7

"Hey, Bax." Ashley shut her front door as I closed mine. She'd lived across the hall from me for years, but we'd never spontaneously run into each other in the hallway.

"Hey."

She slung her backpack over her shoulder, scrunched her face, then dropped her bag to the hallway's hardwood floor and patted it down. She mumbled something to herself.

"What's wrong?"

"Forgot my charger. Be right back." She trampled back inside, leaving her front door open. "Mom! I lost my freakin' charger."

I checked my phone; we had time. Once we started walking to school, I'd tell Ashley what happened with Scarlet. She and Jason wouldn't be crazy about letting Scarlet into our djinn situation, but she'd seen too much for me to keep denying it. They'd understand that.

What they wouldn't understand was how I broke our No Djinn Rule and summoned Janni without them to find out my presentation date. The anxiety over my presentation dissolved after I saw my date since I'd have time to prepare, but a pang of swelling guilt replaced it. Not sure which was worse.

Ashley's mom poked her head out of the doorway. "Hello, Baxter!"

Mrs. Bryant oozed happiness. Her curly brown hair matched Ashley's but with swirls of gray, and her round cheeks always seemed flush. Shorter and broader than Mom, Mrs. Bryant wore her pants super high. Jeans, dress slacks, it didn't matter. I even saw her in a suit once with her pants hiked up.

"Hi, Mrs. Bryant."

She cuddled her coffee cup with *I'm the cool parent* scrawled across it. "How's your mom?"

"Good. Busy. How's Mr. Bry—" The words dropped out of my mouth before I could swallow them. The harmless act of asking about someone's husband had a massive impact in this case. I'd been careful to avoid the topic since Ifrit attacked Mr. Bryant for questioning me about Nick's death. Mr. Bryant had survived—thank God—but with broken bones, internal bleeding, and a few missing teeth.

The nightmares about Mr. Bryant's attack were the most horrifying ones that haunted me. Every few nights, I'd be Mr. Bryant as Ifrit threw him down four flights of stairs at the police station. Submerged in his head, I'd feel bones break until the pain jolted me awake, sweating and shaking in bed.

Mrs. Bryant put a hand over her heart. "He's getting better every day. The guys at the station have been so kind. I can't think of a day when at least one hasn't stopped by. Oh, and that pie your mom brought over last week. If you ask me, she should quit her job and become a baker."

"Yeah, she's an excellent baker." I peeked over her shoulder and across the Bryants' living room. I spotted a foot in a cast at the end of a bed through the ajar bedroom door.

Mrs. Bryant followed my line of sight. "You should say hi. He'd love to see you. He's getting stir-crazy cooped up in this apartment all the time."

My stomach lurched into my throat. "Huh? *No!* I mean, no."

She stepped aside as if I hadn't responded, holding the door open with a broad, welcoming smile. "The doctors say he's in the home stretch, which means his mind doesn't want to lie in bed all day, even though his body isn't quite ready to return to his old routine. And I'll tell you a secret." She leaned closer, and the scent of cinnamon engulfed me. "I appreciate the visitors as much as he does. He's driving me nuts!"

"Oh my God, Mom! Where is it?" Ashley hollered from somewhere in their apartment. "I've been looking for about a hundred years! Did you take it?"

Mrs. Bryant walked away from the open door. "Why would I take it? Tom! Baxter Allen wants to say hi. Go on in, Bax."

Go on in? I wasn't prepared for that. I couldn't look him in the face after I caused his injuries. What if he could read the truth on my face? He had a long career as a detective. The city paid him to sniff out lies.

"Baxter? Send him in!" Mr. Bryant called from the bedroom.

Dammit.

Mrs. Bryant disappeared down the hall to help Ashley.

Like Mrs. Bryant's attire, their apartment's outdated décor didn't match Mr. or Mrs. Bryant's actual age. Knickknacks adorned every one of the ornate and numerous end tables, and the green and brown living room furniture and thick white curtains shrank the space.

The cinnamon scent on Mrs. Bryant wafted through the cluttered apartment.

The floorboards creaked under each step closer to Mr. Bryant's bedroom, and nervous anticipation swelled in my core. I didn't know what I'd say to him. *Sorry my djinn pretended to be a friend at work and tried to kill you* didn't feel appropriate.

I tapped the door open. Compared to the rest of the place, way less clutter littered the small room. Just a simple bed, walnut dresser, and two matching nightstands. When he saw me, Mr. Bryant turned off the TV on the dresser.

Blankets had been pulled up to his midsection, and one foot stuck out of the covers in a thick cast, toes exposed. I couldn't figure out how he got the white T-shirt on with both arms in casts. The bruises on his face had faded from what I saw in my nightmares, but white gauze covered his nose, and a few butterfly bandages held together cuts on his cheeks. My stomach did that thing when you were at the peak of a rollercoaster about to drop.

"Um, hi."

He smiled, exposing a chipped front tooth. "Hey, Bax. How are ya?"

I expected him jaded and bitter, not in positive spirits.

"I'm fine. How are you?" I boomeranged the stupid question back.

"Preparing to climb Mount Everest." He chuckled, then stopped himself with a wince. "Getting better every day, honestly. I think I'm losing one of these arm casts soon and will get a sling instead. Excellent news there. Oh, and your mom's pie. Man, you're a lucky guy."

I picked at my thumb cuticle, fidgeting. "How much longer until you're back on your feet?"

"Well, I can walk around now with only one leg in a cast. I'm slow going but getting faster. At least I can finally make it to the bathroom."

I glanced at his arms, both in casts, trying not to think about the logistics.

He grinned, reading my mind. "It's surprising what you can accomplish if you want to. Let me tell you, Baxter, there's nothing more important than a woman who will stick with you through something like this. Or a man. Whatever. A person who'll help you in ways you never thought you'd need—or want—help."

I didn't need that image in my brain.

"So you tripped?" I shouldn't know all the details. I should pretend I'd heard about his accident from Ashley, not by reliving it when I slept.

"Do me a solid, will you?" He nodded at the nightstand.

I picked up the water glass. "This?"

"Please."

I held the glass before him, and he sipped from the long yellow straw. He swallowed as I set it back. "Everyone keeps asking me what happened. Hell, I'd be asking myself. What you're looking at is a heck of a trip down the stairs. I swear someone pushed me, but my suspect was out to lunch with her girlfriends when I had my…accident. So yeah, I guess I tripped. Doctors think the fall jostled my brain and I imagined the details." He scowled. "That could be true, but no one *trips* down four flights."

"Bax?" I turned around. Ashley stood in the doorway holding her white tablet charger. "We're gonna be late."

"Right." My cheeks grew warm as if she'd caught me snooping through her stuff. She probably thought I had a lot of balls visiting the man I almost killed while acting like I didn't know what happened. I didn't want to see him. Ashley's mom forced me. I couldn't refuse.

"Thanks for stopping by, Baxter. Tell your mom hello."

"I will. Glad you're feeling better." I pushed around Ashley to get out of the Bryants' apartment as quick as possible and avoid Ashley's judgmental glare, no matter how justified.

In the hallway, Ashley called after me, "So what was that like?"

I sped ahead of her down the stairs. *What was that like?* She knew what it was like—horrible.

"Baxter!"

I jumped the stairs two at a time, skipping the broken one, and shoved open the door to the street. A guy in a charcoal suit ran into me. "Watch it!"

Ashley had every right to yell at me, but what did she expect me to do? Tell her mom I'd rather stand in the hallway than say hi to her injured dad? She had to have known the last thing I wanted to do was see her dad like that.

A car honked at someone nearby. I found myself almost at a run.

"Baxter!" Ashley sounded out of breath as she struggled to catch up with me.

I didn't want to see her face covered with disdain, thinking, *You have some nerve pretending to care about the guy you nearly killed.* And she'd be right. I had no right to visit him. God, I sucked.

Ashley grabbed my shoulder and spun me around. "Wait a minute, Baxter. Jesus!"

"What?" We were both panting. "I know I shouldn't have visited him, but what did you want me to do?"

All the pain I'd caused her dad crushed my insides. He'd been doing his job, and Ifrit attempted to murder him to protect me.

"Your mom cornered me into saying *hi*. I didn't want to. I swear. What do you think it was like? I didn't take some kind of sadistic pleasure in it." The words flew out as fast as I could say them to the door of Blaze Antiques. I couldn't look her in the eye.

"You need to slow down." Ashley brushed her thick hair behind her ear, exposing her smiley-face earrings. "I asked because I was legit concerned about how you were feeling about it. Was it weird to see you next to him? Yeah. But I can't imagine how you felt. Now I know, loud and clear. And yes, it would have been rude if you were at my place and didn't say anything to him."

My shoulders dropped. "I'm so, so, so sorry, Ashley. I'm sure you were thinking—"

"Stop it." Ashley stepped back. "Stop telling me how I feel, Baxter. This is about you. And I understand. What happened wasn't your fault. I've moved past it, and so should you. Beating yourself up for it all the time doesn't do any good. It's probably the source of your nightmare situation."

I let out a puff of air, still unable to meet her eye to eye. I didn't deserve her as a friend. "Okay."

"Now, let's get to school." She walked beside me as she changed the subject. "Last night, I researched how to locate a summoned djinn. Didn't turn up much. And by not much, I mean nothing. But when I searched *powerful djinn*, I found all kinds of stuff on Marids."

"New djinn?"

"The only kind more powerful than Ifrit. They're the worst of their kind. Where Ifrit is all smoke and fire, Marids are all water and air. They don't obey any master when released and do what they want. Their hobbies include torturing humans and tormenting other djinn."

"And you're saying?"

Ashley shrugged. "I didn't learn anything about our current Ifrit problem, but at least it isn't a Marid problem."

"Could be worse, I guess." My stomach grumbled as the smell of frying bacon rolled out of Kathy's Diner on our left. I'd forgotten to eat breakfast.

"So, um," I started, wanting to test her reaction, "Scarlet came by my place last night."

"What?" Ashley stopped walking, and a woman in a long coat, yelling at someone on her phone, brushed by us. She shot Ashley a grimace as she detoured.

"She demanded I tell her everything. Wouldn't take no for an answer."

Ashley raised an eyebrow. "Well, your cover story at West End Coffee won't win you any acting awards. Remind me to never ask you to fake an alibi. So, what happened?"

"I told her everything."

"Even about Nick?"

I nodded.

Ashley's stoic face didn't indicate any kind of adverse reaction to inviting Scarlet into the Djinn-verse. "And?"

"She was relieved she wasn't going insane."

Ashley started walking again, and I followed. She

74

scratched her head. "Does she know about our recent problem?"

"Yeah."

Ashley shrugged. "Well, maybe the more people on guard for weird stuff happening, the better. The internet produced a whopping fat nothing last night."

Interesting. She had a good point. I'd expected a more annoyed reaction from her over telling Scarlet. Maybe Jason would respond the same way.

"In other news, I keep seeing Ifrit."

"Again?"

"At school yesterday. And it felt real."

We rounded the corner to a crowd of kids on the sidewalk in front of Truman High, gathered under the three-story leafless maple tree.

"Jason thinks if someone stole the box from you, you may know them. And if that's true, you're in the thief's mind, which means you need to watch out for purple-eyed people. You could be Ifrit's next target."

"I hadn't thought about it like that. Wait, when did Jason say that?"

"Text last night." She bit her bottom lip and shifted in place. "I-I had a question about our Spanish test."

They had Spanish together, but as far as I knew, they never texted each other at night.

"What's going on here?" Ashley pointed to the cluster of people as she walked ahead.

The typical group of students milling around, stalling before entering school, seemed different. Students and teachers had their heads down, sullen. Someone in the center of the crowd spoke, but I couldn't make out the words.

Oh no.

Something had happened. Ifrit struck. He targeted someone at our school. Of course a stupid classmate stole the box.

I jogged past Ashley, closer to the crowd, straining to hear what the group discussed. Were they gathered around an injured student or a dead one?

Jason hovered on the edge of the group. I smacked his shoulder with the back of my hand as I whispered, "What's up? What happened? Did our friend do something?"

Jason smacked me back. "No. Relax. Dedication of a bench."

"A dedication?"

Principal Clark's voice weaved through the crowd. "With this bench, we will remember our classmate, friend, son, and brother with fondness and love. We will always keep Nick Ruiz in our hearts, minds, and prayers."

"A bench?" I whispered to Jason.

"Yeah. The stone one at the base of the stairs. They bolted a plaque on it."

The group fell into a moment of silence. I followed suit and hung my head. After a few seconds, the teachers and students gave sad, solemn applause. Nurse Masson and Mrs. Bronson whispered to each other as they walked up the stairs back into school.

As the crowd cleared, an older man and woman stood beside Mr. Clark. The woman cried, leaning her head on the shoulder of the man with bright blond hair and a perfect smile. Had to be Nick's parents.

Mr. Clark shook Mr. Ruiz's hand. Behind them, Scarlet dabbed her eyes with a tissue as she stared at the bench, Casey's arm around her waist.

Ashley leaned over to me. "Telling her the entire truth last night may not have been the best timing."

"Well, I didn't know about this." The dedication might have prompted her to confront me in search of answers. Hopefully, it didn't just make her feel worse.

"What happened last night?" Jason asked.

"Tell you in a sec."

I approached the bench as the crowd dispersed. It had always been an unremarkable stone bench few people used. For most of the year, the masonry cooked or radiated cold, making it a year-round uncomfortable place to sit. But its position next to the stairs leading to the main entrance of Truman High ensured it received its fair share of dings and chips as kids trampled by it. Now it'd be a memorial we'd pass daily for Truman High School's fallen hero. A shiny bronze plaque on its back with Nick's name, birthdate, and day of the accident shimmered in the sun. Beneath those facts, a quote read: "Always in our hearts."

Up ahead, Cassie escorted Scarlet into school as the two whispered to each other, holding hands. Neither saw me.

Jason tugged on my sleeve. "What happened with Scarlet last night?"

"She came by my place and demanded answers. I couldn't keep lying."

I waited for Jason's disapproval, but it didn't come. "How'd she take it? You told her the Nick part?"

"Yeah." We started up the stairs to the school's entrance. "She left a little in shock."

"I bet."

The bell rang as we entered school.

"Continue this later? I can't be late for first period."

Jason fist-bumped me.

"Sure. Good luck in Spanish. Ashley said you have a test you were helping her with last night." I couldn't help myself, wanting to see if Jason had the same sketchy reaction as Ashley.

Like her, he tensed for the briefest second, then changed the subject. "Thanks. See you at lunch. I want to hear more about the Scarlet stuff."

Chapter 8

"I'm home! You at work?" My voice echoed in my empty apartment. Mom always told me if she'd be around when I got home from school, but I never remembered, so she'd plaster a reminder note on the fridge door. I dropped my jacket and backpack, then went to grab an apple from the kitchen counter as I checked.

"Aunt Jo?"

"Baxter!" My aunt sprung from the kitchen table, arms outstretched, gold bracelets clanging against each other. It always amazed me how much she resembled Mom with the same brown eyes and freckled nose, only she kept her hair shorter, with just enough length to bob with every step. Her heels clicked on our dark gray linoleum as she hurried to greet me.

Aunt Jo squeezed me as she patted my back. Lavender—her trademark scent—enveloped me, reminding me of our holiday visits.

"What are you doing here? I thought you weren't coming in until Thanksgiving." Her shoulder muffled my words as she held me tight with her hand on the back of my head. A typical greeting from Aunt Jo included a good smothering.

She finally released me but held me at arm's length. Her gaze bounced over me, and she shook her head with a click of her tongue. "You've gotten so big and so handsome. Those shoulders! I bet the girls go crazy for you. Sara, when did he grow up, and why didn't you tell me?"

My face warmed, and I rolled my eyes with modest embarrassment. Aunt Jo possessed a superpower for making everyone feel like the most attractive, witty, and important person who ever walked the planet, and it never came across as phony or insincere. Mom said ever since she could talk, Aunt Jo had owned every room she entered.

"Why the surprise pre-Thanksgiving visit? Not that I'm complaining. Mom, did you—" Mom sat at the kitchen table with red and puffy eyes, an empty wine bottle, two full glasses, and a mountain of wadded-up tissues.

"Mom?" Panic swept over me, erasing the comfort of Aunt Jo's greeting. "What happened?" I could count on one hand the number of times I'd seen her cry. For real cry, not because of a sad movie or book or something.

Ifrit. Oh no.

Aunt Jo stepped aside as Mom hugged me. She squeezed me, but not as tight as her sister.

"You're worrying me, Mom."

When she let me go, she wiped her eyes with the sleeve of her white T-shirt and brushed her hair behind her ear. "Well, hon, the hotel laid me off."

At least it wasn't djinn-related. I masked my relief. "You've worked there for a hundred years."

"Ten years." She grabbed a tissue from the box on the table, turned her head, and blew her nose. She tossed the used tissue onto the pile with the others. "Mr. Amari said they cut staff across the board. I'll get a severance, but it's only a few months' salary."

Aunt Jo rested her right hand on my shoulder and her left on Mom's. The enormous diamond on her ring finger glimmered. Even without the sunlight streaming in, it would have been impossible to miss.

"I happened to call right after that asshole fired your mother. Since I'd just arrived at the airport on my way to New Orleans, I changed my flight and headed here instead. I still have to be in Louisiana by tomorrow night, but I figured you guys could use some extra love."

Even though Aunt Jo only visited around the holidays, she and Mom talked on the phone every few months. Mom said they used to be closer, but Aunt Jo lived in Chicago with a demanding job.

"You flew in at the last minute?"

"Honey, there's no way I'll ever use my frequent flyer miles even if I lived three lifetimes. Plus, when you travel as much as I do, the airline is very accommodating with last-minute itinerary changes. Your mom sounded so upset, and then she told me about those kids jumping you and your recent…episode at school. You two have had so much going on I felt it required a spontaneous visit. We'll still come back at Thanksgiving. Anita is excited to see you both."

Mom grabbed her sister's hand from her shoulder and clasped it. "I told Jo she overreacted."

Aunt Jo spun around and snagged her glass of wine from the table as she kicked off her brown high heels. "To be honest, Baxter, the real reason for my visit is because I want to hear everything about this new guy your mom is dating. She said you've met him, so I want the details she won't share. Spill the gossip!" She draped an arm over my shoulder and escorted me to the kitchen table.

The mention of Max's name created a reluctant smile on Mom's face. Aunt Jo always knew how to lighten the mood.

"I don't have anything negative to say. He's pretty cool."

Aunt Jo tapped one of her unchipped manicured nails on our chipped kitchen table. "Your mom paints him as a perfect picture."

I should have been comforting Mom, not engaging in girl talk about Max, but she enjoyed it, acting embarrassed but with a sheepish grin.

"I'd love to give you the dirt, but I didn't see any. At least not yet. I'm still waiting for the background check."

"Baxter!" Mom smacked my shoulder, then rinsed out her wineglass and filled it with water.

"I can't wait to meet him." Aunt Jo sipped her wine.

"Can we talk about something other than me?" Mom emptied the drying rack next to the sink, stacking the plates before storing them in the cabinet. "How's Anita?"

Aunt Jo leaned back in her chair, taking another drink of wine. "Fabulous. She's in Denver this week. Oh, get this, she wants to upgrade our apartment. Doesn't think our place works for us anymore. She wants something with more room if you can believe that. I disagree. I mean, we're never there with our work travel schedules, and we don't need more square feet. It's just more for our cleaning service. Unless you two ever visited, then we'd need a few extra bedrooms. Chicago is such an amazing city, Baxter. You'd love it."

We'd never visited Aunt Jo. She always came to St.

Louis. Mom never said it, but thanks to Ifrit, I knew we never visited because of Ben. A billion people lived in Chicago, but the idea of running into my dad terrified her.

Mom listened to her sister while her mind seemed to be processing other things. She'd probably cried all morning, though she'd never admit it. She always tried to be strong, even though sometimes, I wish she'd be herself.

The hotel had no reason to fire her. She never showed up late, and every time they called her to fill in for someone, she did. I'd never watched her do her job, but I could testify in court about her dedication. At least she still had her job at Zia's Candles.

"Listen to me rambling on and on." Aunt Jo got up from the table, wineglass stem balanced between her fingers. "Let's eat dinner out. My treat. How about that Mexican place you both love at the end of the block? Oh, those soft tacos. Nothing in Chicago comes close to those."

I glanced at my phone. "It's four o'clock."

"I'm so sorry, Bax." She frowned and plunked back down in her chair. Resting her elbows on the table and her chin in her hands, she stared at me. "If you have a schedule to adhere to, we can sit here and stare at the clock until you deem it an appropriate time to dine." Her mouth curled into a smile.

"Is it ever too early for chips and salsa?" I joked with a shrug.

"Now you're talking, Baxter. That's why you're my favorite nephew."

"I'm your only nephew."

Aunt Jo sprung up and tousled my hair. "So

intelligent, too! Can't get anything by you." She glanced down at her crimson blouse. "Let me freshen up real quick." Aunt Jo never needed to freshen up. She rolled out of bed dinner-ready, which drove Mom crazy.

"Josephine, don't freshen up, or I'll have to." Mom ran her hands over her white T-shirt, failing to brush out the stubborn wrinkles. "My eyes are puffy, my mascara is—"

"Stop it, Sara. Besides, what do you care? You've already landed Mr. Perfect." Aunt Jo wheeled her carry-on luggage into the bathroom. "Baxter, put on some tunes while we're getting ready. Pick something you're listening to. I like to keep up with trending music. It keeps me young."

After the bathroom door clicked closed, I turned to Mom. "I'm sorry. They suck."

"They do. I just needed to get out a few tears. Working at Hotel St. Louis wasn't a dream job or anything, but to pack up your things and leave in front of everyone stings—a lot. I'll find another job. There are hundreds of similar jobs around here."

I hugged her.

"Besides, catching up with Jo in person will be a nice break. I promise, one day of sulking, then I'll be good as new."

I grunted. "Take a week of sulking if you need it."

"Oh, Bax." Mom patted my shoulder. "Be a kid. Let me be the grown-up."

"Sara!" Jo hollered from the bathroom through the closed door. "Where's your hair dryer?"

"Hair dryer?" Mom rolled her eyes. "That's not freshening up!"

"I'll turn on the music."

****

An odor slunk into my nose, dragging me from the depths of dreamless sleep. It had a rich, charcoal-like quality, pungent and repulsive. The alarm in my brain buzzed me awake.

No, no, no!

I shot up in bed, eyes wide, searching the darkness. My blankets fell to my lap. The thundering of my heart pounded in my ears. I hated that familiar odor.

In the corner of my bedroom, blanketed in shadows, Ifrit's eyes glowed bright purple as if floating in the dark. The flicker of the flame in the back of his throat cast shadows, making his sharp teeth appear to quiver in his mouth. He stepped into my room and into the city lights from outside, filtered through my closed blinds, and his form solidified around his glowing eyes and mouth. He exhaled a puff of smoke as he lifted Janni by the neck.

The small furry djinn squirmed under Ifrit's flexed forearm and tense biceps. The short black hair on Ifrit's arm bristled in the darkness. Janni whined, his tiny pink hands tugging at Ifrit's hand around his neck, his ears flat against his head.

"Janni?"

"Hello again, Baxter Allen." Smoke swirled at Ifrit's hooved feet, catching the moonlight as it curled in on itself.

"How did you get to him?" I crawled to the end of my bed, wanting to save Janni but fearful any sudden action might cause Ifrit to flick his wrist and snap Janni's neck. "He's supposed to be safe from you in the vortex, and I didn't summon him to this world."

Ifrit's laugh gurgled from his chest before erupting from his mouth. "I waited hundreds of years to be free.

Now, twice in one month. I cannot recall having two masters in such a short period of time."

Janni's eyes glowed brighter than Ifrit's as he tried to break free, punching at the hand around his neck.

So someone summoned him, releasing him back into the world. His box wasn't lying dormant in a landfill somewhere.

Crap.

"Put Janni down. I'll do whatever you want." I swung my feet over the edge of my bed but stayed seated, wanting to avoid a defensive reaction from Ifrit. After everything Janni had done for me, including helping me escape the vortex, I couldn't allow anything to happen to him. Especially because helping me landed him atop Ifrit's Most Wanted list.

Ifrit extended his arm to the side to keep Janni out of my reach and leaned forward, his muzzle coming close. I held my ground, closing my eyes to protect them from the sear of his hot breath. A drop of his drool oozed onto my bare shoulder, warming my skin, but I fought the urge to flinch.

"You and the Janni banished me," he grumbled into my ear, "but this time, there is no moon to save you." He stood back up, puffing out his chest.

Janni's eyes glowed brighter, and he emitted another whimper as he struggled in Ifrit's clutch.

"You can't touch Janni when he sleeps inside the vortex. Those are the rules." I faced the demon, pretending I wore more intimidating clothes than just pajama pants. Reaching into a pile of laundry on the floor. I quickly pulled on a T-shirt with *Huh?* scrawled across the front. Not sure that strengthened my image, but I squared my shoulders anyway.

"Put him down. Right now."

With a flick of his wrist, Janni vanished.

I scanned the darkness. "Where'd he go? What did you do?"

Ifrit chuckled. "You always fall for my illusions, Baxter Allen."

I sighed with equal amounts of relief and irritation. "Who summoned you out of your box? Did the person who released you send you here?"

"No one sent me. I serve my new master, but I am here of my own volition. My new master inspires my actions as a master does, but I will always be connected to you. Whenever I am in this world, you will know it. I am a part of you for the rest of your mortal days."

I planted my bare feet and balled my hands into fists. "So you're taking a break from your new master to mess with me? Awesome."

"Although luck seems to favor you, Baxter Allen. I led you right into the clutches of your attacker in an empty room, and he did nothing. So disappointing."

"My attacker?" What was he talking about? "Oh, you mean Malcolm? So that was why you chased me into the locker room. You'd hoped he'd beat the crap out of me again."

"Human behavior confounds me."

I'd had enough. I needed answers. "Tell me who your new puppeteer is—the person you're serving."

Ifrit's head jerked toward my bedroom door. His purple eyes narrowed. "Josephine Allen hears us." He growled low like a threatened dog. "She comes."

"Aunt Jo? Leave her out of this." I moved between him and the door as if I could stop him from launching himself at her. "How do you know her name? Your master knows us?"

My door opened a few inches. "Bax?" Aunt Jo whispered through the crack. "Are you talking in your sleep?"

Oh no.

I spun to command Ifrit to leave, but he'd already vanished.

"Hold on!"

"Everything good in there, Baxter?" She kept her voice soft to avoid waking Mom.

I fanned the air in front of me with an old T-shirt from the floor, trying to dissipate his scent. No way it'd work quick enough. I was screwed.

"Shit." I flung the shirt around a few more times as the door opened farther.

"Baxter—"

Aunt Jo peered in from my doorway in a long green nightshirt and oversized pink glasses. She glanced at the shirt I'd been waving around. "What are you doing?"

I gave her an awkward smile, tossed the shirt into the corner, and dove under the covers. "Hi. Hey. What's up?"

She sniffed. "Your room reeks like—"

"What smell? What's up?"

Think, Bax, think.

As much as djinn entered and exited my life, I needed to invent a few solid alibis for their scent. No reason I should be scrambling every single time.

Aunt Jo examined my room, looking for anything awry. "My tiny bladder woke me up when I heard you talking in here. You sounded upset."

"No. A friend from school texted. He had a fight with his parents and wanted to talk."

Aunt Jo scowled. "It's two a.m. What kind of family fight happens at this hour?"

I scanned my dark room as if the damp towel on the floor from my shower or the old globe on my shelf would inspire an escape lie. "Truth is that my friend passed an impossible level in a video game and wanted to brag." I twirled my sheet in my hand, faking humility. "Let's not tell Mom. I'm not supposed to be on the phone this late."

With a raised eyebrow, Aunt Jo sat on the edge of my bed. "Video games at two a.m. on a school night? I'm not a parent, but don't you all have bedtimes or anything?"

"*You all*? We're not some kind of alien lifeform." I scratched my head and laughed. "Do you interact with any kids besides me?"

"Why would I subject myself to less interesting kids than you?"

"I'll go back to bed. I promise."

Aunt Jo brushed the hair off my forehead with two fingers. "I still don't quite understand how a call from a friend produced whatever that smell is. Your mom said you've had a rough couple of weeks."

"Yeah. Just a lot going on."

She watched me, her brown eyes magnified under her glasses. Without makeup, she looked even more like Mom. "Sara said things were back to normal, which is good."

"Yeah." I had hoped they stayed normal, too, but that wasn't in the cards.

Aunt Jo scanned my room. Her stare lingered on the lone trophy on my shelf from Little League soccer years ago. "She said she thought you were on drugs."

"Oh my God. I'm not on drugs."

She sniffed. "If you are, I've never smelled whatever is happening in here. And I've done my share of experimenting, believe me. Whatever's in here smells more like burnt skin. Oh Jesus, Baxter, you aren't burning yourself, are you? I saw a movie where this kid—"

"No!"

Her gaze dropped to my arms. "I mean, if it's something—"

"Stop it!" I held out my arms, rotated them, then lifted my shirt, flashing her my stomach. "See? All good."

I didn't need that idea floating around. Mrs. Bronson had enough on her plate with me. We didn't need to add self-harm to the list.

"Seriously, Aunt Jo, Jason texted me, then I opened the window, but the trash people hadn't taken the dumpsters away yet, so instead of letting in fresh air, I let in garbage air, which is what you're smelling. If you think it smells like burnt skin, then a serial killer must be using our dumpster to stash body parts."

After a pause and another sneak peek at my arms, Aunt Jo patted the comforter over my leg. "You sure you're okay? For real. You had your mom worried."

"She worries too much."

"She worries for both parents."

"Unnecessary." I scooted up against my headboard.

"But she does."

Both parents. I only had one and only wanted one. "Aunt Jo, did you know Ben?"

She shifted, tugging on her green nightshirt as if it began itching her skin. She and I never discussed Ben or why we never visited Chicago, but now that I knew the

90

truth, we didn't need to keep tiptoeing around the subject.

"Sara said she told you about Greg. Or rather, Ben. I still think of him with the fake name she gave him."

"The fake name didn't help. I found him anyway." Thanks to Ifrit.

"You were bound to somewhere along the line."

"Do you ever run into him in Chicago?"

"Of course not. Chicago's an enormous city."

"If she hid here, but you stayed in Chicago, did he ever confront you about where she'd gone?"

She paused, then shook her head. "No. But remember, I didn't know him that well. Your mom and I are four years apart. She married him and had you all while I was at Northwestern."

"I thought maybe if he was that mad she walked out on him, he might."

"Baxter, that was a long time ago. Ben's an abusive jerk, but he's not stupid. Confronting me would call attention to him. I'm sure he's moved on by now. I've been trying to convince your mom of that for years. No judgment from me, he was a bad guy, but this isn't a revenge movie. Ben's probably tormenting a new woman by now. God help her."

I wished I could believe Aunt Jo, but through Ifrit's eyes, I'd seen Ben practically salivate at the idea of finding us, even after all these years. I saw him pack his gun, ready to confront Mom. He still kept a picture of us in his wallet. Ben wasn't a typical deadbeat dirtbag. I bet he figured if he confronted Aunt Jo, she'd tip us off and force us deeper into hiding. He'd never let it go.

"I'm glad you stopped by for a visit." I rubbed my eyes, drowsy.

Aunt Jo tousled my hair, and we hugged.

"You get some sleep, Baxter. I hate that I have to leave already tomorrow, but New Orleans calls. I'll be back at Thanksgiving, though. Especially now. I think your mom needs family around. Plus, I want to meet Mr. Perfect." She winked.

"I'll see you before I leave for school, then?"

"Wouldn't miss it." She stood up and straightened the comforter where she'd been sitting. "'Nite."

Aunt Jo closed my door, submerging me back into the darkness of my room. I pulled the covers up, needing to sleep, but Ifrit's scent lingered in the air, and the shadowy image of him about to kill Janni burned in my mind.

Chapter 9

Truman High Commons, or as the students referred to it, THC, swarmed with kids lounging on clustered navy-blue couches, feet up, phones out, tablets on, and in rare cases, books opened. Sanctioned school signage and teachers refused to refer to the Commons as THC, keeping it a school mystery if the administration understood why freshmen always giggled the first time they heard the acronym.

Vending machines lined the west wall of THC, windows lined the east, and a coffee bar sat along the north wall—a generous Ruiz family donation. It consisted of a long counter with a neon-yellow lancer—my school's mascot—on its face, five coffeepots, stacks of paper cups and plastic lids, and rows of sugars, creamers, and tea bags on its top. A far cry from West End Coffee, but it'd become a welcome student body hub over the past three years.

Because it lived in a place called THC, a common theme ran through all the crazy concoctions students invented with the limited coffee supplies. Rob's Big Blunt consisted of half coffee, ten vanilla creamers, and two sweetener packets. Casey's Jolly Joint's recipe was coffee with four hazelnut creamers, one sweetener, and one sugar, just to name two customized drinks. Eddie's Edibles was this year's favorite. No one knew Eddie's recipe but him, and frankly, his drink had become the subject of more dares than enjoyment. Ashley tried it and claimed it contained more sugar than anything else.

The cushion swished as I plopped onto the couch across from Jason. Ashley shared Jason's couch but focused on her tablet as Jason skimmed his phone. When he heard me, Jason grabbed his tea.

"Got your text. They laid her off out of nowhere?"

I tossed my phone onto the table between the couches. "Yeah. She was so upset, my aunt detoured here on her way to New Orleans to cheer her up."

"I didn't know you had an aunt." Ashley shoved her tablet into her backpack.

"She lives in Chicago and is super cool." Jason met Aunt Jo once for a twenty-minute conversation, and from then on, he raved about her awesomeness. She made that kind of impression.

"Your mom will get another job for sure," Ashley said. "There are more freakin' hotels in this city than people."

"It still sucks."

Scarlet poured herself a coffee at the bar. Her fuzzy orange sweater's wide neckline exposed her left shoulder. Her girlfriends orbited her, all talking at once, with Casey's voice rising above the rest. Something about Brad Crafton. Casey always talked so fast that I could never tell by her tone if she was excited, annoyed, or angry.

I still couldn't believe Scarlet listened to me admit my crush, then never acknowledged it. But if she liked me back, she would have said so when I told her. That was the harsh truth, whether I wanted to admit it or not.

As the group of girls finished at the bar, drinks in hand, they moseyed around, searching for a cluster of couches to continue their discussion. Scarlet paused near us.

"I'll catch up." Her friends moved on, not missing a beat in their chatter, while she joined me on my couch. She crossed her legs at the ankles. "Hi, guys."

Ashley and Jason stared at her as if they were watching a cow driving a bus down Market Street. They both knew about Scarlet's visit to my apartment, but none of us—me included—expected our threesome to grow to a foursome.

"Um, hi?" I tried to hide my surprise and play it cool. Not sure if it worked.

"About Monday night." She shifted in her seat as her gaze darted around to see if anyone was watching. Then she leaned toward me. Her strawberry-scented shampoo tickled my nose. With each scoot of her jeans on the cushion, she narrowed the gap between us.

Was she closing in to discuss djinn or my vulnerable admission? I thought she would ignore everything I'd said about my crush, but maybe she needed time to think about it. It was a lot to process in the middle of all the djinn-Nick swirl. I had caught her way off guard. I shouldn't have expected much at that moment.

Her face drew closer, in extreme slow motion. The noise of THC faded into the background. Her pink lips, shining under the fluorescent lights, smiled with what appeared to be excitement, not a trace of anxiety over a djinn who could destroy humankind.

Holy shit.

She'd considered our conversation and wanted to proclaim her love in front of the entire student body. No way. That didn't happen in real life.

As I closed my eyes, waiting for her lips to graze

mine, she whispered, "Any progress on the…thing?"

She checked over my shoulder to ensure no one heard.

"Huh?" My face burned, my cheeks likely redder than the blood rushing underneath them. "You mean…" I swallowed my heart back into my chest.

Hopefully, Scarlet didn't notice what Jason and Ashley undoubtedly saw all over my face.

"The *thing*." She stressed the word with a giggle, oblivious to how I had interpreted her gesture. How many times did she need to make it clear she wasn't into me? I fell for it every time like a desperate idiot.

"Ifrit?" I didn't whisper back, and it came out too loud, considering how close she sat.

Scarlet nodded with eagerness. Her emerald eyes twinkled with the excitement of a kid about to open her birthday gifts. "Of course! There's nothing else in this world I'd call a thing more than that. I didn't want anyone to hear me mention it."

From the corner of my eye, Jason and Ashley watched Scarlet, not me. Maybe my reaction to her sitting so close wasn't as obvious as it felt.

I scooted away from Scarlet, needing some breathing room. "No. No ideas where to even start." I shrugged. "Dead end."

"Well, I want in. I've decided I want to help wipe it out."

"You *decided*?" Ashley's voice carried across THC, but in a school she'd attended for a year and a half, her voice garnered little attention anymore.

"Wipe it out?" Jason's eyebrows scrunched together.

"Yeah." Scarlet fiddled with her thin gold necklace,

sliding the charm back and forth on the chain. "I want to, you know, join the team. Fight the djinn. Be a djinn fighter."

Oh boy.

I shot Ashley and Jason a stern glare to let me handle Scarlet and I jumped in before they could react to her coining the phrase *djinn fighter*. "I don't think so."

Scarlet sat back against the blue cushions and folded her arms. "Why not? I want to be a djinn fighter."

Even though Ifrit killed her ex-boyfriend, and I'd told her about the other people he'd hurt, she somehow missed the life-or-death nature of our situation.

"Please stop saying djinn fighter, and Scarlet, this isn't some exciting game. He ruined my life and others' lives. He's dangerous. You, of all people, *know* that."

She unfolded her arms and leaned forward again, this time with an assertiveness I'd never seen from her. "I'm not stupid, Baxter. Believe me, I am very familiar with the damage he caused."

"And you still want in?" Jason couldn't remain silent. Volunteering to be a part of my dangerous mess seemed unfathomable to the three of us.

Scarlet ignored Jason, keeping her focus on me, unblinking. "I want closure. Complete closure. I want to know he's gone. Forever. I want to see him disintegrate, melt, or whatever he does when he dies. In fact, I want to kill him myself."

She wasn't in it for excitement. Scarlet Lane wanted revenge. I never expected telling her the truth would incite a burning vengeance.

Ashley leaned forward, elbows on her knees. "Just so you have all the information, we're flying blind, Scarlet. Meaning, we don't know how to banish him this time without the super blue blood moon. He will hurt people. If you pop up on his radar, he may attack you or someone you love."

"Yeah. Bax walked me through the collateral damage from last time."

I glanced at Jason and Ashley. She shrugged, speechless, and Jason stared at Scarlet as if she'd spawned a second head.

"Okay. You're in." I started the shit show, so if Scarlet needed to be involved to move forward with her life, then I'd give it to her. She understood the risks.

Scarlet clapped. "Super! What do we know? Catch me up."

She really needed to tone down the cheerleader enthusiasm.

"Well, right before you sat down, I was about to share the latest. Ifrit visited me last night. For real. No imagining. No vision. And we had a conversation."

"He what?" Jason and Ashley asked in unison.

"A conversation?" Jason added.

"He appeared in my room to scare me. He pretended to kill Janni, admitted he tried to force a confrontation with Malcolm that failed, and said we'd always be connected even though his new master inspires his actions."

"*Inspires* is a strange choice of word," Ashley said. "Interesting that's what he calls yanking thoughts out of people's minds."

"He even cracked a joke about how we didn't have moon power this time, so he'd be sticking around for a while."

"Did he say anything else?" Ashley started typing on her phone. "In particular, about his master's identity?"

"I tried to get him to tell me, but no go. Then my aunt interrupted because she heard me talking and he vanished. Although…"

"What?" all three asked at once.

"This is weird. He heard Aunt Jo coming before I did and said, 'Josephine Allen approaches.' He knew her name and didn't seem surprised she was there."

Jason scratched his cheek. "So that means his new master knows you and your aunt. We've had no indication Ifrit is an all-knowing spirit."

Ashley looked up from her phone. "So you've met whoever stole the box, but they don't seem to be out for you. Otherwise, Ifrit wouldn't be showing up to tease you or lead you into risky situations. He'd come straight after you.

"Good call." The crease in Jason's forehead popped out.

Ashley bit her lip as she thought. "I'm going out on a limb here, but is your mom's layoff at work connected? I mean, it could be someone who knows you and Aunt Jo and wanted your mom to lose her job. Ifrit doesn't always go for the kill. He's showed us he enjoys tormenting people in the past."

Jason fell back onto the blue couch. "You don't think it's Ben, do you? He has a vendetta against your mom and he'd know your Aunt Jo."

I willed myself to not throw up in the middle of THC. "But that would mean Ben came all the way here, waited for me to use the bathroom, and stole the box from my bag. No way he knew what that random, crusty box could do. He'd have gone for the apartment keys."

Ashley typed on her phone. "Let's see if Ben has a

police record in Illinois. We never followed up after Janni called the cops on him. Maybe we didn't throw him off your trail as well as we thought."

Scarlet shook her head. "You guys called the cops on a guy named Ben? I'm so confused."

Ashley didn't draw her attention from her phone. "Welcome to the group."

"I'll fill you in later." I shot Ashley a scolding glare she didn't see.

"Okay." Ashley read from her phone. "The State of Illinois charged Ben Allen with a class C felony for stealing copper piping from his job."

"Is that bad?" I sat forward.

"Reading as fast as I can…" Ashley flipped screens. "Wow. Class C could mean prison time. Damn. Stealing copper is a big freakin' deal. Turns out he got community control probation."

"Which is?" Jason read over Ashley's shoulder.

On her own phone, and not to be outdone, Scarlet beat her to it. "You wear an ankle bracelet and can't leave your neighborhood. And you definitely can't leave the state."

"Same as what I read," Ashley unnecessarily confirmed. "So Ben's stuck in Illinois."

"There's one other thing." I hesitated, formulating my thought.

Jason rubbed his head. "I literally just cringed when you said that."

"Remember when we were checking West End Coffee Halloween night for the box, and I did that double take at the guy leaving when we arrived?"

Jason nodded. "Kind of, yeah, like you recognized him."

"Turns out he's Warren's son. He came into town to help at the store. He looks like his dad, which caught my eye."

"Warren's son visited West End that night?" Jason grunted. "I mean, West End is close to Warren's Cosmos, so it wouldn't be unusual for someone to go to both places."

Ashley gasped. "I told you we shouldn't take Warren off the suspect list. You guys have talked about djinn under the guise of your little story since this all began. He knows all about Ifrit."

I shook my head. "Which means he also knows how dangerous Ifrit is. And he helped us banish him, or at least, gave us the idea for it. Look, I'm just telling you what I saw. I don't believe Warren convinced Scott djinn are real, then sent him after the box. It's too much. Besides, when I met Scott at Warren's, he didn't recognize me."

Jason nodded in agreement, Ashley scowled in disagreement, and Scarlet's gaze darted between us in confusion.

The bell rang.

As we stood up, Ashley said, "Okay, so it isn't Warren's son, and there's no way Ben can leave Illinois. We remain clueless about who stole the box."

"I'll swing by Warren's after school and see if I can learn more about Scott. Just to be sure."

Before Jason or Ashley could respond, Scarlet said, "Sounds like a plan," prompting Jason and Ashley to give her *Oh really?* sideways glances.

****

On my way home, I tightened my jacket as snow flurries started falling again. Time to break out the winter coat. I hated wearing coats, which drove Mom out of her mind. Sure, coats kept me warm, but at the expense of wearing chunky, bulky armor. Every fall, I put it off for as long as I could.

I inhaled, taking in the brisk air laced with car exhaust. The thief knew enough about the box to steal it, and he or she knew me well enough to stalk me, waiting to grab the artifact from my unsupervised backpack.

Scarlet? She'd met Ifrit, knew of our connection, and she happened to be near West End Coffee when she stumbled into Janni and us. But she also pledged to help us find the box instead of staying off our radar. That made no sense. We weren't begging her to join our squad or anything.

The green-and-white striped awning of Warren's Cosmos flapped in the breeze up ahead. Warren's story about playing poker against a Moroccan crime lord ranked as one of his best. Maybe Warren would share another epic tale while I tried to learn more about Scott. I agreed with Ashley it seemed suspicious he swooped into town when the box disappeared. I'd never seen him work at the store any other time. But that meant Warren conspired with him to steal it, which I couldn't believe.

The tiny silver bell jingled against the glass door, announcing my entrance.

"Hello, Bax—" Warren broke off into deep, chesty coughs.

"You feeling all right?" I passed through the aisles of comic books. A floor-to-ceiling picture of Purple Hawk hung on the far wall. She stood with a wide stance, face suspicious, watching me with her golden saber at the ready.

"Fine, fine." Warren sipped a glass of water. A few

drops dribbled down his chin's scruff and onto his black Ocean King T-shirt, but he didn't notice. The water splotch matched the growing sweat circles under his armpits, even though a chill hung in the store's air. Warren's skin looked pale, and a faint pink hue tinged his nose and ears.

I grabbed a pack of gum and slid it on the counter toward him, my new tradition that replaced comic book purchases. My dentist would be thrilled.

Warren cleared his throat before pounding a fist on his chest with a wince. "A little cold. Got it in the lungs. No fever, though, so I ain't contagious."

"That sucks."

Warren's son appeared from nowhere and cleared Warren's water glass. I eyed him as he honed in on our private conversation. Warren never needed help running his business. During store hours, he sat at his counter, a fixture to greet people and direct them to where they wanted to go. He manned the operation solo. Maybe as he grew older, he wanted to train Scott to take over the store, but that'd be decades away.

"Hey, Scott."

"Hey, Bax. I'll refill you, Pop." Scott's hair stood straight up—the mark of someone who compulsively dragged their hand through it—and his wire-rimmed glasses slid to the tip of his nose. He pushed them up.

"Thank you, son." Warren's gravelly voice sounded rocky. "We unpacked the new Ocean King issue today, Bax." He pounded the counter with the palm of his hand to emphasize his excitement. "Gonna be gone by tomorrow, I'm sure. Interested in one of the first copies?" He winked.

That was the guy I needed to see. The guy trying to

get me hooked again. "I told you, I'm done with comics. For a while, at least."

His shoulders jerked as he stifled a cough. "Why don't you give me an update on the djinn problem? The story, I mean."

Scott sauntered away at a slow pace—listening in?

"So you're staying with your dad?" I kept my voice casual as I changed the subject.

"Nah. His place is too small for guests. I'm at a hotel on the other side of town. At least for now. It's kind of a dump but cheap. If I end up staying much longer, I'm gonna upgrade."

"Where is your place, Warren?" I'd never asked him that.

Warren pointed to the ceiling. "Upstairs. When Scott relocated to Memphis, I realized I didn't need much space, so I moved into an apartment on the fourth floor. Pretty convenient commute, if you ask me."

Scott smiled with a shake of his head. "Not much space? It's barely bigger than a studio apartment, Dad."

"Well, when you and Cheryl make me some grandkids and come visit, I'll expand."

"We're working on it." Scott laughed as he grabbed his box and hauled it to a nearby shelf to unload it.

They didn't seem like a father-son team scheming to steal an ancient artifact. And Scott didn't seem interested in hearing me answer his dad's question about my djinn problem. Plus, with Scott staying at a hotel, it made sense that he might visit West End Coffee, a few blocks over, on his way back there.

"Anyhow, so about your story, Bax. I always appreciate a fantastical tale."

"We still can't find the box. My characters can't

figure out who stole it."

"No idea where to even start, eh?"

I shook my head. "No. Any suggestions?"

"Sorry, Bax. I'm no expert on djinn or thieves."

Warren's glassy eyes blinked several times as he cleared them. He didn't look well.

"You should take a sick day, Warren. Let Scott run the store so you can rest."

He waved his calloused hand. "Nonsense. Stop trying to escape. You haven't even paid for your gum. I can't give it to you for free every time, you know." He chuckled a deep rumble.

"Right. Sorry." I threw a few dollars onto the counter. Telling a story lit Warren up, so instead of running off, I decided to see if he wanted to talk. Maybe it'd help him feel better.

"Warren?"

"Yes, sir?"

"How did you lose your fingers?" I pointed to his right hand.

"Two stories in two days. May be a record." He held up his missing digits, wiggled them, then turned his head to cough. "You want to know? For real?"

I nodded with an eager smile, ready for a new tale. "I do. If you're up to it."

"Of course I am." His cracked lips spread into a grin, and he leaned back on his stool, which squealed under him. He opened his mouth to start, then stopped. After grinding his fingers on his chin's stubble, he smiled again, but more to himself than to me, and his eyes grew glassy again.

Something's going on with him.

For a minute, I thought he wouldn't say anything,

but then he did.

"I was around ten years old. So to you, a hundred years ago. I experienced some finger pain. Strange, huh?"

I nodded.

"Mother and Dad set up an appointment with Dr. Benson, our family's doctor. Dr. Benson ran all kinds of tests, favoring blood tests the most. That crazy doctor sucked all the blood out of me. Reminded me of the time the FBI exposed me to a horrible biotech weapon the government created."

"What?" I grinned, leaning forward on the counter.

"Haven't told you that one? Thought I had."

I shook my head.

"Another time. Anyway, back to Dr. Benson and my finger pain. Each needle prick filled a new vial. Dr. Benson must've taken a million vials of my blood, draining me faster than a ravenous vampire. A few weeks later, he called us back to his office."

He paused as if someone had frozen him in place, all except his fingers, which tapped the counter. His eyes stared through me.

"Warren?"

With a subtle shake of his head, he continued as if the pause never happened. "Mother cried the entire drive to Dr. Benson's office. She tended to be the more negative one in my family. I remember once I ran a slight fever, and my mother told everyone I'd contracted Hibernian fever despite Dr. Benson's diagnosis of a sinus infection. Mother had a dramatic way about her. Fortunately, my dad had the opposite disposition. He always told her to relax and that boys got sick—the natural order of life."

Something about Warren's serious tone changed the story's sentiment. His eyes didn't twinkle like they did right before the climactic punch line or twist. He must have been feeling horrible. Scott should've told him to stop working. Warren teetered on his stool as if on the verge of passing out.

"So we marched into Dr. Benson's office, and he cut to it, which he liked to do—a real straight shooter, which explained why Dad preferred him over other docs. He gave us the results of the tests. Turns out, I had lung cancer at ten years old."

He paused again, causing me to shift in place, waiting for the twist. I didn't want to disturb the zone Warren seemed to be in by saying anything.

"Anyway, lung cancer can sometimes spread to your fingers or toes. Dr. Benson put me through all kinds of treatment. He seemed to have a different treatment for every vial of blood he'd drawn. He poked and prodded and injected and radiated me. At the end of the process, I survived but lost part of my lung and these two fingers."

He wiggled his missing digits as if I needed a reminder.

I waited for how his treatment helped cure his type of lung cancer. Or how he received the first robot lung. Or how Dr. Benson grew his removed fingers into new creatures. Something.

But all Warren did was wipe his red, watery eyes. Story over.

"I-is that true?" My voice came out in a whisper.

Warren straightened in his chair and forced a smile. He grunted. "I've never lied to you, Bax."

"Warren, I…"

Scott set a fresh glass of ice water on the counter.

"Dad, I think it's time for a break. I'll watch the store."

Warren didn't argue. "Fair enough." He put a hand next to his mouth as if telling me a secret, even though Scott stood beside him. "This one is a mother hen, always picking, picking, picking. Always going on about my hydration and rest."

"Someone has to." Scott gave his dad a warm smile, took his forearm, and helped him off his stool.

"Have a good one, Bax." Warren let his son guide him as he lumbered into the back room of Warren's Cosmos.

I watched the storage room door swing shut, wondering what had just happened. I waited to ask Scott if Warren was okay, but he never returned. After a few minutes, I scooted the gum and my money closer to the register—I didn't want either—and tried to ignore the avocado-sized knot in my stomach.

Chapter 10

Jo's phone vibrated on the white marble bar top, scooting a few inches. She flipped it over to read the text.

—Plane leave yet?—

Jo smiled at her fiancée's need to stay atop of both their travel schedules. Instead of returning a text, she called Anita, who answered before the first ring finished.

"*Hola, mi amor.*" The sound of Anita's voice relaxed every muscle. She hated when long periods passed without seeing each other, but the life of a cochlear implant regional sales vice president required lots of airplane time. Airplane time which paid for their apartment on Michigan Avenue.

"Hi, babe."

"You're still in St. Louis? Did your flight get delayed?"

"Yeah. Storm near New Orleans. The airline hasn't canceled yet, so that's positive. I'm killing time at the bar." As Jo swirled her glass of cheap white wine, she caught a man in a designer suit a few stools over checking her out. He wore a smug grin and nodded when their gazes met.

Smooth, dude.

"I think a guy is about to hit on me," Jo mumbled into the phone as she turned away.

"You are a committed woman!" Anita feigned anger.

"Well, I don't wear my ring when I travel." Jo stared at the four-carat engagement ring on her finger. "I like to see if I still have it. See if I can attract that exclusive airport bar tail."

Anita laughed and then clicked her tongue. "Trust me, you still got it."

"I miss you." Jo frowned, even though Anita couldn't see her.

"I miss you, too."

Someone kicked up the seventies rock on the bar speakers as the bartender signaled to Jo's half-eaten club sandwich. Jo waved for him to take it away and gave him a thank-you smile. "When do you head to New York?"

"In a few. I'm packing up now. How's Sara?"

Jo examined her nails, noticing another chipped one. It must've happened in the security line.

"She's upset. Glad I detoured. I think it meant as much to her as it did to me. Girl, Bax is all grown up. We need to visit more often. He's a man all of the sudden."

Something shuffled in the phone's earpiece. Anita must've dropped it. "Sorry. Back. You know I adore Sara and Bax, but we only get to see each other a few days a week. I don't want to share our precious time with your sister and nephew."

"Two more years."

"That's the plan."

Their engagement agreement: Jo would retire after two years of saving money. Anita would keep working since she earned more as a district president. They'd adopt a kid—a girl—and Jo would be a stay-at-home mom. Anita wanted a bigger apartment, but she wanted a house out in the suburbs. Naperville, maybe. She suggested moving to St. Louis to be closer to Sara and

Bax, but as much as Anita loved them, she'd never leave Chicago.

A stay-at-home mom. Not where Jo envisioned she'd be ten years ago. Hell, not where she thought she'd be five years ago, but the idea excited her. She'd had enough airport life and hotel stays, even if she may not quite be ready for book clubs and carpools.

"Well, I need to use the restroom before they call my flight. Love you."

"Okay. Love you, too." Anita hung up.

Jo waved to the bartender for her check. The man from down the bar had slid closer when she'd looked away, sitting two stools from her. Not too invasive, but enough to send a signal. He had thick hair swept to the side, a dark shadow accentuating his jaw, and perfect eyebrows. Even though she hadn't dated a man in ten years, she knew better than to trust a guy with perfect eyebrows. Trimmed well and without those weird curly hairs—a good sign. That meant he took care of himself. But each hair the same precise length, both eyebrows mirror images, and the ever-so-slightest traces of eyebrow coloring? Run away, run very far away.

"Work or pleasure?" He grinned, showing his glowing white teeth. Too white for her taste.

God, no wonder she preferred women; she nitpicked men to death.

Jo shot him a hurried but annoyed grin. "Work. But detoured for a personal visit."

"Ah. This is home for me. Off to Albuquerque in an hour. Allow me to buy you a drink."

She glanced at her phone to check the time. "I appreciate the gesture, but I'm engaged." She flashed him her ring.

"I'm already married." He showed her his platinum band. "Let me rephrase my offer. Can Reed Investments buy you a drink?" He slid a pamphlet toward her.

He wasn't hitting on her after all. Maybe she didn't still have it—that was disappointing.

She had no desire to sit through a pitch. "Look, you seem like a nice guy—"

"Let me get to it. I'm not trying to irritate you or pick you up. Do you work with a financial advisor for your personal investments?"

"We're doing this at an airport bar?"

He laughed again. "You are no-nonsense, I can tell."

Jo fought back an eye roll. She led a team of sales reps and understood the courage needed to sell to strangers, but she also learned and coached her team to read the potential client and estimate if they had a shot or were wasting everyone's time.

He kept at it. "How about we talk, and then I set up an hour with you and your fiancée?"

"I don't live here. I live in Chicago."

"With technology, location is irrelevant."

"My fiancée handles our finances, and she's happy with our person."

"Let me buy you one drink. Then, if you don't like my pitch, we'll shake hands and part ways. You can keep the drink." He flashed his white teeth again.

She checked the airline app on her phone. Another thirty-minute flight delay. She had time. "As long as you understand the odds of this leading to a sale for you are nonexistent."

"I appreciate your honesty. I'll consider it practice."

Jo sighed. "Chardonnay."

The man signaled to the bartender, who rinsed off a

glass and filled it from an opened bottle.

"I'm Parker. Parker Lewis from Reed Investments." They shook hands. "I started Reed Investments with a few friends after graduating from college. We've been serving high net worth clients for over twenty years—"

"How do you know I'm high net worth?" She sipped her wine.

He smiled as his gaze flickered to the luggage near her barstool. "I can spot a seven-hundred-dollar bag when I see it. My wife has a similar one."

Damn.

Bags were her guilty indulgence. She didn't need a seven-hundred-dollar bag but had to have it.

He didn't pause, diving into his story and business. Jo remained polite, nursing her wine. She hated everything about finance. Didn't understand it. That was why Anita handled all of it. She didn't even know how much they paid in rent. She should be more involved, but Anita made it easy to opt out.

Nearby, an older woman stuck her hand against the grated door of an animal transporter underneath her table. A tiny tongue lapped at the woman's fingers. Dog? Cat? She couldn't tell. She and Anita should adopt a cat. With their travel schedules, a dog wouldn't work, but a cat might.

Shit. Don't be impolite. Focus, Jo.

She redirected her attention to Parker, who continued to drone on and on and didn't seem to notice she'd zoned out.

"—so we leverage industrial-scale, conservative investments, with a smattering of riskier global options."

Did he just use the word smattering in a sales pitch?

Her phone vibrated.

Thank God.

"Hold on a sec." She held up a finger to pause him, picked up her phone, and turned away to answer it, pivoting on the stool. "Hi, Sara. Everything okay?" She stepped away from the bar to hover over an empty table nearby.

"Figured you'd be on the plane already, so planned on leaving you a voicemail."

"Delayed another thirty minutes. Gotta love New Orleans weather."

Sara chuckled. "I just wanted to say thank you for coming by. I enjoyed the spontaneous, in-person catch-up."

Jo fiddled with the salt shaker on the table, aligning it with the pepper. "I told Anita the same thing. It's getting too long between visits."

"You're still coming to town for Thanksgiving?"

"Wouldn't miss it. Anita's coming, too."

"Perfect!"

Jo paused. She'd wanted to bring up her conversation with Bax during her visit, but never found the right time. He finally knew the truth about Ben and would love Chicago. Sara needed to live her life again, free from fear of her dickhead ex-husband. Although legally, the two were still married.

"You know, you're always welcome in Chicago. It's magical during the holidays. We could window shop and see the sights. Bax would love Field Museum. We could ice skate…"

Silence.

"It's been a long time, Sara. Chicago's a massive city. The odds of running into Ben are slim. I've said it before, and I'll say it again, he's moved on. He was an asshole, but not a deranged psycho. There's nothing to worry about."

Silence.

Did she hang up?

"I know," Sara muttered.

Way to go, Jo.

She'd ended their delightful visit on a down note.

"Sara, I love you. Whatever you're comfortable with, I'll support that decision. No pressure. But if things keep progressing with Max, you'll want to cut ties and live in the now." She drummed her nails on the tabletop.

Sara let out an enormous sigh. "I've been thinking about calling a lawyer to see what kind of divorce options I have."

"You have? You didn't tell me that!"

"Because I knew you'd flip out and ask me for daily updates."

"I'd be doing it out of love."

"I want to do this at my speed."

"Fair enough. Take your time. Chicago will be there for the foreseeable future."

"You're at the airport, so I won't keep you, Jo. I just wanted to say I appreciated the visit."

"Well,"—Jo turned her head away—"you're not bothering me at all. I'm getting a sales pitch for financial services at the bar by a big fat douchebag."

Sara chuckled. "Uh, he obviously doesn't know you. You don't even know how much a gallon of milk costs."

"Shut up!" Jo laughed. "But you're right. I'm guessing five cents? Talk soon."

"Love ya."

Jo hung up and returned to the bar, grateful her call ended on an upbeat tone.

Parker remained smiling as if he'd paused his face when she stepped away. "Everything okay?"

"Yeah." She shoved her phone into her purse. "I'm sorry, but I should go. I need to visit the ladies' room before we board."

Parker raised his hands in an admission of defeat. "I gave it a shot."

"Let me buy my wine. You didn't even finish your pitch." She dug into her bag for her wallet.

"Don't be silly. How about this, you give my card to your fiancée and I'll buy the drinks?"

"Deal." They shook hands.

She swallowed the last of her wine in two gulps.

Jo clutched her bag under her arm and extended the carry-on handle, wheeling it behind and out of the bar. A woman's voice over the loudspeaker announced the last call for Aero France, Flight 279 to Paris.

Jo spent too much time at airports around the country, but no matter where, all airport pedestrians traveled at two speeds: meandering or sprinting. And the sprinters always dragged too much luggage and too many kids behind them as they barreled through the terminal. That'd be her one day. Too much baggage, kids, and a cat carrier.

She cut across to the bathroom, avoiding a collision with a man jogging by with two pumpkin seats swinging at his side. As the man passed her, his wake created a tidal wave of lightheadedness that washed over Jo, causing the floor to sway like a boat deck. She gripped the handle of her carry-on to steady herself.

Strange.

With a deep breath, she pushed forward toward the bathroom.

The dizziness lingered. The chatter, airport announcements, and clanging of the nearby coffee vendor became distant, then near, then distant again, as if someone was adjusting the volume of her surroundings, making them loud, then muted, then loud again. She stopped to collect herself.

The women's restroom to her right jumped farther away, across a vast expanse of travelers bustling in both directions.

Focus, Jo.

She'd drunk three glasses of wine in an hour and a half, not enough to make her so tipsy. She'd splash some water on her face and regroup. Jo tripped on her heel as she crossed the threshold into the bathroom, recovering before completely falling.

Bleach and lemons overpowered the air in the bathroom, and the silence boomed in her ears. She dropped her carry-on, which toppled over onto the black-and-white tiled floor with a thud. She leaned on her palms, resting on the chilly porcelain of the sink as the room swayed around her.

Jo stared at her reflection in the mirror, trying to focus on her image to anchor herself. Her face blurred and then sharpened. She touched her cheeks, but her fingers were numb on her face, even when she dug her nails into her skin.

She needed to call for help but couldn't quite remember how to speak.

Leave the bathroom, Jo.

She needed to pass out where people could see her and call for help. She readied herself to push off the sink and stumble back into the terminal walkway, checking the doorway in the mirror.

Yellow tape crisscrossed over the bathroom's entrance. She squinted to read the black letters forming a pattern on the tape. *CLOSED FOR CLEANING.*

What?

She'd just walked through the doorway. Even if she somehow had broken through the tape, someone re-taped it since she'd been inside? How long had she been in the restroom?

Steadying herself on the sink again, she stretched toward her purse to get her phone. She closed her eyes, afraid the checkered floor tiling would induce a fresh bout of dizziness. If she released the sink from her grip, she knew she would never get back up.

She couldn't reach her purse.

New plan.

She'd break through the cleaning tape and pass out in the terminal. It was just tape. Then, someone would see her and get help. She just needed to make it through the bathroom's entrance.

Focus.

She'd burst through the tape like a marathon winner. First place! She snickered. Hilarious.

Her eyelids became steel covers she fought to keep open, her legs melted, and the room rocked like a raft in a hurricane. She stumbled away from the sink, losing her steadying grip. Two steps backward toward the stall. She held her arms out like an acrobat on a tightrope, struggling to keep her balance.

Hands grabbed her underneath her arms, preventing her fall. She threw her head to the side, no longer controlling her neck muscles. Him. Parker Lewis with perfect eyebrows.

When did he slip into the women's restroom?

And his eyes…purple?

Losing her ability to stand, Jo collapsed into his arms, but instead of laying her down, Parker used the momentum from the catch and sprang her back up, tossing her forward toward the sink she'd been clutching seconds before.

Unable to use her muscles, she watched the sink's hard edge coming closer and closer until her head cracked against the porcelain.

****

"Bax! Wake up!" Mom shook me.

I opened my eyes. "Mom?"

Tangled hair hung over her pale face. She gripped her phone in her left hand.

"What's wrong?" I didn't need her to answer. Images from the dream lingered in my mind.

"I'm running to the hospital. Aunt Jo had an accident at the airport. She passed out and hit her head. She's at St. Bernard's."

"Let me get dressed." I untangled my legs from the covers.

"No, hon. You have school. I'll text you when I learn more. They're not allowing visitors yet, but I need to be there when they do."

"Um, okay." I rubbed my eyes. "Is it serious?"

Mom turned away, tugging on her shoes as she leaned against the wall. "I'm sure she'll be fine. They're running tests."

I wiped the gunk from the corners of my eyes. Ifrit would only attack Aunt Jo if his master wanted to punish Mom or me, but which of us? That answer would be a clue to the thief's identity.

We had to figure out who Ifrit was working for—soon.

Chapter 11

"It's all a bunch of bullshit," Calvin Wolk said as he texted on his phone. We were supposed to be discussing *The Scarlet Letter* in small groups, but as soon as we circled up our desks, two of my three discussion partners began doing other things.

"You'd better not let Mrs. Macklind catch you on your phone." Ellie filed her nails, not paying any more attention to our assignment than Calvin despite lecturing him.

Jason attempted to keep us on task. "Are you saying this assignment is bullshit or something on your phone is?"

Calvin dropped his phone onto the desk and blew his long hair out of his eyes, irritated at the interruption. "Both. What are we doing?"

Jason tensed, having no tolerance for kids who didn't take school seriously, especially when it impacted him. "We're supposed to be talking about the themes we're considering for our presentations."

Ellie jumped in, suddenly engaged in the discussion. "My theme is how the town treats Hester like a slut while respecting her baby daddy. Why? Because he's a man. Guys are playboys and girls are sluts. It's a pathetic theme as old as time."

Jason typed a note on his laptop. "So your presentation is how the people of Salem treated men and women differently for the same offense?"

"Obviously." Ellie returned to examining her nails, admiring her work. "I mean, that's the number one theme, right?"

"How's it going?" Mrs. Macklind stood outside our small circle of desks. Calvin slid his phone under his tablet and Ellie dropped her nail file to her lap.

Jason answered on our behalf. "We're discussing how the town treats Hester like a pariah and reveres Dimmesdale because he's a pastor, even though they both had the affair."

Mrs. Macklind nodded, folding her hands behind her back. "That is true. But in the town's defense, they didn't know about Dimmesdale's involvement. A related question you could discuss is how did Hester and Dimmesdale cope with the town's treatment of them?"

Mrs. Macklind's amber eyes locked on me, causing me to shift in my chair. I'd been unable to make eye contact with her since I'd peeked at the presentation schedule. "Um, well, in the book, Dimmesdale's guilt ultimately killed him because he kept his love a secret. He couldn't handle it. Hester wore her red *A* with a sense of pride."

"Pride or responsibility for her wrongdoing?" She rested a hand on my shoulder, drawing the jealous gazes of both Calvin and Jason but making me shudder under her touch. Janni must've not replaced the list in the same spot, and she noticed. Had she figured out what I'd done?

"Is it better to own your choices with everyone hating you or hide your mistakes and allow people to revere you?" She drummed her fingers on my shoulder.

"Hester doesn't have a choice. I mean, she can't hide a daughter." Ellie fiddled with her novel's worn cover.

Mrs. Macklind patted my shoulder and withdrew her hand. "See how the themes build on each other? Isn't it fascinating?"

Not sure I'd considered that *fascinating*.

She proceeded to the next group, closing with, "Keep up the robust discussion."

Knowing I wouldn't present next Tuesday didn't relieve any of the swelling guilt every time I sat in American Literature, although I appreciated having the additional time. I had more pressing issues than worrying about two Puritans who couldn't keep their hands to themselves back in Salem a few hundred years ago.

Jason's phone vibrated in his bag. In a very un-Jason-like move, he checked it while Mrs. Macklind talked with the group next to us. The crease on his forehead exploded, spreading like cracks from an earthquake.

"What's wrong?"

After making sure Calvin and Ellie weren't paying attention, Jason leaned over and whispered, "Remember Dr. Bashir? The professor my dad works with who helped us translate Ifrit's incantation?"

I nodded.

Jason started to elaborate but noticed Calvin watching us with a curious eyebrow raised. He grabbed my sleeve and tugged me out of my desk. We stepped away from our study group.

"Dad says Bashir is asking where we found the picture of the incantation. Someone discovered an artifact with a similar inscription, seven lines long, so he thinks there may be a connection."

"Are you kidding me?" I lowered my voice before continuing. "Another incantation? We don't need this right now. Tell your dad to tell Bashir not to rub any purple jewels. No, don't rub *any* jewels. No, wait, don't touch the thing at all."

"How do I explain that?"

Right, it sounded suspicious. "Okay, this doesn't mean there's another djinn. Sumerian is an ancient language. I'm sure a Sumerian person scribbled a seven-line poem unrelated to djinn at some point in history. The poem Bashir found could be about a breakup, unrequited love, nature, or something else poem-ish."

Mrs. Macklind called to us from across the room. "Mr. Allen and Mr. Franklin, does everyone in your group have their themes worked out?"

The world couldn't handle two djinn. It sure as hell didn't need a third. We needed to learn what Bashir discovered and warn him not to unleash anything. But how did we do that without revealing our current situation?

"Let's get the details before we panic." We slunk back into our chairs. "Lunch is in fifteen. Let's call your dad and find out what Bashir knows."

****

Despite my stomach roaring with hunger, we skipped lunch. We needed privacy—as much as possible during a high school lunch period—so we met at the curb in front of school. The ground froze my ass, but neither of us wanted to use Nick's memorial bench. In fact, no one had used it since the dedication. It felt like sitting on a gravestone.

"I can't believe Ifrit attacked Aunt Jo." Jason retracted his hands into the sleeves of his baggy red sweatshirt. "Glad she's okay."

"Me too. Mom said she whacked her head on the

sink several times, so she's in a lot of pain but will heal. I'm gonna visit her after school and see what she remembers. Maybe she noticed something I didn't that'll give us a clue about Ifrit's new master."

"Let's hope."

"Right now, let's figure out this thing with your dad and Bashir. Call him."

"I'm not sure what to say."

While I never thought fast on my feet, Jason might be the worst liar in the history of lying. He'd get so nervous he couldn't spit out the right words, or he'd fumble them into complete nonsense. Once, his mom asked if we'd eaten two cupcakes she'd baked for Michelle's birthday. Jason, with a deadpan, straight face, responded, "Us? No. Why would we? I think her birthday ate them."

"Take a deep breath and focus, bro. Let's strategize before you call your dad. Ask him questions to learn what you can about Bashir's discovery. You're into academic stuff. Just be interested in the artifact. Then, when he asks about your project, tell him we found the picture online from a museum, and you can't remember which one."

Jason shook his head. "He'll ask me to check my citation on the reference page."

I rolled my eyes. "Only your dad, the professor, would ask that."

"I'm not wrong."

I started typing on my phone and scanned the screen. We needed a decoy museum. Somewhere to point his dad and Bashir. "Here. We found the pic at the *Museo Nacional de Antropología*. It's the national museum of Mexico."

"Why there?"

"Because it has a butt load of artifacts. And if it's in a different country, it'll be harder for your dad or Bashir to hunt down information."

Jason glanced at my phone to read my screen. "Man, djinn have made you a smooth liar."

"Thank you, I think? Let's get this over with."

Jason dialed his dad and hit the speaker button.

Dr. Franklin answered on the second ring. "Hey, Jason. You got my text?"

"Yeah."

"So Dr. Bashir called me. He's the professor who helped you and Bax translate—"

"Yeah, yeah. I know."

I motioned for Jason to keep calm and stay focused. He brushed me off.

"Anyway, he said a colleague found an artifact at a dig in Minnesota with markings very similar to the Sumerian text Bax shared with him."

"Weird."

"Or kinda cool. This is an ancient text. And a Sumerian artifact in North America is unprecedented. Dr. Bashir said this discovery's inscription contains the same pattern and line count, so he thinks they're part of a larger story or book of poems."

"What does he need from me? From us?"

I put a hand up to remind Jason to calm down again.

"He wants to find out where your poem originated and see if there's a connection. He still has a copy but said Bax told him you'd downloaded the picture from a museum somewhere, so he wants to examine the source records."

I held up my phone so Jason could read the name.

"Oh, okay. We found our poem on the *Museo Nacional de Antropología* website."

"Is that in Spain?"

"Mexico."

"Excellent. He'll be thrilled. What a discovery. What if you and Bax helped assemble a book of prayers thousands of years old?"

"That would be so super cool." Jason couldn't have sounded less impressed.

"All right. I'll let you get back to school. Thanks, son."

"Bye, Dad." Jason hung up. "Shit. An archeologist found another djinn."

I stood up, needing to warm up from the frozen ground. "We don't know for sure. Your dad didn't mention a purple jewel."

Jason stood and brushed off his pants. "He has an item with a seven-line Sumerian poem on it. Why didn't I ask him to describe the item? Dammit!"

"You had enough to focus on. I forgot, too. Let's worry about the djinn we know. We'll deal with any new djinn later."

Jason grumbled, "I don't like how the Djinn-verse is expanding."

Chapter 12

The St. Bernard Hospital complex sprawled across endless city blocks. Determined to maintain its status as a leading medical institution while preserving its historical aesthetic, the campus consisted of glassy, modern towers next to landmark brick buildings with tubular walkway connections on and aboveground like a hamster cage. Inside, however, easy-to-read signs dangled from the ceiling, pointing to every hallway leading out of the bustling main entrance, making navigation relatively simple.

I checked the text from Mom on my phone—3-1454—then scanned the signs for patient room numbers. Down the hallway to my left, I passed open doors with pale people, hair disheveled and gowns crooked, getting poked and prodded. I hadn't spent much time in hospitals, so in my mind, attractive staff tended to beautiful patients who never appeared sick in between romantic liaisons with each other. And the hot doctor always stumbled upon the cure for a rare disease at the end of an episode. Turned out, TV didn't reflect reality.

As it swept me to the third floor, the elevator car floated on air, unlike the creaky elevator in my building that thumped, jerked, and moaned its way upward as it gasped its dying breath. The doors swished open, and I stepped into the hallway, only to jump back into the elevator to avoid a group of people in black scrubs racing alongside a wheeled bed. A woman with long braids tied back called over her shoulder, "Excuse us!"

Polite, even while saving a life.

The signs guided me through endless corridors. I turned right, turned left, and stayed straight. The twists and turns didn't seem to have a pattern, and the uniform white walls and floors made navigation impossible without the signs. I expected to run into an old man huddled in the corner, who, after fifty years of trying to visit a loved one, gave up and surrendered to live out his remaining days in the continuous halls of St. Bernard's.

The door to room 1454—Aunt Jo's room—was ajar. I snuck a peek inside like a creeper, afraid I'd open the wrong door and scare the crap out of someone in the middle of a sponge bath.

All clear.

I pushed open the door while knocking. A woman with legs as long as Mrs. Macklind's and thick, bronze-tipped curls cascading down her back stood beside the bed, holding Aunt Jo's hand. When she heard me, she whirled around, startled at first, but then a bright smile bloomed across her face as she released her fiancée's hand. "Baxter!"

Anita's heels clicked on the white tile as she trotted toward me, flinging her arms around me and burying me in her chestnut suit jacket. She and Aunt Jo had been dating for a few years, but I didn't see her often. However, that didn't stop her from always acting like we were family reunited after decades apart. Aunt Jo called it her *Cuban dramatics*, but Anita would dismiss that with severe annoyance and respond, "In Cuba, *la familia es familia!*"

Anita held my face with smooth hands and gazed

into my eyes. Her long nails pressed into my cheeks. "So handsome, Baxter. Jo said you grew up, but you've become quite the man."

My neck heated. "Nice to see you, too."

Anita's hands dropped from the sides of my face to my shoulders, and she guided me to the bed. Her musky perfume overpowered the room. "It's so terrible what happened to my Josephine. Horrifying!"

Mom always said only a person with a huge personality could handle Aunt Jo's already oversized one. Anita Rodriguez might be her soulmate.

Covers stretched across Aunt Jo's torso, tucked in under her armpits. A massive brown-and-purple bump adorned the middle of her forehead, and bandages wrapped her nose. Wires draped from machinery behind her and disappeared under her blankets while IVs dripped fluid into tubes plugged into her arms. She noticed me and smiled, the effort of which caused her to flinch in pain, which dulled her bright eyes. I'd never seen her so vulnerable and didn't like it.

"Hi, Aunt Jo."

She reached out for my hand. "Bax, you didn't need to come here. It's a school night." She patted my hand, sandwiched between hers. "You missed your mom. She and Max went to the cafeteria to grab a bite."

"Max is here?" Must be getting serious if he was visiting Mom's sick family.

"You guys weren't exaggerating at dinner last night. Few people return from the dating pond with a catch like Max." Aunt Jo laughed, then cringed and stopped. "Every muscle in my face hurts."

Anita tried to distract her. "He's so charming!"

"Enough about Mom's new guy." I changed the

subject. "What happened, Aunt Jo?"

"Some salesman attacked me. I turned my back for one minute to talk to your mom on the phone, and he spiked my drink. I tested positive for GHB. Asshole."

Anita grumbled something in Spanish, then said, "Who secretly gives someone date rape drugs at the airport? Did he intend to haul you out of there over his shoulder, right through security?"

Someone who wasn't interested in date rape. Ifrit wanted to send a message. I just needed to figure out if he intended the message for me or Mom. Of course, I couldn't let on I knew any details. I had to hear it for the first time. "He drugged you?"

"Yeah. So by the time I detoured to the ladies' room, I passed out. Whacked my head on the sink. But the weirdest thing…"

Uh-oh.

"Baby, you were delirious." Anita twisted the charm on her thin gold bracelet. "Who knows what you—"

Aunt Jo pointed at me. "Bax, I swear, right before I blacked out, someone taped up the bathroom entrance. Like they do before cleaning or repairs. I didn't walk through any tape going in. And somehow, that shithead beat me into the ladies' room to wait for me. I don't understand how he knew I'd stop at *that* restroom. Thank God a lady heard me scream and called security. Though, I don't remember screaming."

"Again, you were delirious!" Anita grabbed Aunt Jo's other hand, so we hovered on each side of her bed. "I'm sure the drugs scrambled your senses. A woman heard Josephine hit the sink, but when she opened the stall door, the rapist had run away."

"Oh my God, we don't know he was a rapist, Anita."

"He stole nothing from you. Why else drug you?"

"I guess, maybe." Aunt Jo sighed as she squeezed my hand. Like all of Ifrit's victims, she recognized missing pieces of her story, gaps that rationality couldn't fill. "The cops said camera footage didn't show any man entering the restroom. And the woman who saved me said she didn't see any tape over the door. It's official: I'm crazy."

"Or someone drugged you, which, oh yeah, is what happened." Anita brushed Aunt Jo's hair behind her ear with her red fingernails. "It doesn't matter. What matters is arresting that predator who spiked your drink while you talked to your sister for twenty seconds."

"Oh, Bax." Jo squeezed my hand harder. "I didn't tell your mom the part about suspecting the man drugged me when I answered her call. Let's not tell her. You know how she is. She'll spiral and blame herself for calling. She already told Max if I hadn't come to visit, I'd have never been in the airport bar, blah, blah, blah. My sister is ridiculous."

Aunt Jo knew Mom well. "I won't. So how much longer will they keep you here?"

"Not much. They said likely tomorrow sometime. Fractured my nose, and I have a massive bump on my head, but nothing permanent, thank God. They just want to flush all the drugs out of me." She lifted her arm with the IVs attached.

"That's good news at least." Ifrit's attacks had grown bolder. He attacked Aunt Jo in the middle of a crowded airport. Luckily, the lady in the stall saved Aunt Jo. Who knows how far Ifrit would have gone if she hadn't interrupted?

"Speaking of which"—Aunt Jo released my hand—

"why don't you catch up with your mom and Max if you don't mind, hon. I'm super tired. The doctors had been keeping me awake because of the concussion, but now I can sleep. And I need it before they kick me out of here. Thank you for coming by, kiddo."

Anita came around the bed to my side and patted me between the shoulders. "Always a treat seeing you, *sobrino*."

"Same here, guys."

I hugged Anita, glad Aunt Jo had someone with her even though I hadn't known Ifrit to strike twice, at least not in my experience. But I'd never seen anyone interrupt him either. If he intended the attack on Aunt Jo to send a message, he'd consider it a success and leave her alone. Then again, rationality might not predict the actions of a timeless demon.

Guided by the signs high on the white walls, I retraced my path through the hallways to the elevator and descended to the first floor where the sounds of clanking silverware, banging plates, and a myriad of voices let me know I'd arrived. The scent of fried chicken weaving through the smell of bleach reminded me of Truman's cafeteria on steroids. St. Bernard's eatery extended forever in all directions, with six-person round tables speckling it like a million stars.

Mom and Max had chosen a table near the soda fountain, so I spotted them right away. They stared at each other, hands folded together. They leaned forward as if the table created too much separation between them. Max said something while Mom gazed at him as if he was telling her the most exciting story in the world's history.

Man, she is into him.

"Come on!" a voice boomed from my right.

A man padded in endless layers of ragged clothes and shredded gloves shook his fists at the young cashier. Four pieces of white bread lay on the counter where the man's tray should have been.

"You have to pay for the bread." The cashier, twenty years old at most, ordered the much older customer in a weak voice. "You know the rules, Hank."

The homeless-looking guy spoke through a thick, unkempt beard with wiry hairs pointing in all directions. "I'm hungry and don't have any money. Not to mention, I sit outside all the time and leave your patients alone."

The cashier sighed. "Leaving our patients alone is not a reason to pay you off with free food. You're not even supposed to be outside. Look, Hank, I'm on a scholarship. I can't break any rules, or I'll lose my job. And if I lose my job, I lose the scholarship."

"Pssht." The man waved his hand, shooing an invisible bug away, the frayed ends of his coat sleeve followed his gesture. "You can spare a few slices of bread."

The kid shook his head. "It's not mine to give."

A hospital security officer approached them with an overabundance of confidence for a short, stubby guy. His tight uniform shirt stretched over his enormous belly, and the badge he wore caught the cafeteria lights. "Come on now, Hank. You can't come in here unless you can pay. There's a soup kitchen on Bayless."

"Well, if it isn't everyone's favorite sheriff of Mayberry." The homeless guy's booming voice attracted the attention of nearby diners.

"Who?" the cashier asked.

"Before your time, kid," Hank muttered.

To de-escalate the situation, the security guard lowered his voice and raised his hands. "I'm asking you to leave, Hank."

The homeless man noticed the eyes on him. He grumbled, then sighed. He waved to a toddler watching with wide, curious eyes. "Okay, fine. You win."

As Hank sauntered away, he swiped one piece of bread and shoved it into his pocket. He tried to be sneaky, but the cashier and officer both saw him. They said nothing about it.

A hospital, of all places, could spare a few slices of bread. Besides, wouldn't they need to treat him if he starved?

The cashier wiped his hands on his apron. "I feel bad, but he comes in all the time. Tony says we can't give him any more food until he pays."

"I get it." The officer coughed into his elbow nook. "You know, Hank's been living outside of here for as long as I can remember. Poor guy."

Hank lumbered through the massive lobby, his oversized pants dragging on the floor as he shuffled to the exit with a limp. Visitors parted around him like he carried a contagious disease, but he ignored them. He waved to a nurse, who waved back. "Hi, Hank."

The exit doors swished open, and I followed. I stayed a safe distance behind, tailing him with the stealth of a veteran private eye. But, unlike a detective, I couldn't explain why I followed my target.

Hank hobbled down the sidewalk to a shadowy corner where the hospital entrance section of the building met its east wing. Tucked behind a few tall, leafless bushes, protected from the gusting winds and other natural elements, a flimsy cardboard box, big enough to fit Hank, swayed next to a shopping cart covered with a tattered gray blanket.

With a loud grunt, Hank collapsed to the ground. The layers of clothing made it difficult to bend and sit—a minor inconvenience for warmth. He tore the bread into bite-size pieces, savoring each delectable chunk.

A rock formed under my ribs. Homeless people weren't new to me, but I'd never seen one trying to scrape together something to eat by begging for bread slices and then denied.

Thanksgiving was a few weeks away, a holiday to celebrate everything we had, while people like Hank couldn't even score bread from a behemoth hospital complex. It didn't seem fair.

Ever since I'd banished Ifrit, I'd spent most nights reliving the killings and beatings I'd inspired. And when I used Janni, I used him for my own gain, like finding out the date of a stupid book presentation in American Literature. I should have been using Janni to do good and inject positivity into the world. That might end the crushing guilt keeping me up at night.

I jogged across the street, running in front of a car that honked. Ducking into a dark corner across from Hank, away from the glow of the parking lot lights and out of everyone's sight, I dug the ring out of my pocket like a superhero about to change into my alter ego.

The purple jewel ignited as I rubbed it, so I buried my hand inside my coat to make sure no one saw. Soon after the icy shudder finished raining down on me, Janni appeared.

"HOW CAN IT SERVE? WHY IS BAXTER HIDING IN SHADOWS?"

"Janni, we're going to do something good for once.

Do your invisible thing and take a few bucks from the cafeteria register in the hospital. Just a few."

Janni vanished without question. I expected a follow-up from him about my motives, but he just jumped. I'd give the money to Hank. It wouldn't change his life forever, but it'd buy him some food. Like the mayor said over and over when she scrambled to win the election—it was a redistribution of wealth. The hospital fortress would survive without a couple of bucks. If I had any money on me, I'd use that, but I didn't.

I'd use Janni for the greater good.

Janni reappeared with a stack of twenties and held them out to me, the wind flapping them in his pink hands.

"That's more than a few bucks, Janni."

"WHAT IS A FEW, BAXTER ALLEN?"

I stared at the glowing hospital towers looming over the shorter buildings nearby. The place had tons of money and I was using it to give a guy a break. I took the money. "Fair point. You can go. Thanks."

Janni jumped.

I jogged across the street but kept a safe distance on my side of Hank's bushes, not wanting to run up on him. "Excuse me. Hank?"

The homeless man looked up, his skin cracked and weathered. Pink tipped his bulbous nose, and red veins streaked the whites of his eyes. "I ain't bothering no one, kid."

"I know." I held up my hands in surrender.

"And I ain't got nothing, so keep walking." He rolled to his side to hoist himself to a stand, struggling to get up under the weight of his layers of clothes.

"I heard your conversation in the cafeteria."

Standing, Hank raised one of his bushy eyebrows.

In a strange way, he reminded me of Warren in an alternate universe. "And? What's it to you?"

"Here." I held out the money.

His gaze flipped from me to the cash and back to me. "This a joke?"

"No. It's so you can buy food." I shifted, still extending my arm, even though he didn't reach for my hand. "Please take it."

Hank's attention lingered on my hand. "Where'd a kid get that kind of cash?"

"My parents won't miss it. We're rich."

He took the money. "You sure?"

"I am."

He stared at the bills. "Bless you, son. Thank you. Thank you very much."

He shoved the cash into his tattered coat pocket as I nodded. "Have a nice Thanksgiving and Christmas. Or Hanukkah or whatever."

"You, too. What's your name, son?"

"Bax."

"You have a blessed holiday, too, Bax."

A bounce worked its way into my step. I could change the world bit by bit using djinn magic. I could improve people's lives. That money would buy a ton of bread at the cafeteria or maybe a warmer coat at a thrift store.

St. Bernard's glass doors swished open, letting me back in to join Mom and Max. The inside warmth washed over me as my mind rambled through various good deeds Janni and I could accomplish. Like real-life superheroes, we'd use magic to make the world better. Janni could turn invisible and find kids in trouble, then we could save them. Mom's life would've been completely different if she'd had someone like me looking out for her during her broken marriage with Ben.

As I entered the cafeteria, the portly security officer still stood beside the cashier, but the kid patted his apron and pants as the officer shook his head and scowled.

"I swear the money was here!" The cashier's voice cracked, his face blotchy with panic. "You didn't see me take it!"

The guard examined the counter and the floor under the kid. "The drawer's missing three hundred dollars."

I'd given Hank three hundred dollars? That's more than I intended. I should have counted it.

"I reported it! Why would I report it if I stole it?" The cashier flapped his apron and pulled his pockets inside out.

"Perhaps you handed it off to a friend when I stepped away." The officer's voice remained calm, unlike the cashier's.

"Again, why would I report that if I did? I'm telling you, the money was here, then gone." The cashier slammed the drawer shut with a bang.

A tall, thin guy in a black chef coat and pants approached. He had grease spots on the front of his jacket. "What's up, Kyle?"

"My drawer's short, which I told Rob about." He pointed at the security guard. "But he thinks I stole it."

The security guard shrugged. "Kyle says the drawer's missing money, but no one has been near it but him. I'm asking him questions, is all."

"And I've answered them!"

"Calm down." The chef folded his arms. "How much are we talking?"

"I didn't take it." Tears welled in Kyle's eyes. "I

swear."

The officer chimed in. "About three hundred."

"Dollars?" The chef shook his head. "Jesus. That's not a few coins short." He used a key to open the drawer. "All your twenties are gone. The entire stack."

"I am aware!" Kyle yelled. "I. Reported. It."

"Keep your voice down, son," Officer Rob mumbled.

"I didn't steal anything."

"I need to call human resources," the chef said. "Why don't you clock out, and I'll text you tomorrow."

"No, you can't. If you fire me, I'll lose my nursing scholarship. Plus, I'll never be able to work here with a termination on my record. Not as a nurse or anything."

The chef patted Kyle's shoulder. "You're not fired. Maybe the money will turn up." He winked at the cashier, giving him a last chance to make things right.

"I don't have it! And if I did, why the fuck would I report the missing money to Officer Idiot?"

"Easy, son."

"Your drawer is empty"—the chef shook his head—"and the register is your responsibility, whether you stole or lost the money. Now, take your apron off and clock out. I'll text you tomorrow to come in and talk to HR."

"You've got to be kidding me." The cashier ripped off his apron and threw it to the ground. "This is so fucking stupid!" He stormed off, almost toppling a slow patient with a walker.

My sense of pride and newfound purpose dissipated under the explosion of guilt in my gut. Janni could provide Hank with food or a new winter coat, but someone like Kyle would pay the price. My heroic plans to change the world dissolved into a dumb, childish fantasy. Djinn magic was a curse, not a superpower, and I was just an average kid stuck in a world of magic beyond his control. Djinn magic always had consequences. Ifrit told me that himself when he held me captive in the vortex. Why did I think I could outsmart magical beings who'd been around for millennia?

I could blame Ifrit for all the damage he caused when he ripped thoughts out of my mind, but in this case, I caused the damage.

Chapter 13

Mom had forgotten her cell phone at home—again. Not having anything better to do on a Saturday morning but obsess over who stole Ifrit's box and beat myself up over getting a student nurse fired, I decided to deliver Mom's phone to her before she gave herself a heart attack, thinking she lost it on the street. Knowing her, she didn't even realize she'd forgotten it. Something I couldn't fathom.

Zia's Candles' pink awning flapped over the sidewalk of Euclid Avenue, and miniature pine trees grew out of the massive stone urns at its entrance. Millions of candles dotted the display window corner to corner, with imitation fall leaves clustered between them as seasonal decoration. The designer clothing boutiques and other specialty stores around Zia's embellished their storefronts with pumpkins, cornucopias, and turkeys, building excitement for the upcoming Thanksgiving holiday. Mayfield's Women's Wear had already strung up white twinkling Christmas lights.

My phone vibrated in my pocket. Jason.

—See you online later. 3:00. Archer Annihilation.—

Nothing sounded better than losing myself in a medieval world where swords, bows, and magic coexisted with robots and machine guns.

I didn't see Jason much at school yesterday, so I didn't tell him how I'd broken our No Djinn Rule. Sure,

I'd had the best of intentions, but I still broke our pact. Jason didn't seem to suspect anything, but he'd figure it out. He always did.

I responded, *Sounds good*, and dropped my phone back into my pocket.

When I looked up again, I saw him. Every muscle in my body turned to stone. To focus, I lifted my hand to block the late morning sun from my eyes.

Ahead, in broad daylight, the old man hunched over a thick, waist-high walking stick in the middle of the sidewalk in front of Zia's entrance. His red-brick-colored coat absorbed the bright daylight while the sun washed out his pale features, making him appear faceless.

The few early shoppers strolled by him, unphased by the strange loiterer. Could they see him? No one walked through him, like a ghost or a vision, but no one seemed to notice him either. And it wasn't like he blended in with the other people who spent their Saturday mornings on Euclid Avenue browsing expensive candles, trying on fancy suits, or perusing Simmon's Jewelers for a gold watch.

What was he doing outside of Mom's work?

I willed my legs to work again and approached him, slow step after slow step.

His face sharpened as I got nearer. He tilted his head to the right and grinned, his lips a shadowy line on his white face. He lifted the heavy sleeve of his thick coat, too heavy for his feeble frame, and from the end of his sleeve, one of his overgrown nails wiggled at me, beckoning me closer.

Ifrit assaulted Aunt Jo in the middle of an airport and now appeared in his old man form on a public street with pedestrians around. But could anyone else see him, or was he in my head like when he chased me through school?

I had to get to Mom, not comfortable with the old man standing between us. Closer to him, the purple of his glowing eyes broke the whiteness of his face, and his crooked yellow teeth became visible.

"What do you want?" I kept several arms' length from him, hoping his response would prove him real or in my imagination.

A man and woman holding hands passed by, glancing at me before diverting their eyes away from the crazy kid talking to no one. They didn't see him.

The old man inhaled a jagged breath, then exhaled steam in the frosty air. His words, though mumbled, exploded in my head. "I am free."

"Yeah. Good for you. Stop bothering me and my family. Leave us alone." A burnt skin scent wafted off him—the djinn's trademark.

His laugh vibrated his chest as his shoulders quaked, but his face showed no smile.

An older woman in a lime-green overcoat touched my arm. "Are you ill, son?" Her eyeshadow matched her coat.

"Huh? Yeah, fine."

When I looked back, the old man had vanished. No trace of him. Even his odor had dissipated.

"You sure?" She dropped her hand from my arm as if realizing the inherent risk of touching a crazy person.

I pointed to where he'd stood, hunched over his walking stick. "Did you see an old bald guy in a reddish-brown coat?"

She turned to double-check as if she might have missed him. "Well, I came from that direction, but no.

No one caught my attention."

He appeared only in my mind, but it made no sense. He showed up, laughed at me, then vanished. And why at Zia's, unless he was plotting something against Mom? I needed to check on her.

"Can I call you some help?" What an admirable lady. Most wouldn't have stopped at all.

"No. My mom's working in there." I thumbed toward Zia's.

The woman pulled her coat tight. "Okay, then. Have a nice Thanksgiving, sweetie."

I pushed open the door to Zia's Candles. Unlike entering Warren's Cosmos, entering Zia's Candles overwhelmed customers in a blanket of flowers and spices as they stepped through a portal from a dingy street into a fairy's garden. Glass shelves of all sizes covered the walls, and candles of every color filled the hundreds of racks. Vines of purple flowers draped from the ceiling in white pots, and the bright pink carpet matched the awning outside.

Mom pointed to a far corner, directing a middle-aged woman in a beige leather jacket. The woman asked a few follow-up questions. People who shopped at Zia's settled for nothing less than the perfect scent.

From over the woman's shoulder, Mom winked at me as she answered the woman's questions. I scanned the store, but no sign of Ifrit or the old man, and Mom's customer had bright green eyes. Safe for now.

I picked up a thick, ivory candle in a stout jar. Enchanted Rainforest. Unable to resist, I opened the lid, needing to smell the distinct scent of an enchanted rainforest. Turns out, it resembled not-very-enchanting wet grass.

"Thank you so much for coming in." Mom waved to the leather jacket lady, who continued to browse in a far corner.

"Well, hello, Baxter. What are you doing here?" She hugged me. "What a surprise."

"Forget something?" I handed her the cell phone.

"Oh, shoot!" She patted her jeans pocket. "You didn't need to come all the way here for that."

"But what if someone broke into our apartment, held me hostage, and demanded a ransom? I couldn't call you to meet their demands."

She blew out a breath and shook her head, a slight grin on her lips. "Well, this visit got dark quick. What are you doing today?"

I shrugged. "Hanging out with Jason later."

"Oh, Jo texted. They got back home safe and sound. Said Anita didn't let her out of her sight the entire time they were at the airport. I wish they would have stayed with us last night instead of rushing from the hospital right to the airport, but you know how the two of them are, go-go-go."

I released a cleansing sigh. They'd be safer from Ifrit in a different city, far away from me, and by the time they returned for Thanksgiving, I'd hopefully have this mess sorted out. Not hopefully. I would.

The door opened behind me, and a small electronic chime sounded. "Be right back, Bax. Welcome to Zia's. Can I help you?"

I roamed farther into the store, sniffing candles while Mom helped the customer. Jarred candles, bare wax candles in holders, tall ones, and short ones, all with specific names like Evening Sunset Musk, Ocean Waves, or Sweet Home Comforts. After hundreds of people sniffed these, someone had to have gone in for a whiff and dropped a booger.

Gross.

I stopped sniffing.

A gust of winter wind whipped through the store as the door opened again, blending the hundreds of scents. Candle shopping seemed to be the thing to do on a Saturday morning. But the new customer differed from the other two middle-aged women.

Malcolm?

Bumping into Malcolm Reardon at school always jolted me. Seeing him at my mom's job felt like worlds colliding, creating a monstrous black hole. I ducked behind a shelf like I'd seen something I shouldn't have.

I watched him from between the shelves like a creepy stalker. He unzipped his thick camouflage hunting coat and checked his phone before shoving it back into one of the coat's million pockets.

"Welcome to Zia's!" Mom greeted him from across the room. Apparently, she didn't think it odd a teenage boy shopped for candles on a Saturday morning. And Malcolm, of all teenagers—a kid who looked like he graduated a decade ago and dedicated his life to intimidating teachers and students. The same person who beat her son senseless a few weeks ago. But she didn't know about our drama. I'd told her my story about a gang jumping me.

Malcolm sauntered down a row of display shelves. He kept glancing back at Mom, busy with her customer in the incense section. He fiddled with his thick coat, zipped it all the way up, then hiked up the collar. Every move screamed suspicious.

With a glance back at Mom again, Malcolm shoved

a small, jarred candle into his jacket with a lightning-quick swipe, then spun on his heel and eased back toward the door, smooth and steady.

Are you kidding me?

Still busy with the other customer, Mom didn't notice.

The old man.

Ifrit chased me into the locker room to confront Malcom. Was the old man appearing outside of Zia's Ifrit's attempt to lure me in so I'd be near Malcolm again? Couldn't be. I was already going to Zia's, old man or not.

I'd spent my entire high school career hiding from Malcolm and his buddies before all hell broke loose and Ifrit plunked me smack dab into the middle of their radar. Thanks to Scarlet, he and his thugs ignored me again, but I couldn't let him get away with this. I couldn't allow Mom's boss to fire her for stealing like the hospital cashier's boss. She needed her job at Zia's Candles now more than ever. We needed it. I refused to let Malcolm ruin that, whether Ifrit staged this whole scene or not. I had to step in. If Malcolm beat the shit out of me again, at least I'd have done the right thing. I'd messed up enough lives already. This time, I'd ensure things stayed right—without the help of any djinn magic.

I held in a massive gulp of air, then marched outside after him.

Here we go.

More people strolled between the shops than a few minutes earlier providing excellent cover if things got ugly. Malcolm wouldn't kick the crap out of me in plain sight of all these people.

"Hey, Malcolm!" I shouted over the rumble of light

traffic. My call snagged the attention of a few pedestrians—perfect.

He'd already speed-walked halfway down the block. When he heard me, he turned around and held his hand up to his forehead to block the sun, squinting.

My stomach spun in my gut, but I forced myself onward. Confrontation was not my thing—never had been. Especially confrontation with the monster named Malcolm Reardon, the guy who almost killed me less than a month ago. I squeezed my eyes shut to stop the tingling in my jaw as I remembered his fist crashing against it. Or the toe of his tennis shoe driving deep into my gut. Or his piss in my mouth, mixing with my blood.

All over a ten-dollar candle?

Yes. For Mom.

I marched closer to him, and he lowered his hand as he recognized me. He sniffed snot back into his throat. "What do you want, Allen?"

Please don't throw up. Please don't throw up.

"The candle you stole. Give it to me." I'd somehow kept my voice firm and wobble-free.

"What candle?" He stepped forward, a reminder of how he towered over me and had shoulders twice as wide. "Be careful with the accusations, man."

"My mom works there. I saw you take it. Give it back."

He inched closer. "Your mom works where?" His nostrils flared.

My hands trembled, and I tightened my abdomen, ready for a punch. "Zia's. The place where you stole the candle just now. The one in your coat pocket."

"You'd better watch your mouth." Here it came. Malcolm shifted his right foot back a few inches, bracing himself to deliver a hard right. I turned my stance, ready to block.

Block, yeah, right. I'd be lucky to slow his fist. I'd lose the fight over a candle and end up with a cracked skull again. My confidence shook.

"Just give the candle to me. Please. I don't want them to fire my mom. Steal something from somewhere else."

Malcolm's eyes flickered to Zia's storefront, half a block behind me. "Your mom works there?"

"That's what I said." My eyes wanted to shut in anticipation of the fist about to fly. I concentrated on keeping them open.

Malcolm raised his arm, and I flinched, but instead of winding up, he pulled the purple jar out of his coat pocket and handed it to me.

It worked?

I took it in a shaky hand. "Thanks." Not sure why I thanked him for giving back what he stole, like he did me a favor.

Without another word, he turned to go. No punching, no yelling. He just started walking away.

How long had I lived in fear of this guy?

After he'd gone a few steps, my new confidence fueled words that escaped my stupid, stupid mouth. "Why a candle?"

What is wrong with me?

Malcolm stopped and turned back around.

I readied myself to run, but he stayed in place.

He spit on the ground. "You don't know shit about me, bro. So you'd better stop while you're ahead. Promise to Scarlet or not, I *will* fuck you up."

I swallowed. "Sorry. Candles just don't seem like

your thing."

Malcolm glanced around us, then shoved his hands into his pockets. I relaxed my stance. "The candle is for my mom. I gave it back because I don't want them to fire your mom over a gift for mine. Feels a little too ironic. So don't get all high and mighty."

If Jason and Ashley heard him, they'd debate if his comment fit the definition of ironic. I wasn't sure it did, but I didn't need to get into a definition debate with him. The bottom line was that Malcolm had a soft spot for moms, even if misguided.

He walked away, and I kept my stupid mouth shut.

Malcolm turned out to be an actual person with a mom and not the spawn of Satan. He wanted to do something for his mom in the only way he understood, which didn't make him a saint or anything, but I appreciated the non-bully side of him. I'd never understood why Malcolm picked on kids, drank from his silver flask during lunches, or stole on Saturday mornings, but a sad reason for his behavior drifted somewhere in his empty head.

The door to Zia's swung open. "Baxter, I thought you'd gone home without saying goodbye."

"You're busy in there."

"It's Saturday. But I hit a lull. You chillin' out here in the cold?"

I groaned. "Please don't say chillin'. And no, I saw a guy from school shoplifting." I handed her the candle. "He apologized."

Mom turned the candle over in her hands. "What? You don't need to be playing security guard, Bax."

I shrugged. "I knew him. Besides, I didn't want you to get in trouble."

Mom wrapped an arm around my shoulders. "Let's hope I'm in good enough standing that one vanishing candle doesn't get me canned. Although, with my luck at jobs lately, who knows?" She hugged me. "Thanks for bringing my phone, too."

Over Mom's shoulder, a car's engine revved, its tires squealed on the pavement as its driver pounded the accelerator to the floor, launching it forward. The black sedan tore down the street toward us.

"These cars." Mom only heard the car and didn't see it behind her.

Time slowed as the car sped up. Each second, the gap between us closed. The sedan didn't follow the road, but I couldn't tell if it headed toward us with intent or if it was driven by a careless driver who'd correct course at the last minute. Ifrit paranoia clouded my judgment. Or was it clouded? The old man appeared outside Zia's a few minutes ago. Had Ifrit started taking so much pride in messing with me, he was sending warnings before striking?

Moving to the right, the car jumped the curb onto the sidewalk. It barreled right for us.

Holy shit!

I shoved Mom toward Zia's glass storefront, diving behind her. She tripped on her feet, and I stumbled over her. The car's engine roared louder.

We smashed against the glass display window, face-to-face with a rainbow of candles.

Behind us, the car had lurched over the curb, caught air, and crashed on the sidewalk just past us. It rolled a few feet before slamming into a tree planted between sidewalk slabs. The tires squealed as the driver tried to reverse, but the sapling had snagged the bumper.

As if on command, all other sounds disappeared, leaving only the hissing of the car's engine as it released smoke from under its hood.

"Baxter, oh my God, are you all right?" Mom scrambled to her feet, realizing what had happened. "Baxter?"

"Yeah. Fine. You?" I stood.

"Jesus Christ!" She brushed off her pants. "Let's check on the driver."

Of course, Mom's first concern would be if our attempted murderer had a cut or bruise.

I suspected they'd be uninjured, confident the driver wouldn't be a kid who'd lost control or a person distracted by texting. It would be some manifestation of Ifrit. Seeing the driver might help me determine if the murder attempt targeted Mom, me, or both of us, depending on his form.

"Stay here."

Mom picked up her phone from the ground, and I limped to the black sedan. I must've scraped my leg when I dove.

The driver poked his head through the door's open window, leering. Despite the accident and smashed front end of his car, his greasy hair remained in place, his dark black sunglasses still rested on his nose, and his button-up starched dress shirt was wrinkle free. Not a scratch on him. Not even a bloody nose from hitting the yellow airbag, which had deployed from the steering wheel.

But his violet eyes burned behind his sunglasses, casting a purple glow on his eyebrows and cheekbones.

When the old man appeared outside of Zia's, it had nothing to do with Malcolm. Ifrit revealed himself as a warning. He'd attacked Aunt Jo in a public airport and then Mom and me on a public street. He'd grown confident or reckless, and I didn't know which.

The driver revved the engine as Mom approached from behind. "I called the police."

The car reversed, breaking free from the tree, then drove over the curb with a loud clank and sped off down the street, almost hitting a family on the crosswalk.

An older couple tapped Mom's shoulder. "We couldn't get the license plate but saw everything," the old man said. "I can call an ambulance."

"No, no. We're fine." Mom rubbed my arm. "Right, Bax?"

"Yeah."

We were fine—until Ifrit tried to kill us again.

Chapter 14

Scarlet slid into Jason's desk as kids meandered into Mrs. Macklind's classroom, scanning their notes and hoping she didn't pick them to present first on day one of the dreaded presentations. Glad I wouldn't be the first sucker. I couldn't imagine not knowing when it'd be my turn. I had enough in my life without having to deal with fighting off an episode before every American Literature class.

Scarlet leaned across the aisle. Her red hair fell over her shoulders. "Nothing yet? No signs of...*him*?"

So much had happened since Scarlet joined our squad, and I hadn't talked to her in a week. I didn't know she expected me to keep her up to date and figured she might lose interest at some point. "Yeah. He attacked my aunt at the airport and tried to run me over with a car last weekend."

"What?" Her mouth dropped open. "Oh my God, you didn't tell me!"

When did we talk all the time like legit friends?

When Cassie spotted Scarlet talking to me, she didn't hide the mixture of confusion and revulsion that flashed across her eyes, outlined by multiple shades of glittery brown eye shadow.

"It all went down quick. Um, you're giving Cassie a panic attack because you're not in your spot." I nodded toward her seat up front.

Scarlet waved off her friend. "What's next?"

"I don't know. We've hit a dead end until we figure out who has the box."

Jason cleared his throat, standing beside his desk with his hands drawn up into his sweatshirt sleeves.

She glanced up at him, then stood. "Well, keep me posted."

"Okay."

"Promise?"

"Yeah. Sure."

Scarlet joined Cassie at her assigned desk as Jason fell into his. "What'd she want?"

"She doesn't want to miss any djinn action."

"She can have it," Jason grumbled. "No new assassination attempts?"

"Three days later, I'm still alive to talk about it."

Jason and I hung out after the incident at Zia's. Sharing my near-death experience helped me avoid telling him about breaking our No Djinn Rule at the hospital. Mom and I had just survived a hit-and-run. I didn't need a lecture. Besides, I'd learned loud and clear how even charitable deeds came with consequences in the Djinn-verse.

"Students, let's get started!" Mrs. Macklind announced as she closed the classroom door. Her silky yellow blouse quivered as she wrote *Themes of The Scarlet Letter* on the whiteboard in red marker.

"You think you'll present first?" Jason whispered as the chatter faded.

"Who knows?" I kept my eyes pointed at the whiteboard, but Jason's heavy gaze weighed on me.

"You seem calm, given the whole speaking-in-front-of-people thing may happen in less than a minute."

I hated having a best friend who knew me so well.

"The odds of me going first are slim." I chuckled.

The bell rang, saving me from digging deeper into my pit of lies.

"Good afternoon." Mrs. Macklind clapped, drawing the focus of the class. She held her paperback copy of the novel with a million yellow and pink sticky notes poking out of its pages. "Today's the day. As promised, two of you will give your presentation on a theme that resonated with you about *The Scarlet Letter*. I assigned names at random, so I hope everyone is prepared. Your presentation will be one-quarter of your grade for this novel, along with the quizzes and our test."

The class shuffled. A few scribbled on their note cards, and others focused downward, hoping no eye contact would change the predetermined order.

Who will be the lucky —

"Baxter Allen. You're our first presenter."

I coughed, gagging on air as I almost fell out of my desk.

What the hell?

I'd heard her incorrectly. Had to have. Or she'd made a mistake. Why didn't she follow her own predetermined order after she'd assigned everyone at random? She must've been misreading her list.

The gaze of every student stabbed me from all directions. A few classmates sighed in relief that Macklind hadn't chosen them first. My heart rate cracked like lightning.

"What?" That was the only word I could spit out. I'd misheard her. She hadn't called my name.

"Yes, Mr. Allen. You're up. Being first is always difficult, but I'm sure you'll survive. Let's get to it.

Chop, chop." She stepped aside, motioning to the front of the room, welcoming me to my humiliation with her perfect, illuminating smile.

I had done no preparation. I thought—no, I knew—I had plenty of time to prepare. It felt like an unexpected slap upside my head.

Jason whispered. "You got this."

I pretended to shuffle papers, swallowing the shooting vomit in my throat, hoping an earthquake would tear the school apart. My heartbeat exploded, and orange spots popped into my peripheral vision—an episode brewed in my core.

No! I'd beaten my VS!

Gathering random papers that had nothing to do with my presentation but hoping it would create the illusion I'd prepared, I forced myself to stand.

Think, Bax.

Hester and the town preacher had a kid. Her husband found out and tormented the dude out of anger and jealousy. I needed a theme. Having an affair? Hester had to wear a red *A* on her dress to show everyone she cheated on her husband. Shame? Guilt? Pride? Sin? The words all spun in my head, curling over each other like a thundercloud.

"Baxter?" The patience behind Mrs. Macklind's pleasant voice thinned.

Orange spots multiplied in my vision, leaving me a narrow tunnel to guide my slow steps toward the front of the room.

Someone giggled. They'd seen this play out before. Poor Baxter Allen would pass out and embarrass himself—again.

I had to forget about the presentation and focus on

not losing consciousness. Shouldn't be difficult since I didn't pass out anymore. I'd beaten it in the djinn vortex, a place *way* scarier than American Lit. Why did I even use Janni to find out the date? I didn't need his help.

Although, if I passed out, I'd escape the presentation. Which was worse, failing the project or utter humiliation? Everyone had finally stopped calling me Flower after the last time. I didn't want to give the Truman High student body any reason to resuscitate my stupid nickname.

I slowed my breathing as I dragged my iron feet up the aisle, trying to ward off the orange curtain descending across my vision.

"Baxter, we have a lot to cover today. Let's hurry it up." Mrs. Macklind took a few long strides down the aisle toward me as if preparing to catch me from falling.

Gathering my breath, I inhaled and blurted, "I'm not prepared."

Inhale. One, two, three, four.
Hold. One, two, three, four.
Exhale. One, two, three, four.
I closed my eyes.
No passing out, Bax. No passing out.

"That's unfortunate…are you feeling well?" I couldn't see Mrs. Macklind with closed eyes, but she sounded nearby.

Inhale. One, two, three, four.
Hold. One, two, three, four.
Exhale. One, two, three, four.

My heart rate slowed. I opened my eyes. No orange spots. Clear vision.

Episode averted.

Yes!

My pride was short-lived, however. I'd failed my presentation.

"Why don't you see Nurse Masson? Will someone please go with—"

"I don't need a nurse, but I'm not ready." How many times did I need to say it?

"Not ready? Baxter, we talked about—"

"I know!" I snapped.

She didn't back down, waiting for me to address my behavior before she did.

"I'm sorry. Like I said, I'm not prepared, Mrs. Macklind." My soft voice masked my inner fuming at her betrayal. She must've figured out someone saw her list. She must've been able to tell and re-randomized the order.

"Come see me after class." She spun, heading back to her desk as students whispered about my failure. I avoided eye contact with Scarlet and Jason.

"Mr. Wilcox, you're next."

Paul Wilcox jumped up and hastened to the front of the room, clearly not wanting Mrs. Macklind's disappointment at me to rub off on his grade. He unfolded his notes and read.

I hated prepared students.

"What happened?" Jason whispered.

I still didn't look at him.

I had a solid B, which would fall to a C.

Seething, I didn't pay attention to Paul's presentation, Jason's inquisition, or Mrs. Macklind's warning for everyone to be prepared after Paul finished. I should have winged it. It wouldn't have been hard. Talk for a minute or two about a theme that resonated with me. There couldn't be a wrong answer since it was based on my opinion.

You're an idiot, Bax.

Macklind rambled on and on for the rest of the hour about Puritans in New England or something. She also introduced our next novel, *Fahrenheit 451*. I couldn't wait to see who had an affair in that one.

The bell blasted. I sprang out of my desk and marched to Mrs. Macklind's, ready to listen to her lecture and get the hell out of her classroom. Scarlet hovered in the doorway with a sympathetic smile as kids shoved their way out of American Literature. That smile was the single worst part of my episodes—the *poor Baxter* look of pity.

Mrs. Macklind folded her hands on her desk. "Bax, what happened?"

You screwed me. That's what happened. "I forgot."

"I'm surprised."

"Me too."

She watched me, waiting for an excuse I didn't offer. "By not presenting, you're forcing me to give you a—"

"I'm not sure what you want me to say. I get it. I failed this project. Can I be dismissed?" My eyes clouded with frustrated tears. What did she want from me? I wished she'd stop pouring salt on my gaping wound. It stung enough. Let me leave with my remaining dignity.

She nodded, waving me off with a jangle of her thin gold bracelets.

I bolted, bulldozing past Scarlet and Jason down the hallway, shoving people aside. I wanted something to go my way. I didn't deserve vasovagal syncope. No other kid on the planet worried about passing out in front of their classmates. I had a whole other level of teenage stress.

Through the main entrance, I stumbled down the stone stairs, past Nick's memorial bench, and across the brown lawn of Truman High. I jogged around to the back of school to the small brick bungalow at the edge of campus.

I hunkered behind the house where students met to complete transactions prohibited on school grounds. The owners had no idea their fenceless and overgrown yard provided an ultra-convenient, safe zone for nefarious student activities. Thankfully, no one else occupied the safe zone, so I could wallow by myself.

I dug the ring out of my jeans and picked off a piece of lint between the jewel and the band. If Macklind changed the order on me, then I'd summon Janni to fix my grade. Simple as that. She can't change the rules on me. I had djinn magic.

The purple jewel caught the sun, glistening. I didn't rub it, though. I just stared at it. If I hadn't used Janni in the first place, I'd have been prepared for my presentation. But then I'd have had to deal with my VS on top of preparing.

Or would I have? I'd beaten it in the vortex. I'd even beaten it a few minutes ago on my march of shame. With focus and calm breathing, my racing heart slowed, and I'd dissolved the orange spots from my vision with no help from Janni.

Mrs. Macklind altered the presentation order, but my failed attempt at cheating was what pissed me off. I'd rationalized using Janni as an accommodation for my VS, but it was straight-up cheating.

I rested my head against the house's cool brick and shoved the ring back into my pocket. Mrs. Macklind should give me a failing grade on my American Literature presentation because I didn't do the work. And I deserved a failing grade in life for using my VS to justify my despicable actions.

"Baxter?"

Startled, I looked over, jumping to my feet. Scarlet buried her hands into the pockets of her pink coat as she watched me. "What are you doing out here? You don't strike me as a guy who spends a lot of time behind the house next to school."

"I'm not. I don't." I brushed the dead grass from my jeans. "Just needed a break from everyone."

"Jason and I waited outside of class to see if you were all right, but you sped off like a fugitive. He's checking THC. I happened to see you bolting out the front door."

"I'm fine." I was a deplorable human, but fine.

Scarlet shrugged. "Macklind might let you redo it."

I shook my head. "That's a nice thought, but I don't deserve a redo."

"If she knew about your aunt and the car thing, she'd understand why you weren't prepared."

No way. I couldn't lie to cover my cheating. I'd sunk low enough. Besides, my failure had nothing to do with Aunt Jo or Ifrit's attempted hit-and-run. "I could have prepared. I just didn't."

"Okay." Scarlet shrugged again. "On the bright side, it occurred to me when I was walking over here that at least we now have two leads to figure out who has Ifrit's box."

"What do you mean?"

"Well, you guys said when you tried to use Janni to follow Ifrit's energy to its source, he couldn't because no one had summoned him yet. But this time, he showed up at the airport and at your mom's work, so Janni should be able to sniff out his trail, right? He could lead us to Ifrit's new master."

"Holy crap! You're a genius!" I dragged a hand over my head. How had we missed that? It'd been a few days. I hoped the trail hadn't faded.

Scarlet grinned with pride. "About time I started pulling my weight on the team."

"I'll talk to Jason, and we'll try after school."

"Perfect! Text me where you're meeting."

I hesitated. I'd imagined only Jason, Ashley, and I would meet up, but I couldn't cut her out, especially since she'd come up with the idea. "Yeah, okay. Sure. I will."

Hopefully, we hadn't waited too long.

Chapter 15

Jason's building resembled a three-story horseshoe on its side next to Pine Avenue. Its long legs extended to the street; its entrance nestled behind a small rose-filled courtyard in the horseshoe's crook. Like many older buildings, it had stone letters above the front door proclaiming it *The Esquire*. My apartment had seven more floors than Jason's but no name or rose garden, so having both made the building much fancier than mine. Jason hated it whenever I called his apartment by its name, so I did it often.

I pressed the buzzer.

"H-ey." Static broke up Jason's greeting.

"I'm here." The door clicked open.

The small lobby smelled like an old building—hundred-year-old wood and stagnant air. I passed the wall of mailboxes and leaped up the left stairwell two stairs at a time, then down the hallway. Jason's algebra book propped the door open for me, so I let myself in and snagged his book from the doorway letting it click shut.

Jason's parents kept the place cool year-round. Not freezing, but like an eternal October evening. And a spiciness always lingered in the air, not overpowering, but tinging the apartment with a soothing aura.

Whenever I stopped by, the Franklins always seemed to be expecting guests with no piles of bills or junk mail strewn on the table, no dirty dishes in the sink, and no clothes on the floor. Another trait on the long list of things Mom admired about the Franklins.

I dumped my jacket and backpack near the door to show them how most people lived, which I was sure they appreciated.

Jason and Ashley sat on one of the dark brown suede sofas, unusually close together, but each on their devices. Scarlet stood across from them in front of the matching suede chair, studying the poster-sized oil painting of a pride of lions on the wall. She ran her finger along the thick brass frame, entertaining herself while my friends buried their heads in their screens as if they'd been hanging out in silence the whole time.

"You guys been here long?" I set Jason's algebra book on the coffee table.

Scarlet and Jason replied at the same time, but with different answers.

"Kinda."

"Not really."

"Scarlet said you were thinking we could ask Janni to track Ifrit's energy." Ashley stood up from the couch and dropped her phone into her pocket. "We should have thought of that after the attack. Either attack. I hope we haven't waited too long and Ifrit's energy already dissipated, or whatever it does."

Scarlet didn't correct Ashley, so I did. "Actually, Scarlet suggested it."

Ashley shrugged. "Either way."

"Should we start at the airport or Zia's?" Jason looked at me, then Ashley. Scarlet faded into the background.

I'd never seen my friends act so rude. I couldn't afford the time to address it and start a whole thing at

Jason's, but I'd say something later. Scarlet didn't deserve the cold shoulders. She'd done nothing to them.

I—very intentionally—spoke to all three of them as I took the ring from my pocket. "Zia's was the most recent, so we should start there. I've been thinking, Aunt Jo mentioned Ben, and then the next day, Ifrit attacked her. Two days later, Ifrit tried to run over Mom. This all in addition to Mom's layoff. I can't shake the feeling it's Ben."

Ashley scratched her elbow. "Did you ever learn anything about Warren's son?"

"I don't think he makes sense as a suspect."

Ashley shrugged. "Well, Ben can't leave the state, so that's not a case-closed situation. But aside from us, Warren is the only other person you've told about Ifrit. He could have said something to his son and triggered his curiosity."

I ran a hand through my hair, and one of my fingers hung up in a tangle. "All I found out is that he's married, has no kids, and is in from Memphis to help his dad. Said he's staying at a hotel across town because Warren's place is tiny. Didn't say where, just that it's a dump, so he intends to upgrade if he stays much longer. I don't think it's Scott, though. He'd have no reason to go after Mom. Plus, he wouldn't know Aunt Jo or where Mom works."

"So we have one suspect with no connection to your family"—Ashley sighed—"and one suspect who can't get into the state."

"We can speculate all day long." Jason wiped his glasses with the hem of his shirt. "Let's get moving before we lose the trail. Dad's working late, Mom's at a board meeting, and Michelle's at Grandma's. We should be alone for a few hours."

Jason gathered his thoughts as he rubbed his chin. "We also need to think about what we do next. Once we discover who the thief is, do we steal the box back? If we do, Ifrit will come for it on behalf of his master. He hates the vortex and will do whatever he can to stay in our world."

"What are you saying?" Scarlet stepped forward.

"He's saying we're about to start a freakin' war with Ifrit." Ashley, always the blunt interpreter.

Preoccupied with determining the thief's identity, I hadn't considered what followed. Last go around with Ifrit, we'd spent our energy trying to stay away from him. Now, we planned to run right into his clawed hands. But we had no choice. Ifrit would keep coming for Mom and me until we stopped him.

All eyes rested on the ring in my hand. "One step at a time. Let's see who we're dealing with first."

I rubbed the purple jewel. It lit up, casting its violet glow around us and cascading me with icy tingles. My shoulders trembled, never used to the sensation. Scarlet sniffed the air and grimaced.

Newbie.

After a minute, Janni waddled out from behind a waist-high wooden statue of a giraffe in the corner. He paused, glanced at it sideways, eyed it up and down, then touched it but yanked his hand back as if the statue burned red hot. He gave the fake giraffe a low growl. For a creature who'd been around for millennia, he found the strangest things intimidating.

Janni shook his head to refocus. "HOW CAN IT SERVE?"

I kneeled in front of him. "Remember how you

found Ben by following Ifrit's energy up to Chicago?"

He nodded, but his ears fell flat against his head. "UH-OH."

"I need you to do that again. We need to figure out who is summoning Ifrit. The thief summoned him within the last few days, and his master is here in town—we think."

Janni's nose twitched.

"He attacked us at Zia's Candles. See if you can follow the energy traces or whatever."

Janni's purple eyes glistened. "IT WILL TRY."

"That's all I'm asking."

He jumped, vanishing before us.

"How did you guys banish Ifrit last time?" Scarlet sat on the couch, crossing her legs at the ankles.

Ashley answered. At least they were speaking to each other. "Every djinn has an incantation—or ancient poem—on their artifact or vessel. For Janni, it's on the ring. For Ifrit, it's on the box. We read the incantation during the super blue blood moon a few weeks ago, which powered it enough to suck him back into the vortex."

Scarlet had Astronomy with Ashley and me, so we didn't need to explain lunar events. She recalled our chapter on lunar anomalies. "But isn't the next super blue—"

"Yeah," I interrupted, "a hundred and fifty years from now."

"So then how will—"

"We don't know!" Jason yelled, throwing his hands in the air. "Sorry."

Ashley rested a hand on Jason's shoulder and used a foreign-sounding, soothing tone. "We'll figure it out."

Where'd that voice come from?

A wave of burnt hair odor filled the room as Janni reappeared on the glass coffee table.

"IT FOLLOWED ENERGY FROM ZIA'S TO THE SUNRISE HOTEL."

I sprang to my feet. "Where's the Sunrise Hotel? Can you identify who has the box?"

Ashley moaned as she typed it into her phone. "Uh, it's a crusty hotel in a sketchy neighborhood."

"Ideal place for a probation jumper to camp out," I said.

"Or a dump Scott would want to upgrade out of." Jason raised an eyebrow.

I ignored him. "Did you see them, Janni? Did you see who stole the box?"

"NO ONE IN ROOM WHERE ENERGY LED."

I swallowed, my throat tight. "We need to check it out. Stalk the place. See if Ben"—I glanced at Ashley—"or Scott return."

"If it's Ben," Jason said, "he might recognize Bax. We should go without you to do the recon."

I shook my head. "No way. You might need Janni, and he only listens to me. He's our defensive magic."

"I have an idea." Scarlet sat on the couch, stroking a tan pillow like a pet. "Why can't you just give the ring to Jason? Can you, like, transfer ownership?"

Scarlet's question caused us all to turn to her. Would that work? Can we bounce around djinn ownership?

Janni answered. "IT SERVES BAXTER ALLEN. IF BAXTER ALLEN READS THE INCANTATION AND GIVES JASON THE RING, THEN JASON SUMMONS IT, IT WILL SERVE HIM."

"So the incantation is a reset button, I guess."

Ashley typed on her phone as she talked. "Makes sense in an ancient magic kind of way."

A strange pang stung me in the gut. I couldn't give up Janni. Not even for a few hours. I'd grown attached to the ring and to him. And if I did, Jason might somehow figure out I'd misused Janni. I had to tell him what had been going on. He and Ashley were in this mess because we're friends. I owed them the truth.

Jason must've heard my mind grinding. "Let's not. It's fine. But I don't know if you should go."

I shook my head. "Ring transferring aside, you can't identify Ben. I know what he looks like from Ifrit's visions."

"That's true."

"Well," Ashley jumped in, "if we're doing this, I'd recommend we do it before it gets dark. Otherwise, our evil djinn will be the least of our worries in that neighborhood."

"Let's go."

Chapter 16

"This definitely qualifies as a dump." Ashley's joke fell flat. "What does Scott do for a living?"

The bright pink and green of the Sunrise Hotel's flickering neon sign on its roof didn't invoke the hopeful summer morning sentiment it intended. Pretty much the exact opposite. The seven-story espresso-colored brick building butted up against the cracked sidewalk, flanked by a gas station with barred windows on one side and a liquor store with boarded-up windows on the other. A homeless woman—I thought—slept under a mountain of blankets in the nook between the liquor store and the hotel.

The four of us gathered across the street in a tight cluster, more out of place than the billboard one block away featuring a glistening penguin advertising a world-class zoo. Not sure the residents in the neighborhood cared much about a must-see tourist destination.

"Guys," Scarlet's voice wobbled, "we shouldn't loiter. I mean, no judgment, but this place is rough."

"Fuck you!" A man's voice bulleted through the air, causing all of us to jump.

Three guys in their twenties strolled down the street, talking and punching each other like teenagers. Despite the forty-degree weather, one sported a sleeveless shirt, and another didn't wear a shirt at all, with dozens of tattoos inked across his torso and arms. They drank beer out of cans twice the size of regular cans, and one smoked a cigarette, exhaling from his nose. As they walked, they hurled trash from the ground at the buildings they passed.

Still more than a block away and on the Sunrise Hotel's side of the street, they didn't notice us watching them like petrified animals wearing hoodies and sunglasses—our failed attempt at spy attire.

A car backfired a few blocks over, and we jumped again.

"Over here." I signaled for everyone to follow. Not wanting to duck into a dark alley in this neighborhood in our typical fashion, we hunkered in front of a shuttered drugstore. I unzipped my backpack. "Hey there."

Janni's purple eyes glowed in the darkness of my bag.

"Is he okay?" The entire trip, Ashley had lectured me about shoving him into my backpack, but if we needed him in a hurry, I couldn't afford the time to summon him and wait for him to appear. Not sure how Janni could help if we got into trouble, but having his magic on our side felt safer.

"He's fine, Ashley."

"HOW CAN IT—"

"Shhh!" I put a finger over my lips too late. Janni's voice skyrocketed through the air like a bullhorn. The three guys, now across the street from us, glanced toward the source of the odd sound.

"Oh, crap," Jason said. "Do we run?"

The shirtless guy smiled, exposing a top row of gold-plated teeth. He didn't point at the backpack but at Scarlet before he shoved his other hand down the front of his pants and started playing with himself. His buddies doubled over with laughter.

Scarlet's face burned bright red as she turned away, letting her hair fall over her face and focusing with too much intent on my backpack.

Screw those assholes. Scarlet was only in high school. Not that they cared. But I couldn't sit there. It might have looked like harmless heckling, but if the three of us squirmed along with her, it wasn't very harmless.

I stood. Time to show Scarlet the actual hero of Truman High. Not some super athlete, but the guy willing to get his ass kicked by three grown men who likely carried illegal weapons in their baggy pants.

"Bax, what are you doing?" Jason didn't tear his gaze from the gang across the street.

The sleeveless guy joined his friend, rubbing his chest while he licked his lips. The third one mouthed, *I love you,* to Scarlet.

"Don't, Bax. It's fine." Scarlet's voice trembled.

"It's not fine. They're being gross. And rude." I focused, taking in a breath. I summoned the most resounding, most intimidating tone I could muster. If this one shot at telling them off backfired, we'd all be in deep shit.

As I opened my mouth, ready to holler, *Keep moving*, the leader removed his hand from his pants, emitted a loud hoot at the sky, then slapped his friends in their stomachs and continued walking. The other two followed.

I exhaled, blood rushing from my head and back to my wobbly legs.

Thank God.

"They're leaving," Ashley told us as if we hadn't had our gazes glued on them.

I willed myself not to pass out with relief.

Neither Jason nor Ashley—both of whom saw me ready to take a stand—said anything about my brave, or dumb, attempted hero maneuver. No teasing, no mocking what I would have said, no nothing. The only comment about the incident came from Ashley. "Jerks," she said as she rested a comforting hand on Scarlet's shoulder.

Scarlet sighed. "Can we hurry this along? I want to go home." Her cheeks remained pink.

I always imagined an idyllic life for a girl like Scarlet. From my experience at Truman, everyone wanted to date her or be her friend. With straight As, she even charmed teachers. Hell, an upperclassman with superhuman football abilities fell head-over-heels in love with her. But her reaction to those assholes didn't appear to be the first time she'd encountered asinine behavior.

"Scarlet, if you want to—"

"Nothing happened. It's fine. Let's get this over with." She didn't look me in the eye.

Ashley nodded at me in agreement, her hand still on Scarlet's shoulder.

All right then. I squatted in front of my backpack. "Go see if anyone returned to the room where you traced Ifrit. Hurry."

My bag deflated as Janni jumped.

Jason refocused on our task, sensing we all needed a redirection. "What if Ben is there? Or Scott? Are we barging into a sketchy-ass hotel to confront them?"

"That's exactly what we're doing." I didn't hesitate. "They need to understand what they've done by summoning Ifrit."

"You think they'll listen to you?" Ashley's hair blew into her face, but she ignored it, letting it whip her forehead. "Don't forget, you're attempting to reason with a convicted felon who hates your mom or a guy who knows precisely what Ifrit does and stole the box anyway."

"I'm open to other ideas! In a perfect scenario, they stepped out and left the artifact, so we can use Janni to break into the room to steal it back."

Scarlet buttoned her green coat tight. "It's getting dark." Her gaze darted around us, anxious about running into another gang of assholes.

Janni reappeared in my backpack. "NO ONE IS IN THE ROOM."

Damn it.

"Did you see the box?"

Janni shook his head.

"Okay. So we wait for him to return with the box then." I watched my friends, gauging their reactions. We were so close; we couldn't bail now.

Scarlet was the first to protest. "Wait out here? Until after dark? No way."

"MASTER OF IFRIT HAS CHECKED OUT. NO RETURNING."

"What? How do you know?"

"ROOM IS EMPTY. CLOTHES GONE. BOX GONE."

"Shit!"

The blue sky started melting into orange as the sun fell below the tops of the buildings. Before my next question, I waited for a city bus to roll by. "Where did Ifrit's master go?"

Janni shook his head. "IFRIT ENERGY LED

HERE."

"So"—Jason rubbed his eyes—"the last time Ifrit appeared in this world, he appeared in there?"

"YES. CAN IT LEAVE NOW?"

The question we all wanted answered.

"Great." Jason put his glasses back on. "We're back to waiting for Ifrit to strike again. How many horrible things need to happen before we can confront Ifrit's new master?"

I kicked the brick wall of the vacant drug store. "He can't hurt anyone else."

"Yeah, but we're out of options here." Ashley checked her phone. "And it's getting late."

"Has the hotel cleaned the room yet?" I asked my backpack.

"ROOM IS MESSY."

"Perfect!"

"Where are you going with this?" Jason glowered at me.

"Housekeeping hasn't been there. Let's see if there are any clues about the thief."

"Clues?" Ashley's voice rose an octave. "Hey, Nancy Drew, what do you think you'll uncover in there?"

"Who's Nancy Drew?" I hated Ashley's cryptic references. Not the time.

"Read some classics, Bax. I'm saying we aren't gonna stumble onto a forgotten driver's license lying around."

I sighed. "How do you know? Maybe there's a signed room service ticket or something. Then at least we'll solve the mystery. I need to do something. What if something happens during the next summoning? Ifrit already beat up Aunt Jo. He's circling Mom. He tried to run us over with a car. He might be successful next time. I can't take the chance. And right now, looking for clues is all I got." Without waiting for a response, I stood up, grabbed my backpack with Janni, and stomped across the street. "With Janni's help, we'll be in and out of his room in two minutes."

About halfway across, at the yellow dotted line, I paused, thankful to let a plumbing van pass while hoping my friends caught up. The idea of breaking into a hotel room and walking home alone afterward sounded like two horrible ideas. But I'd do it if they left me with no other choice.

After the van's noise died down, the street quieted. No footfalls. They were leaving me.

I stepped onto the curb outside the Sunrise Hotel, resisting the urge to check and see if they'd disappeared.

"Just you and me, Janni," I said over my shoulder. "Let's do some breaking and entering."

He squirmed against my back. "IT IS NOT LIKING BACKPACK. BESIDES, BAXTER ALLEN KNOWS JUMPING AND STAYING IN THIS WORLD MAKES IT VERY TIRED."

"I'm sorry. After we check the room, you can jump back into the ring and sleep or whatever you do in there."

Janni sighed loud enough for me to hear.

"Wait!" Jason called, followed by the trampling of several pairs of tennis shoes across the street.

Thank God.

He grabbed my shoulder and spun me around. "I hope you know what you're doing."

"Janni can open the door from the inside. Easy. No breaking into anything."

"Of all places to *investigate*." Jason looked up at the outside of the seven-story hotel.

I met each of their pleading gazes to leave. "We'll be quick. I promise."

"Well, I'm not walking home alone, so I guess I'm in." Scarlet's words didn't have an ounce of sarcasm.

They followed me into the Sunrise Hotel through the barred glass door. Opening it triggered a chime that started at a high pitch and ended at a lower one, pinging a sad welcome. No staff lingered anywhere in the lobby or at the front desk.

In fact, it didn't appear any staff had greeted customers in years. Stacks of papers, several empty cans of soda, and an old-fashioned register like Warren's sat on the mahogany counter. The crimson lobby wallpaper, cherry wood floors, and dark wood counter created a dismal entrance. Missing bulbs appeared like black dots on the dusty crystal chandelier above us.

Ashley whispered with an uncomfortable laugh. "This place doesn't even seem to be open for business."

I peeked into my backpack. "What room, Janni?"

"FLOOR THREE, ROOM EIGHT."

Jason scratched his head. "I say we take the stairs. Who knows when the elevator last passed an inspection."

"Can we hurry, please?" Scarlet bit a nail.

"Over there." Jason pointed. We followed him up the creaking staircase in the back of the lobby. Up to the second-floor landing, we spun, up another flight, spun again, then stood before a long, carpeted hallway. Stained wallpaper decorated with brown flowers covered the walls between identical doors on each side of the hall.

"Seriously, guys," Ashley muttered, "I bet ghosts murdered at least a dozen people here."

"Room Eight." We didn't need Ashley adding to our jitteriness. I started down the hall, trying to keep everyone on task, even though beads of sweat broke out on my forehead. The hotel would have been the perfect setting for pretty much any horror movie.

I couldn't envision Scott spending a single night in one of those rooms. *Dump* was an understatement. And in my dream, Ben's apartment wasn't as fancy as Aunt Jo's on Michigan Avenue, but it didn't seem like a place where he had to worry about getting stabbed if he closed his eyes.

A door opened without the spooky creaking I expected. We froze, willing ourselves to turn invisible.

A woman in an extremely short purple skirt, an off-the-shoulder sweater, and crazy tall high heels closed the door to Room Six behind her. She attempted a runway model walk with one foot in front of the other, but her struggle not to stumble over her feet ruined her attempt at sexy confidence.

"Hey, kids." She didn't seem surprised by a cluster of clean-cut teenagers in the hallway. "Happy Halloween."

Halloween? She'd missed the holiday by a week. She must have been trying to freak us out because she knew the creep factor of the hotel, or she'd been in her room for a week with no concept of time.

I shook it off, giving her a polite smile as she passed.

"Did she—" Jason started.

"She did." I searched the tarnished brass wall plaques for Room Eight.

Room Six.

Room Seven.

Room Eight.

"Here we are." I lowered my backpack on the crimson carpet and unzipped it. "Janni, open the door from the other side."

He jumped.

I checked up and down the hallway. Scarlet continued to gnaw on her hot-pink nails, and Ashley buried her head in her phone.

"Turns out," Ashley said, "no one's reported any murders from here. At least nothing that made headlines. But I doubt these guests would report it. I mean, if they're all shady, they don't want to call attention to—"

"Will you stop?" Jason hissed.

A scream shot through the air.

I searched for the source. It came from Room Six. Before I could point that out, laughter from inside the room followed the scream.

Jesus.

The door to Room Eight clicked, and the four of us hurried to the safety inside.

Ashley coughed. "Gross."

Stale cigarette smoke and bleach hung heavy in the air. The wall heater clanked and vibrated but didn't circulate much of anything. Beer cans overflowed the small plastic wastebasket, a pile of wadded bedsheets filled the corner, and half a dozen fast food bags littered the floor. The thick curtains kept all light out of the room.

"This place is disgusting." Scarlet flipped the light switch through the sleeve of her coat, not wanting to touch it. I waited for Ashley to make a crack about Scarlet's snobbiness but noticed she avoided contact with items in the room, too.

Jason started poking the trash on the ground with his shoe. "They didn't leave anything I'd consider a clue to their identity. Wait. What's this?"

A piece of paper on the dresser had a note scribbled on it: *Blackhawks Kings Two.*

Ashley leaned over to read it. "A password?"

Jason shook his head. "Hockey. Chicago and LA. I bet the two is how many points he thinks the Blackhawks will win. Our thief is a gambler."

"I remember that from when I saw Ben's apartment in my dream. He commented on losing a baseball bet. What are the odds of someone staying in this hotel following a Chicago team where Ben happens to live?"

"Ben might be our thief." Ashley roamed into the bathroom.

"Chicago is a five-hour drive from here." Jason checked out the wastebasket near the bed. "That doesn't mean it's Ben. Lots of Chicago fans come here for games."

I wouldn't accept it, desperate to make the break-in worthwhile. "But they'd stay here? They could spring for a nicer place if they could afford a road trip and hockey tickets."

Jason rubbed his chin. "I'm not saying you're wrong, but this isn't indisputable proof it's Ben. Just a sign it could be."

"Well, we can't confirm it with DNA, Nancy Drew."

Ashley groaned as she returned from the bathroom. "Don't try, Bax."

"Check this out." Scarlet held a paper between two fingers. "It's a receipt for Warren's Cosmos. Isn't that—?"

I yanked it out of her hand. Sure enough. "Are you kidding me?"

"Score one for Scott being the thief," Ashley said. "Does he have any ties to Chicago?"

"Holy shit, man," Jason muttered. "Do you think Ben was at Warren's? Or did Scott leave that in his pocket?"

After all those years of waiting for my estranged dad to return to Warren's Cosmos, the idea he'd finally done so weakened my knees. Despite the grossness of the comforter, I sat on the bed, staring at the receipt. The purchased item was Comic Book H345KI, whatever that meant. Ben bought something at Warren's. My Warren's Cosmos. Owned by my friend, not his. He didn't deserve to visit that place. My skin crawled, like finding out someone had been rooting around in my things.

Ashley eased the receipt from my hand to read it. "I can tell by your face you're freaking out that Ben was close to home, but Bax, Scott could have forgotten it in his pocket. That doesn't mean the person in this room purchased anything. It just means they had a receipt."

Jason chose his words with care. "Ifrit's master is a person who gambles on a Chicago team, has a vendetta against your mom, knows your Aunt Jo, and recently visited a comic book store in your neighborhood. I don't know, Ash. Only one of those clues points at Scott. I'm leaning toward Ben."

"SOMEONE IS COMING." Janni stared at the hotel room door.

I sprang from the bed, shaking off the disgust that stuck to me from the comforter.

"What do we do?" Scarlet's voice squeaked. "Who is it?"

"IT DOESN'T KNOW THEM." Janni climbed into my backpack. "IT WANTS TO LEAVE."

We had to get us out—fast.

"Janni, you can return to the vortex." My backpack deflated instantly.

I opened the room's door a crack and peeked out. Someone had parked a cleaning cart in the hallway and I could hear banging in the room next door.

I shut our door. "Housekeeping."

"I can't believe they clean these rooms." Ashley scrunched her nose.

"Okay, everyone, act cool." we walked into the hallway single file. As Scarlet eased the door closed behind us, a short man in a white T-shirt and jeans dotted with water spots exited Room Seven. He held a spray bottle and sponge in his rubber-gloved hands.

He grunted a greeting.

"We're staying here. Come here all the time." Jason thumbed behind us with a wide smile plastered across his face.

The man shook his head like Jason spoke an unfamiliar language and returned to his cart.

We abandoned our plan to act casual and hurried through the hall. Midway down the stairs, Ashley whispered, "Sometimes less is more, Jason."

I shushed them.

Once in the lobby, we jogged past the empty front desk and out the main entrance, happy to be free of the horror movie hotel.

Ashley skidded to a stop in the middle of the street. "Wait! Did anyone grab the receipt and the gambling note?"

We all looked back at the looming Sunrise Hotel.

"The cleaning guy has to be in the room by now," Jason said.

"No way we're going back." Scarlet shook her head. "Nope."

"I think we got the information we needed. Let's head home." The trip had been worth it. We had narrowed our suspects from two to one.

But now what?

Chapter 17

Ifrit floated gracefully through the air without touching the ground. He's shed his powerful beast form for a nimble spirit form, free from the constraints of physicality. He glided through the front door of Bax's apartment building and up the stairs as if in the nothingness of his vortex prison.

Down the hall, he paused outside the Bryants' nicked front door. He sniffed, absorbing the diminishing pain from the law enforcer's broken bones and injuries. The human was healing, not that it mattered anymore. Ifrit had a new master to protect from the law.

He turned, slithering across the hallway to the apartment of Baxter Allen. He breezed through the locked door into his former master's home. Ifrit inhaled again, taking in the dreams of Baxter and his mother. Both slept in their beds, unaware he'd let himself inside.

A pile of keys sat on the small end table near their front door. Next to them, a phone charged. Its green battery symbol flashed to its own rhythm. Dark gold glimmered underneath the keys. Through the metal, Ifrit read a golden name tag with a black silhouette of a hotel beside a scripted *Hotel St. Louis*. Beneath those words, black letters read: *Sara—St. Louis.*

Her job.

Ifrit floated deeper into the Allens' apartment. In the kitchen, a note stuck to the refrigerator secured by a ceramic magnet with a jouster—or a lancer—on it. Sara had scrawled a reminder across a scrap of paper: *Jo's Flight—Midwest Air 146, 10:37 a.m.*

A guest arriving.

Ifrit scanned the rest of the kitchen: dishes washed and drying, refrigerator humming, a few bread crumbs on the counter. On the small, round table, exploding from the top of a narrow glass vase, white carnations, yellow roses, and daisies brightened the shadowy darkness. Ifrit kept his distance, careful not to go too close and risk killing the flowers, but he leaned forward to examine the card that had fallen from its plastic clip.

Thanks for being you—Max.

A loved one.

Ifrit pivoted, floating into the Allens' living room, hovering over a wadded-up quilt and a squashed throw pillow. He glided over the furniture, pausing over the small table piled with bills and a math book.

A sleepy moan tickled his ear.

Ifrit stiffened. He must see him.

He drifted to the other end of the modest apartment and its hallway. Three doors, two closed and one ajar. Creeping closer, he peered in through the gap. Baxter Allen slept on his stomach. A series of parallel shadow lines cast from the streetlights through his blinds striped the skin of his back. He had hooked one arm under his pillow, the other straight against his side. A glisten of saliva dripped from the corner of the boy's lips, creating a tiny puddle on his white pillowcase.

The door didn't make a sound as Ifrit melted through it, closer to his former master—the clever child who'd figured out how to banish him. When he'd first appeared to the boy, he imagined being free to travel between the boy's world and the vortex for years, but the kid proved smarter than he'd expected.

Baxter's vulnerable midsection expanded and contracted with his slow, steady breaths. Ifrit inched closer, inhaling the boy's dreams and thoughts. He missed weaving through them, picking and choosing the desires to extract and manipulate.

He enjoyed teenage minds more than those of adults. They contained thousands of erratic impulses, wants, and images fueled by immature irrationality. So much fodder from which to choose. But humans, regardless of age, never appreciated the meticulousness he gave to the wishes he granted. They were never satisfied.

Now he served someone new. An adult who valued his devotion and dedication. Someone who would never banish him, who could never banish him.

If a spirit form could, Ifrit would have smiled.

****

With a sudden gasp, I rolled over and sprang up. Reaching over my shoulder, I swatted at the middle of my back, swearing Ifrit's drool burned my skin. I kicked to untangle the twisted sheets around my legs and checked my torso for injuries, still feeling his breath on me.

I shook my hands, disturbed and grossed out, sure Ifrit had hovered inches over my back like a sick creeper while I slept. He'd been in my home, snooping around in our things, violating my space.

Wide awake, I lay back, pulling the sheets to my chin. I'd never get back to sleep knowing he could come into my bedroom whenever he wanted. And did his visit happen tonight or a few nights ago? Ifrit visions weren't always in real time. The link between us moved faster than reality sometimes, foreshadowing his attacks, and slower at other times, after the attacks happened.

Mom!

I jumped out of bed, tripping on my covers and tumbling through my bedroom door. I paused, scanning the darkness of our apartment. My heavy breathing echoed in the hallway's emptiness. Mom's door remained closed, but that didn't stop Ifrit.

I eased Mom's bedroom door open a crack. She slept on her back, blankets tight, her chest expanding and contracting with normal, relaxed breathing.

A locked door wouldn't stop him, but checking our front door's bolt reassured me. An eerie sense of untouched stillness hung in the room. He'd sniffed around without leaving a trace. Mom's note about Aunt Jo's flight still stuck to the fridge, and Max's flowers remained on the table. No evidence he'd visited.

It could have been a straight-up dream, a conjuration of my stressed-out imagination since I'd never dreamed from Ifrit's point of view. It'd always been from the eyes of his victims. He wouldn't want me to see him snooping around.

Maybe his visit had been an actual nightmare, not an Ifrit manifestation. Reality had become challenging to track.

I sucked in a long, calming inhale of air, needing some sleep. I fell back into bed and under the covers, trying to take comfort in the warm security. I rolled over and a breath caught in my throat. A light cut through the darkness from between the slight opening in my nightstand drawer.

I sprang up again.

No. No. No.

I yanked open my nightstand drawer. Janni's ring threw a purple glow across my room, blanketing the shadows in a violet hue, signaling without question that Ifrit had opened the connection to my dreams.

****

I plopped on the blue couch, releasing an appropriate sigh of air from the cushion. THC bustled with activity and chatter, but Jason buried his head in his laptop. He must not have heard me sit down. We hadn't talked since the break-in at the Sunrise Hotel. All four of us made an unspoken agreement not to speak for the entire walk and bus ride back home, our minds reeling.

Mine tried to process how Ben had escaped Illinois and knew enough to steal Ifrit. The heckling from those thugs had shaken Scarlet. Jason had agreed Ben targeted us but kept replaying our clues in case we missed something. And who knew what Ashley thought about when she wasn't talking.

Jason looked up from his laptop, his eyebrows crunched together. "Uh-oh. You have your something-bad-just-happened look."

"More developments."

He closed his laptop and his eyes, bracing for my news. "Who'd he hit?"

"Me, I think. I had this dream—"

"You know what?"—Jason sighed—"I miss when you used to say that, and it ended with you naked in the auditorium, trapped in a video game, or sprouting wings and flying to Jamaica. Now, it always ends with someone dead or injured."

"Ah, the good ol' days. At least this recent one doesn't end with a corpse or a hospital visit. But way creepier. I dreamed from Ifrit's point of view, not his victim's."

Jason scratched his cheek. "That's a first. Why creepy? Weird, yeah, but what made it creepy?"

"He snooped around in my apartment."

Jason leaned forward. "What?"

"He became a ghost or spirit and floated around my apartment, rifling through our stuff. Then he drifted into my bedroom while I slept and got, like, really close to me. I could hear his thoughts and feel his breath on my back. He'd never been so close, and he seemed to enjoy it. I swear, even though he was a ghost, I could feel—"

"You should stop. Some dreams should be kept to yourself. Even best friends should have some secrets."

"What do you mean?"

Then he grinned, flickering his eyebrows as he winked.

"Oh my God! Shut up, perv. This is serious." I spun a yellow throw pillow at him.

He laughed, knocking the pillow to the couch. "Give me the details."

"He just snooped around, then I woke up."

Jason's phone vibrated on the table. He glanced at it, then shoved it into his pocket. "Ashley's gonna join soon."

She was texting him her schedule?

"You guys sure seem to talk a lot these days."

Jason ignored my comment. "Ifrit might be trying to scare you if he thinks we've figured out Ben's his new master. Maybe he meant the midnight visit as a threat, so you knew he could get to you if he wanted. He's sending a message you're not safe anywhere."

"So you're finally convinced it's Ben, then?"

The phone vibrated in Jason's pocket, but he didn't

check it. She was texting again? Had to be since Jason didn't have an endless roster of contacts.

"Yeah, although there are still gaps in the story if it's Ben, which I can't figure out. How'd he jump parole with enough time to find you before the cops found him? And how'd he know to steal the box, let alone rub the jewel? I mean, the stuff we found at the Sunrise Hotel points to him over Scott, but still..." Jason rubbed his chin. "How much do you remember of the dream besides Ifrit getting a little too personal with you while you slept? What did he rifle through?"

I retraced his steps, recalling the dream's details. "He checked Ashley's place but didn't enter. Then he found our keys but lingered over Mom's hotel name tag."

"Her old job?"

I closed my eyes and let out a breath. "Oh, no."

"What?"

Resting my forearms on my knees, I kept my eyes closed to remember each step of his visit. "Then he read the note where Mom had written Aunt Jo's flight number."

"Uh, two for two. That explains how he knew Aunt Jo's name when he appeared in your room. And then?"

Think, Bax.

"He...he read the card from the flowers Max gave Mom." I opened my eyes. "Oh, shit."

Jason shook his head. "Bro, he's not creeping around your apartment just to sniff you while you sleep. He's gathering intel for his master. But wait, the timing's off."

"What do you mean?"

"You said Aunt Jo flew in spontaneously *after* the hotel laid your mom off. Therefore, the note wouldn't have been on the fridge until after they fired her. So if Ifrit was the reason they let her go, the dream you experienced may not be the only time he's poked around your place."

I fell back on the couch. "He could have seen her badge previously, worked his magic to get her fired, and my dream last night was where he learned Aunt Jo's name and about her visit. Mom stuck that note on the fridge the night she stayed with us, which was also the night he appeared in my room, threatening Janni."

Jason fell back, too. "So we've nailed down when your dream took place, but sounds like that's not the only time he's come creeping around."

I shuddered. "Awesome. Well, if we can rely on my dream as a checklist of Ifrit's targets, he saw the work badge, then he got my mom fired. He saw the note about my aunt's flight, then he attacked her. He saw Max's card—"

"Max is next," Jason said.

My stomach dropped. Mom finally opened herself up to a handsome, successful guy and Ifrit planned on destroying him. Made sense if Ben's thoughts motivated him.

Jason stiffened. "Something else just hit me."

"I'm not sure I can handle anything else."

"If Ifrit was gathering intel, then that means his master may not be Ben. The only reason we nixed Scott was because he wouldn't know your Aunt Jo or where your mom worked. This puts Scott back on the suspect list."

One step forward and two steps back. "I hate to say it, but you're right. And one thing that's bugging me is why would Ifrit show me how he marks his victims?

Never has before. Why start now?"

"We don't know if he's aware you saw him creeping around. What if you weren't supposed to have that dream? The last time he appeared to you, he said you guys will always be connected. I don't think he sends you those dreams intentionally. I think they happen on their own because of that connection."

Not a comforting thought; I'd be forever bound to a djinn. "Well, whether it's Scott or Ben, what do we do about Max?"

Jason picked at a loose thread on the couch, thinking. "We can't warn him. Not sure what we'd tell him, be on guard for purple-eyed people?"

Scarlet walked in front of the coffee bar with her friends. Our gazes stalled on each other for a split second. She waved, but the kind of wave when you noticed someone by mistake and then acknowledged them out of obligation. Not the type of wave you gave someone you were happy to see. I understood how the Sunrise Hotel incident scared her, but I'd warned her about getting involved with the Djinn-verse. No magic carpet flights through a fantastical adventure on this ride.

I returned the wave, but she'd already gone back to her conversation with Latoya, giving no sign she intended to join us. Seemed strange after yesterday. I figured she'd want to discuss our clues and figure out the next steps.

"I guess she's too busy to come over." Jason shook his head at our awkward exchange.

I'd heard Jason's opinion on my relationship with Scarlet enough times, but that didn't mean he and Ashley needed to be so icy toward her. Our trip to the Sunrise Hotel more than demonstrated her commitment to banishing Ifrit.

"I'm sure you're devastated she's not coming over." The words flew out harsher than I intended. "By the way, you and Ashley have made it abundantly clear you aren't her number one fan. Message received. I swear, you two act like we're some kind of exclusive club she barged into."

"No, we don't." He didn't even believe what he said.

"Oh my God! When I met you guys at your place on Tuesday, you and Ashley were totally ignoring her. It was the most uncomfortable scene to walk into. Ashley wouldn't even credit Scarlet for coming up with the idea of tracking Ifrit from Zia's, and neither of you would look in her direction when we were talking."

"It wasn't intentional. We just have nothing in common."

"You guys were rude. She's my friend, like it or not." The last sentence felt strange coming out of my mouth, but I wouldn't admit that to Jason.

He rolled his eyes. "Dude, she's not your friend. She's your crush who started paying attention to you when she found out you controlled a djinn."

Was he kidding me? "Not true."

"True. Has she talked to you about anything *other* than djinn? Any friendly *how are you* texts? Any drop bys when her friends are around? Be honest. She's using you, and you're okay with that because you're in love with her. That's fine. That's your decision, but let's keep it real, bro."

My blood boiled. Keep it real? *He* wants to keep it real?

"Then why don't *you* be honest about having a thing for Ashley? The two of you lurk around, texting, talking, and hanging out like a couple, but you both clam up when I ask if something's going on. Why don't we keep *that* real, *bro*?"

"You're an asshole." Jason threw open his laptop, pretending to type something.

"No, you're an asshole," I said, unable to come up with a better response.

I grabbed my backpack and stormed out of Truman High Commons.

Chapter 18

On my way to the kitchen, I flung my backpack into my room, where it hit the comforter with a squish before rolling to the floor with a muffled thud. I'd stomped home at a speed that qualified as a run, reliving my argument with Jason over and over in my head.

I was an asshole?

Jason acted like he didn't have feelings for Ashley when he did. He needed to admit it. She was just as dishonest, pretending nothing was going on between them. They were both liars. And he had the nerve to say Scarlet was using me. He knew we'd always been friends. Not super close, but friends. Besides, he wasn't comfortable around her because she never paid attention to him. He couldn't handle that I was friends with a popular hot girl. He should have *kept it real* with himself.

I filled a glass with water from the plastic pitcher in the fridge and chugged it. Jason's probably complaining about me to Ashley at that moment, nervous I discovered their secret love affair, and planning their next devious maneuver to throw me off the trail and convince me it wasn't real.

I fell back onto my bed and shoved my headphones into my ears. I tapped my playlist and cranked up the volume when my favorite Drill song started. The crashing guitars dueled over the fast drums and thundering bass line, but even their best song couldn't kill my circling thoughts about Jason and Ashley.

My two so-called friends lied right to my face and didn't even feel bad about it. Jason acted like he was an expert on what girls thought, always telling me Scarlet didn't like me. How would he know? He and Ashley thought they were so much smarter than me, with their perfect grades and advanced classes. That was why they wanted the No Djinn Rule. Because they thought I couldn't navigate the Djinn-verse without them. Neither one hesitated when Scarlet suggested I give Janni over. They'd have loved that.

I pulled the ring out of my pants pocket. Djinn magic had consequences, but I didn't care. I'd take my chances.

Jason and I shared everything. Why was this such a taboo secret? Maybe they were just friends. No, that wasn't true. Otherwise, he'd have said that instead of always changing the subject. Why wouldn't my best friend since fifth grade be honest? Well, I didn't need them to be honest. If I wanted the truth, I could find it.

I rubbed the ring. The chills cascaded over my skin, pricking me like needles. As the pungent odor rolled into my room, I inhaled. Screw their No Djinn Rule.

"HOW CAN IT—"

"Jesus! Do you have to open with the same phrase every time?"

Janni's ears fell flat against his head before he straightened his short spine and squared his shoulders. "WHAT DOES BAXTER ALLEN WANT?"

"Do your invisible thing and read Jason's texts. See if he's texting with Ashley right now."

Janni jumped without question.

They wouldn't admit it? Fine. I'd prove their little secret. Then I'd tell them I knew, and we could all stop playing this stupid charade. After that, they'd have to admit why they didn't tell me in the first place, which was the real problem.

I fell back against my comforter and rubbed my eyes. As I stared at the ceiling, my pounding heart eased. What was I doing? Using Janni to spy on my best friends? They'd be furious and would have every right to be because it was a shitty thing to do.

Janni reappeared on my bed. "I READ THE MESSAGES."

I'd known Jason way longer, but Ashley had been through so much with us. In the past month, she'd put her life on the line to save mine. She and Jason literally dragged me out of the vortex and stood by my side against Ifrit. They were my best friends. Best friends didn't spy on each other or read private texts not meant for them.

My face burned with guilt and shame.

"JASON AND LOUD GIRL ARE SENDING NOTES ON THEIR PHONES."

I buried my head in my hands. Jason called it right. I was the asshole. If I'd acted casual and supportive, they might have admitted it, but I behaved like an obsessed person. Despite our friendship, their romantic relationship—if one existed—wasn't my business.

"JASON AND LOUD GIRL ARE MAKING PLANS FOR TOMORROW."

"Wait, stop. Stop talking, Janni."

"TOMORROW THEY—"

"Stop! Don't say another word."

Janni's ears fell back against his head again. "BAXTER SHOULDN'T SHOUT AT IT." He growled deep in his throat.

Great, even Janni thought I was an asshole.

"I'm sorry for yelling at you." I brushed his arm fur with my fingers, but he yanked away with a pouty grunt. "The whole how-can-it-serve greeting is your thing. I'm sorry."

Janni side-eyed me with his purple eyes.

"Forgive me?"

He turned back to me and sat on my bed, stretching his legs in front of him. "BAXTER ALLEN IS VERY CONFUSING."

"Tell me about it."

"DOES HE WANT TO HEAR WHAT IT READ?"

"Absolutely not. I shouldn't have asked you to spy. Don't tell me anything you read. And in the future, if I ask you to spy on Jason or Ashley, you need to tell me no. I give you permission to disobey."

Janni's chest expanded, then contracted as he exhaled. "CONFUSING INDEED."

"You can go."

Janni disappeared.

I was a complete dirtbag. I'd sworn off djinn after we'd banished Ifrit but kept walking back into the Djinn-verse like an addict—the exact reason we created the No Djinn Rule. Having magic at my disposal was too tempting to abuse. Hell, even when I tried to do good with it, like at St. Bernard's, things went wrong.

I rolled off my bed and headed to the kitchen to get an apple and text Jason an apology. I'd tell him I didn't care if he and Ashley hooked up or not, and I was available if he ever wanted to talk about it. What I should have said at the beginning.

A note from Mom poked out from under the bowl of bananas on the counter.

Bax—

At Max's. There's leftover ham in the fridge. Eat some carrots, too, please. Be home around 10. Do your homework. Love you.

Mom

She'd gone to Max's.

Crap.

Ifrit read Max's note from the flowers, which meant either Max was his next target or he'd attack Mom using him. I'd been so worried about Jason and Ashley, I'd forgotten what really needed my attention.

Dialing Mom, I scrambled to think of what to say. I couldn't tell her to leave without a valid reason, but I couldn't sit around waiting for Ifrit to strike.

One ring.

I could tell her I wasn't feeling well, but I wasn't a baby. She'd recommend I take an aspirin and rest. She wouldn't leave Max's because her fifteen-year-old had a tummy ache.

Two rings.

I'd destroy our apartment and say someone broke in. No, too much. Besides, then we'd be saddled with paying for the damage.

Come on. Answer.

Three rings.

She picked up.

"Hey, Bax. What's wrong? Didn't you get my note?" A gust of wind blew across her phone, fuzzing her last few words.

Outside. Good. I wanted to believe Ifrit wouldn't want an audience for an attack.

"Got it." I crumpled her note in my fist, turning my knuckles white. "So, uh, what are you guys doing?"

"Well, change of plans. Instead of eating at his house, we're walking around Delmar. They strung the Christmas lights up, and it's not even Thanksgiving! Ridiculous. Did you not get my full itinerary?"

"Haha."

A conversation happened behind her. Definitely not alone, especially on Delmar Avenue, and dinner at a restaurant meant other diners.

"Bax, you're acting strange." Mom covered the phone and said something to Max that included my name.

I didn't have a plan, and I couldn't do anything to protect Mom and Max. Ifrit could strike today, tomorrow, or in a week.

"I'm just checking in. You know, we did almost die during a hit-and-run."

"Oh, Baxter, we were victims of a random incident. Those things don't happen to the same people twice. It's like lightning striking. The odds are slim that it happens once, but twice? Hardly ever."

Unless lightning struck under the command of an evil djinn with a vendetta.

"I realize my dating life is an adjustment. Why don't we plan a movie night—"

Oh my God. Is Max standing right there?

He would think I couldn't deal with sharing Mom. Or worse, she would think I wasn't comfortable with her dating. I couldn't let either of those things happen.

"No, Mom. All good. Really. I'm rereading the note. I thought it said Max was coming over here. Not you were going there. Wondered when and started planning where I'd hide for the evening. I need to learn to slow down my reading."

She paused. "Why would I leave you a note if we'd be at home?"

"To warn me? I don't know, you tell me!" I laughed, sounding insane and needing to get off the phone before it woke Mom's instincts, and she turned this into a thing.

"Here's the ham, and I promise to eat a few carrots." I slammed the refrigerator door loud enough for her to hear. "Be safe out there, you crazy kids!"

Max said something in the background.

"Okay, hon. Text or call if you need me."

"Will do."

I hung up. Nothing I could do, and she sounded as safe as she could be. I ignored the unsettled helplessness in my gut. I didn't have any other options.

Plopping on the couch, I started texting Jason about Mom, then stopped. Instead, I texted:

—*I'm sorry for calling you an asshole.*—

I'd talk to him about the Ashley thing in person, not over text.

He responded right away.

—*Me too. Play some AA in a few?*—

I texted back a thumbs-up emoji.

****

Max stood in front of the bathroom mirror, the electric toothbrush humming in his mouth. A line of toothpaste foam dribbled down his chin and landed on his chest. He spat, rinsed, then wiped the toothpaste with a swipe of his thumb, but the white remained.

He leaned closer to the mirror to examine the white speck amid his black chest hair and scraped at it with his thumbnail.

"No way. A gray hair."

With the white hair between his finger and

thumbnail, he yanked. It held steadfast against his skin. "Come here, you little bastard." He secured a better grip and yanked again, plucking it out.

Massaging the sting with two fingers, he held the hair up in front of his face.

"Well, damn."

He flicked it to the floor and smacked the bedroom light switch on. The room was empty. Too bad. Sara warned him she'd move slower than other women. She'd warned him multiple times, convinced he'd be disappointed, like a crazed womanizer. Not sure how she expected him to live a ladies' man lifestyle with his job's long hours and travel.

The mere thought of Sara brought a grin to his face. While he didn't know Bax that well yet, he could imagine a future with Sara and him, even though they'd only been dating for a few weeks.

He hung his pants on a hanger and beat the wrinkles from them with his palm, then shoved them into the small closet where they'd wrinkle again. He kept his wardrobe minimal since the old house had little space to spare. There'd be no way Sara and Bax could live at his place, and Sara's apartment was even smaller.

Okay, man, you're getting ahead of yourself.

Max fell back onto the red comforter and flipped on the TV. Headlines scrolled across the bottom of the screen, while stock prices scrolled on the right side. An attractive Asian woman with cherry-colored lips talked to the camera. The scrolls and rhythmic delivery of the anchor weighed on his eyelids—the red wine and pasta at dinner with Sara didn't help. With as few movements as possible, Max slid under the blankets. He reached for the TV remote.

Smash!

Max shot up in bed and muted the TV.

Glass shattering?

He listened and waited, but only heard silence.

As he unmuted the TV, the floorboards in the hundred-year-old house creaked as weight shifted on top of them. The identical sound he made walking across the room. He muted the TV again.

Max strained to listen for another sound, but his pounding heart thundered in his ears. Maybe he'd imagined the noise. Old houses made noises; it came with the territory. But the creaking of a settling foundation didn't sound the same as smashed glass.

He crawled out from under the covers and stepped forward on the ball of his foot toward his bedroom door. He paused to listen.

A soft, muffled noise floated through the hallway— a cough under someone's hand.

The hairs on the back of his neck stood at full attention. It didn't sound like it came from outside.

Shit. Now what?

As an accountant living in one of the safest suburban zip codes, he'd never dealt with a home invader. He grabbed his phone off the nightstand and scanned his bedroom for a weapon. Nothing in sight.

Golf clubs!

Nope. In the foyer closet.

He stared at his phone. He should call the police. And say he heard something resembling a cough that could also have been a dog barking outside. Or say he heard shattering glass or his neighbor's recycle bin falling over at the curb.

He picked up the lamp, easing the plug from the

wall, careful not to let it tap the floor. It wouldn't do much damage, but it'd be something.

Armed with his phone in one hand and lamp in the other, he tiptoed another long step to his bedroom doorway. He needed both hands on the lamp but wearing only his boxer briefs, he couldn't slide his phone into his pocket. Putting on pants would be too risky—too much opportunity to make noise.

After a shaky breath, he exhaled.

With a quick leap, he jumped into the dark hallway, landing on the balls of his feet. He switched his phone's flashlight on and swept it to his right. Clear. To his left. Clear.

He'd read most burglars would run at the first sign of people at home. Surely, they'd heard him jump, even with bare feet, but he didn't hear anyone scrambling to escape before he could identify them. Thank God he didn't call the police. How embarrassing.

He cleared his throat as loud as he could to alert anyone who'd broken in.

No response.

"Hey!" Max hollered in his most resounding, intimidating voice. "If someone's here, I called the police."

An icy breeze rushed by him, a reminder he only wore his underwear.

Icy breeze.

Someone had broken a window.

Shit.

He dialed nine-one-one on his phone, and the screen lit up his face.

The operator answered after one ring. "Nine-one-one. What's your emergency?" Max lowered the volume.

"Yeah, hi," he whispered. "Someone threw something through my window, and I think they're attempting a burglary—" A stirring in the darkness ahead of him drew Max's attention from his phone.

His eyes adjusted to the shadows, piecing together the form of a man standing at the far end of his hallway watching him.

The man wore tight black pants and a black, long-sleeved T-shirt stretched over broad shoulders. Taller than Max, a rubber mask of a goat's head concealed his identity. The fake muzzle protruded from his face with a small hole in the mouth's tip so its wearer could breathe. The curved plastic horns hugged its head.

As Max's brain registered what his eyes absorbed, the man lunged forward with a few thunderous bounds. He body-checked Max in the torso, knocking the lamp and phone out of his hands. The hardwood floor squealed as Max's bare back skidded across it and into the living room.

Rolling to his stomach, he grabbed the legs of an end table and clawed his way up, hoping to get out from under the man before he pinned him. He'd almost made his way to a stand before the goat man, still on the ground, caught Max's ankle and yanked.

He lost his balance without his foot on the floor and fell forward. His chin smacked the surface of the end table. His teeth bit down hard on his tongue, ringing in his head.

Taking advantage of Max's temporary dizziness, the man yanked Max toward him on his back with one hand. As he slid, Max grabbed blindly for a weapon but could only snag a magazine to defend himself.

He threw it at the goat mask, but the man batted it away.

The man rose before coming down, ramming his elbow into Max's gut. With the wind punched out of him, Max's body curled as he gasped.

The goat man shimmied up Max, keeping him pinned to the ground on his back.

"Hello? Sir? Are you there?" The operator's distant voice came from the phone that had slid across the living room.

"Help! Send the police!" Max shouted as he tried to knock off his attacker. The man in black straddled Max's abdomen, making it hard to catch his breath after the elbow to his gut. Max launched a fist against the side of the man's head, but the goat's head didn't budge.

What the hell?

"What do you want?" Max rammed his fists into the man's iron-tough sides, more granite muscle than human flesh. Pinned on his back, Max couldn't exert much force behind his punches.

With inhuman speed, the man angled himself so his shins pressed Max's biceps to the floor, and he rested his weight below Max's rib cage.

Max flung his legs, trying to get enough leverage to knee the man in the back and throw him, but the burglar pinned him like a ten-ton boulder on his midsection. He sat so high on Max that he couldn't get his knees high enough to make any serious impact.

"Take whatever you want! I don't give a shit. Just leave!"

The man's labored breathing echoed within the thick rubber mask. "After what you've done?" Although muffled under the goat's face, the intruder's voice sounded like a growl.

"What are you talking about?" Max twisted his shoulder but couldn't free his arms from under the man's shins. Max did corporate taxes. He didn't make enemies at work. There'd been no contentious run-ins with anyone on the street. Who'd be so angry at him?

The man raised his fist over his head. Max closed his eyes in dreaded anticipation. The fist slammed the side of his face. Max's vision sparked with white light.

With a grunt, the man's other fist crashed against the left side of his head.

Although he was flat on his back, the room swayed under Max. With his arms pinned against the floor and his legs ineffectual, he lay exposed and defenseless.

"You will stay away from Sara Allen." The man growled so low Max didn't understand how he made out the words behind the rubber mask. "And Baxter. Never see them again. Do not call them…"

He pounded his fist into the right side of Max's head.

"Do not see them…"

He slammed his fist into the left side.

"Do not think about them…"

Max swallowed the blood in the back of his throat as he coughed. He tried to answer the goat man so he'd stop the beating but forgot how to form words.

The man's punches continued.

Left side.

Right side.

Again.

And again.

And again.

Max couldn't keep his eyes open. They rolled back

in his head. The ringing in his ears drowned out the sound of his blood splattering on the floor with each landed blow. His head throbbed, numb to the barrage. His brain flickered like a TV hit by a power surge.

As the intruder leveraged his weight on Max's chest to stand, bloody coughs spouted from Max's mouth. He flopped his head to the side to avoid choking.

Max lifted his hand to his head, needing to feel it, to assure himself it remained attached. He swallowed gulp after gulp of blood, hearing nothing beyond the ringing in his head. He curled into a fetal position, unable to stand or think.

"Tell me you understand. Stay away from them." The goat man kept his voice low, panting his words.

Max tried to nod but couldn't control his head. "I understand." He couldn't hear if the words escaped the bloody cough.

With his boot, the man stepped on Max's side, rolling him onto his back again. Max covered his face with his hands in fear of another pounding. Between his fingers, the goat mask hovered inches from him. Close. Waiting for him to lower his hands.

He complied. The fuzzy image of the goat's head through his tears and blood became a spirit welcoming him to the next world.

"I said yes." Max coughed.

The man in the goat mask stood up and melted back into the shadows from which he came.

****

I launched up in bed. My heart pounded, and my head throbbed as if I'd suffered the beating. My ears rang, and dizziness swayed the room for a second.

I yanked my nightstand drawer open, and it fell off

its tracks and onto the floor, dumping out my tissues, headphones, a book, and the ring.

The jewel glowed bright purple, lighting up my room.

Chapter 19

I leaned against the wall of lockers, my backpack at my feet, waiting for Jason to arrive. The kids milled around me, killing time before the first bell. Malcolm and four other football players hooted and hollered as they passed, amped up as always. It must've been exhausting.

Malcolm glanced in my direction but didn't make eye contact. Fine with me. Besides, he'd returned the candle in a rare show of compassion for my mom. What else was there to say about it? We hadn't bonded and become friends over his shoplifting. And at least our confrontation hadn't broken the peace treaty Scarlet brokered.

Mom didn't say anything about Max's assault before I left for school. She either didn't know, or it hadn't happened yet. Dreams used to be a window into what Ifrit had already done, but Zia's proved our connection also allowed him to foreshadow his activity. I was stuck. I could warn Max if the dream hadn't happened, but even if he believed me by a strange stroke of luck, hunkering down in his locked house wouldn't stop Ifrit. If the djinn set his sights on Max, nothing could stop him.

Jason might have an idea. It'd been a day, and we'd said our apologies. I'd acted like a lunatic. Sure, I wish he'd have told me about Ashley, but he didn't owe me that. I smiled at the idea of Jason and Ashley having a secret affair. The idea sounded so bizarre. Their texts said they were planning to hang out tonight. They didn't need to sneak around behind my back. I refused to lose either of them as friends over my bruised and misguided ego.

"Hey." Jason dropped his backpack on the floor next to mine.

I stepped aside so he could enter his locker combination, happy he smiled at me. We were all good again. "Two things. First, Ifrit struck again—or will soon—and it isn't pretty."

Jason grunted. "Like he ever strikes in a good way. What happened?"

"I dreamed he attacked Max. Ifrit beat the living shit out of him. Posed as a burglar, and as he punched the hell out of him, told Max to stay away from Mom and me. Ruthless, man. Worse than Mr. Bryant."

"At the risk of sounding basic, you're sure it was Ifrit?" He started unpacking his backpack, piling books inside the locker, one on top of the other, spines facing out. Jason might be the only sophomore who didn't toss his books into his locker but stacked them in the order he needed them.

"Well, I couldn't see any purple eyes, but the burglar wore a rubber goat head."

Jason paused with his hand on his Spanish book. "Jesus. That's creepy. He's messing with you."

"Yeah."

"How's Max? Has your mom talked to him?"

"She hasn't, which is why I'm not sure if the attack happened yet."

Jason slammed his locker, snapped his lock, and

turned around holding his Spanish book and laptop. He dropped his voice. "He lives alone. Do we need to call an ambulance or something?"

"Max dialed 9-1-1 in my dream, so the operator heard—or will hear—what happened."

"We should check on him. We can use Janni to pick up Ifrit's trail again. Even if our favorite djinn hasn't attacked Max yet, maybe he cased his place, and there're energy traces." Jason checked his vibrating phone.

Ashley? He didn't say, just slipped the phone back into his pocket.

"Good idea. Do it after school?"

"We should do it as soon as possible. I'm guessing your mom will have heard from him, or not, by then. I gotta run, though. You said you had two things?"

I sighed, nervous. "The second thing I wanted to say is that I wish you would have told me about Ashley—if there's something to tell—and it hurt you didn't. But that's on me, not you. Given how I acted yesterday, I would have thought twice about telling me, too."

Jason's nose twitched, and he rubbed it. He bit his bottom lip. "Man, I'm not sure what Ashley and I are. Nothing, like physical, has happened. But we're starting to talk and stuff over text. We share a lot in common."

"So true." I shrugged, grinning as I looked away. "You're both super big nerds. So there's that."

I watched for a reaction. A reluctant smile flickered on his face. "And when we nerds are running the world, we'll let you stay with us. To help clean the house and stuff."

"I suck at cleaning."

"Your room is a dump. Cleaning isn't the job for you because then I'd have to fire you. Talk about awkward."

The bell rang. First period. I picked up my backpack. "We're good? We need to be since the world needs us to save it." I held out my fist. "Again."

He bumped it. Jason and I didn't fight often, but when we did, it didn't last long.

"Let's save the world," Jason said, "but after school. Mrs. Montego and her Spanish test await me. You know. Nerd stuff. I'll text Ashley."

"Hopefully, Max's will be quick and nothing's happened, and then you and Ashley can hang out afterward. I have to work on my history paper, anyway." As soon as I said it, my neck warmed up to my cheeks and my ears started ringing. I'd never wanted to take back a sentence more.

Shit. Shit. Shit.

Jason stopped walking and eyed me over his glasses. "How did you know we talked about hanging out tonight?"

"Just trying to be supportive of you guys." I couldn't hide the look of horror that blanketed my face.

"Did she say something to you?"

"No." I couldn't look at him.

Stupid. Stupid. Stupid!

"So then..." He dropped his gaze to my pants pocket. "Did Janni spy on me?"

I fought the urge to throw up all over the floor in the hallway. "No. I mean, yes, but I stopped it. I was mad. But then I told him not to tell me anything. I swear. He got out one sentence before I shut him down."

Jason leaned close to me. "You've been using Janni without us, and even worse, to spy on me? And now you want my help?"

"Only once. And again, I stopped him after one

sentence."

"After you found out she wanted to hang out tonight, you decided to stop him."

"No. Janni blurted it out before I could say anything. I swear."

"You swear? Really? I don't believe you, Bax." Jason spun around and stomped off, disappearing into the crowd of students hurrying to their first class.

****

Mr. Buchannan rambled on about black holes. I doubted a zero-gravity void in space and time could save me from our djinn problems like a super blue blood moon did the last time. However, falling into a black hole and letting it rip me apart might be a better alternative to my current friend situation.

I'd avoided all human contact since talking with Jason. I ate half of my lunch outside and threw the rest of it away—wasn't hungry and too cold. At forty degrees, no one else joined me outside, but my stomach wretched at the idea of sitting with Jason and Ashley in the cafeteria. I couldn't face either of them.

The clock clicked by slow second by slow second until the end of the day when the last bell rang. I jumped up and dove into the river of kids in the hallway, weaving through the swarming bodies to Truman High's double glass door entrance. Down the stairs, I sped past Nick's bench and down the uneven sidewalk off the school grounds. I turned left on Pine Avenue at an unintentional jog.

I needed an afternoon to regroup and figure out what to do next. Mom texted me that Max was picking her up from work and they were going to dinner, which meant I'd have my place all to myself, and more importantly, that meant Ifrit hadn't attacked Max yet.

Up ahead, the green-and-white awning of Warren's Cosmos beckoned me—a perfect, momentary distraction. I hoped he had a story ready about Moroccan crime lords or wrestling with dangerous crocodiles in the Amazon, not one about his childhood cancer scare. Plus, I could see if Scott moved out of the hotel where he'd been staying. Hopefully, he'd say no, which meant he wasn't the guest who'd vacated the Sunrise Hotel, and we could take him off our suspect list.

The silver bell dinged as I opened the door and breathed the comforting smell of musty paper. My gaze fell to the empty stool behind the counter. I'd never seen it without the store's owner perched upon it. Never in the history of Warren's Cosmos. I'd been frequenting the place since Mom first let me walk to school, and Warren always sat there ready to greet me, happy to recommend the newest release.

I swallowed, trudging to the counter as if knee-deep in mud. A voice nagged me to turn around and walk back out the door. If Warren wasn't at his store, then I shouldn't be. It felt unnatural.

The comforting, musty air in Warren's Cosmos triggered memories of the mildewy cellar below my building, where scary things haunted every dark nook and shadowy corner. For the first time since I'd walked through the doors of Warren's Cosmos, it smelled old and dying.

At the empty counter, I shoved my hands into my coat pockets, unsure what to do. I'd give it a minute. Maybe Warren had to use the bathroom. He had been sick.

The bulky, old-fashioned register reminded me of

the receipt we'd forgotten at the Sunrise Hotel. Warren could have deciphered the code on it and identified the purchaser. His reaction to my ask might have revealed if he or Scott had anything to do with Ifrit's return. I still couldn't get my head around that, though.

I called to the empty store, "Hello?" Rows of comic books absorbed my voice, reminding me of when I screamed in the vortex.

The storage room door opened and Scott noticed me waiting. "Oh, sorry. What can I do for you?"

Was he not going to even acknowledge Warren's absence? "Where's Warren?"

"Ben, right?" Scott ran a hand through his hair. It remained standing straight up.

Of all the names to mistake mine for, he had to pick Ben. "Bax."

"Right. Sorry." He let out a breath. "Dad's not in today."

The combination of words in his last statement didn't make sense. "I don't understand. Warren's never out. If the Cosmos is open, he's here." I stretched a smile across my face to mask the nervousness in my tone. The echo of Warren's cancer story summoned a queasiness in my gut.

Scott pushed his wire-rimmed glasses higher on his nose. "He's sick."

"Has he ever missed work because he was sick?"

Scott sighed. "Lately, yeah."

"I guess it is flu season."

Warren's son stiffened as if he didn't want to answer me at first. "He doesn't have the flu. Remember the last story he told you? He didn't make that one up."

I'd suspected it was true but chose not to believe it.

"Right, but that's when he was a kid. And he beat it. He just lost a few fingers."

"The cancer's come back a few times since then, but he survived it every time. We're not sure if he can this go-around." Scott's voice cracked.

"Cancer?" The word pierced my ears, stabbing my brain. I shook my head in disbelief. I'd never known anyone with cancer. That disease happened in movies and TV because it never ended well for the character. Years of experimental treatments where they lost their hair and half their body weight.

"I'm sorry." The room swayed under me. "He'll beat it this time, too. For sure."

"We're praying he does." As Scott spoke, his lips remained motionless, and his eyes shimmered with the reflection of the fluorescent ceiling lights.

Warren couldn't have cancer again. He never did anything wrong to deserve cancer.

A glow appeared around Scott as my eyes teared. I turned my head, pretending to be interested in something at the other end of the store, so Scott wouldn't see.

After swiping my eyes with my sleeve, I turned back to Scott and repeated, "I'm sorry."

He nodded but said nothing. There weren't any words to say.

"Can you tell him I stopped by?"

Scott opened the drawer to count money and distract himself. "I'll tell him you asked about his fingers. Right? That's your thing?"

My stomach fell to the floor. I'd never ask him that again, now that I knew the truth. My lifelong tradition of our two questions—one around Ben's search for his missing comic book, and the other about how he lost his fingers—had ended. Neither of them remained hopeful, entertaining questions. They both led to awful, somber answers.

"Yeah, that's our thing, but it doesn't feel right to ask him that anymore."

Scott looked up from the register. "He wouldn't see it that way. Cancer's been part of his life forever, and I bet he never once squirmed when you asked him."

"But I didn't know."

"Maybe that's why he never told you. He enjoyed telling his stories as much as you enjoyed hearing them. He wouldn't want that to stop." Scott closed the register drawer.

"Okay. Then tell him I stopped by. And I'll ask him next time I see him."

Scott smiled. "He wouldn't want it any other way."

I sauntered out of Warren's Cosmos on wobbly legs. Warren wouldn't die. He beat cancer before, and he'd do it again. He was the toughest guy I knew. The experience would just be fodder for more fantastical stories.

My hurried pace quickened into a jog, then anxiety fueled me to run. My skin tingled as my sweat chilled in the brisk air. I didn't know Warren well. I never would have guessed he had a kid until Scott showed up a few days ago. But I couldn't imagine my life without him. He probably didn't even realize the impact he had on me. I should have told him. We were friends. I'd known him as long as Jason. I never told him how much I valued his friendship after all these years.

Stop it, Bax. He's not dead. People survive cancer.

I needed to think positive thoughts. I shouldered open the door to my building and leaped up the three flights, jumping over the broken stair. My legs burned from my sprint home.

I unlocked the door to our apartment and dropped my backpack to the floor, eager to collapse onto my bed. Before I could, though, I saw Mom sitting at the kitchen table instead of at work or out with Max.

Oh no.

My brain couldn't handle anything else on the worst day in the history of days. Another horrible thing would cause it to explode in my skull.

"Mom?" I approached the table cautiously.

"You're home already?" She dabbed her red and swollen eyes with a tissue. I didn't like coming home to her crying twice in a week and a half.

"What's wrong, Mom? Is it Aunt Jo?"

She sniffed. "Max and I broke up."

Crap.

I fell into the chair across from her and grabbed her clammy hand. At least they broke up and she didn't say anyone attacked him. So he survived. "What did he say?"

"He invited me out but then texted me about an hour ago." She let out a sound, half snort and half laugh, sliding her phone to me. I read it.

—I'm sorry, Sara. It's not working out. I think it is over for us.—

Mom grabbed her phone back and reread the text she'd likely read a hundred times. "A fucking text." She glimpsed up. "Sorry for the language."

At least he'd survived Ifrit's attack if he contacted her, but I couldn't tell her that. Without knowing about Ifrit's threat, she'd forever blame herself or think no one would date her again. As much as it pained me, I needed to let her think that until I could banish Ifrit. And after I banished him for the second time, I'd tell her everything, but not before then. If I told her before trapping Ifrit back in the vortex, it'd put her in even more danger since the djinn would see her as an obstacle.

"Maybe he's having a bad day, Mom." I squeezed her hand. "Give it time. He'll come around."

"No, Bax. When you're having a shitty day, you draw the people you love closer, not shove them away."

I tightened my grip, with nothing to say, even though I had lots to say. I'd betrayed my two best friends, ruined Mom's first relationship since Ben, and never told Warren how much I appreciated him. Oh yeah, and an evil djinn hunted Mom, me, and everyone we loved.

Life had become a vise, squeezing my soul. I hated Ifrit. I hated everything about the Djinn-verse. My tears matched Mom's, even though she needed me to be strong.

She waved me to her, and I collapsed onto her lap. The chair creaked under my weight. I was too old to be sitting on her lap and crushing Mom's legs, but she didn't let me go, wrapping her arms tight around my torso.

Her uncontrolled sobs into my shoulder broke me. My tears dripped on her head.

"I'm sorry, Mom. I'm so sorry."

For more than you know.

Chapter 20

—Can we meet at West End Coffee tomorrow morning?—

Scarlet texted yesterday evening while Mom and I binged an awful reality show called *Love, Straight Up.* I texted her back:

—Sure. What's up?—

She answered:

—We'll talk at 10:00.—

Just what I needed, Scarlet mad at me too. I hoped she'd at least explain why she'd suddenly been so standoffish around me.

I didn't have time to speculate about it that evening. Mom needed me. She kept checking her phone, even though she tried to hide it. She waited for an elaboration from Max on his cryptic and abrupt breakup, which she'd never receive. I wanted to tell her to hang tight, that after I banished Ifrit, I'd tell her everything and convince him to reconsider. But of course, I couldn't say any of those things yet.

At least she'd stopped crying after becoming distracted by *Love, Straight Up,* a show about crazy-hot bartenders vying for romance while operating a dive bar in Boston. Mom used every pause to lecture me on how the show exploited the young cast and furthered the dumbing down of America. She reiterated a version of her remark every twenty minutes throughout the three hours we watched it while eating our frozen pizza. I almost called her out about it, but the attractive bartenders arguing over who should bus tables gave Mom something to think about other than Max.

It also gave me a break from dwelling on my life falling to crap again. Not even Ifrit could overpower the mindlessness of trashy reality TV.

Before leaving to meet Scarlet the next morning, I opened my bedroom window and summoned Janni while Mom showered, hoping his stink would dissipate before she finished. Max broke up with Mom, the last clue from my Ifrit vision. I had no idea what he'd do next and couldn't risk leaving Mom alone.

"HOW CAN IT SERVE?"

Janni's bright, innocent eyes brought a much-needed smile to my face. "Can you do me a favor?"

"IT ALWAYS DOES WHAT BAXTER ALLEN WANTS."

I buttoned my coat. "I'm meeting up with Scarlet. Can you turn invisible and hang out here? Keep an eye on Mom? Ifrit's meddling with her life, and I'm worried it'll escalate while I'm gone."

Janni nodded. "YES. BUT BAXTER ALLEN KNOWS BEING IN THIS WORLD FOR MANY MINUTES MAKES IT VERY TIRED. HOW LONG?"

"Not too long. I'll be gone maybe an hour, then you can return to the vortex. But while I'm with Scarlet, come get me if anything suspicious happens. Anything at all."

He nodded again. "IT WILL."

Janni faded, becoming an unusual bend in the background, noticeable only if someone studied the space.

"Thanks, Janni. Again, tell me if *anything* suspicious happens."

I couldn't make out if Janni nodded for a third time, but I interpreted the silence as agreement. Time to meet Scarlet at West End Coffee.

****

I dropped my phone into my back pocket after checking the time: 9:53 a.m. I squared my shoulders outside my favorite coffee shop, ready for whatever Scarlet wanted to discuss. Normally, the anticipation would have overrun me with anxiety, wondering if she'd wanted to proclaim her love for me. However, her text's tone and recent mood rendered that highly unlikely.

The thick caffeinated aroma saturated the air in the coffee shop, and even late on a Saturday morning, the place bustled with customers waiting for their pick-me-up. Medical students and staff from St. Bernard's dominated the coffee shop with their powder-blue scrubs as the aproned baristas scrambled to serve their customers as quickly as possible.

I almost missed her in the crowd but spotted Scarlet at a two-person table. She must've arrived early to secure a window seat.

When she noticed me, she flashed me the smile you gave someone you were about to tell disappointing news. Only my life could earn the we're-about-to-break-up smile when we weren't even dating.

"Bailey!" the barista hollered over the conversations and the spoons clanging inside ceramic coffee cups. "Bailey, you're up! Vanilla cappuccino."

I joined Scarlet at the table without ordering, unsure how long we'd be and not having any money. "Hey."

She swirled the mug in front of her as fresh steam

escaped. She'd gathered her red hair back into a ponytail, showing off silver loop earrings that wiggled with every movement. "Thanks for meeting me."

"What's going on?"

She sipped her coffee. "I'm aware I forced my way into your group and the djinn thing, but I want out."

"Huh?" We didn't need a formal sit-down for this. I didn't mind her being part of it, but as she said, we didn't beg her to get involved. Besides, she'd already started distancing herself from us. I appreciated her desire to formally break up with the team, but a text would have been sufficient.

"It's obvious Jason and Ashley aren't crazy about me, and I get it." She spoke to her off-white coffee cup. "I've barely uttered a sentence to them in the past year and a half of high school. Now I'm barging into your djinn fighter club."

Stop saying djinn fighter.

"If this is about their rude behavior, Scarlet, don't mind them. They—"

"That's not the reason. This will sound crappy, and I don't mean it to, but I'm not sure how else to say it."

"Okay?"

"My mom and stepdad are broke."

My nose crinkled. "You used to live in my building, so I'm aware you don't live the life of a celebrity."

"What I mean is that I need to get a scholarship to get out of here, out of the Midwest. My parents can't afford college, and I want to be a marine biologist. It's always been my dream."

Marine biologist. I never knew. Come to think of it, I never asked. She never asked me what I wanted to do with my life either. When we talked, the conversations stayed superficial. After all these years of denial and arguing with Jason about it, Scarlet revealing her career ambition drove home what Jason had been preaching since I'd met him—maybe Scarlet and I weren't really friends.

Her favorite color? No idea.

TV show? No clue.

Music? Did she even listen to music?

My insides deflated with the heavy realization. I'd been blind to reality. Naïve. I knew nothing about Scarlet Lane, the girl who I often dreamed about, the girl who—at a minimum—I'd defended as a close friend.

Our talk turned out to truly be a breakup conversation, even though she didn't realize it.

I smiled, not wanting to intensify the awkwardness. "I guess you'll need to live on a coast. No oceans in these parts." I forced a chuckle. "But I don't understand how hanging out with us relates to earning a scholarship and attending a coastal college."

Scarlet leaned forward. "Really, Bax? We broke into a hotel room. What if someone caught us?"

Bingo.

It wasn't about creepy dudes harassing her or Jason's and Ashley's rudeness. She risked too much battling Ifrit. I tried to warn her. Everyone thinks djinn are all about granting wishes with sparkling magic. That was what Ashley used to think when she forced her way into the Djinn-verse. Hell, I thought the same thing until I soon learned the opposite.

Scarlet dipped the tip of her finger into her coffee and swirled it. "Everything about Ifrit is scary. I never planned to see the inside of the Sunrise Hotel. Ever. And those guys outside…you saw the way they gawked.

Fortunately, that was all they did. Otherwise, that interaction could have ended very differently."

"I'm stuck in the middle of the hurricane, and can't leave." I paused. "But you can and should. For real. No hard feelings."

She sighed, slumping over a bit. She must've expected an I-told-you-so moment, but that wouldn't do any good. Besides, I had enough people mad at me.

"The idea of djinn seems exciting, but it's terrifying, Bax. I hate bailing on you. But I-I need out." Scarlet's eyes glistened in the bright café lighting.

"Scarlet, it's fine. I understand. We're cool."

"I'm a jerk."

I wanted to put my hand on hers to comfort her, but figured that'd be crossing a line. "Please don't cry about it. And definitely don't worry about it. You have the chance to leave, and you should take it. I'd be a total shithead if I thought bad about you for escaping the disaster I've unleashed on the world. Besides, the oceans need you. They're in rotten shape these days."

She faked a scowl at me before her face softened.

"Again, I'm sorry." Scarlet stood, gathering her coat and bag. "See you at school." She threw her purse over her shoulder, then opened her mouth to speak but stopped herself. With a quick turn, she weaved through the crowd and out the door of West End Coffee.

After all these years, Scarlet Lane dumped me. We'd see each other at school, but no more meeting at coffee shops or THC. She'd obliterated our only legitimate connection. She'd return to Casey and the other popular girls, throwing me a smile here or there. We might say hi but that'd be it. I could blame Ifrit for ruining it, but I wasn't sure we ever had anything. Not for real, anyway.

The customers of West End Coffee escaped the freezing morning to order their hot drinks, talk, laugh, study, and gossip. Time passed as I watched them enjoy their djinn-free lives. I'd lived a regular life a few short months ago, but it felt like another lifetime.

"I saw Scarlet walking out." Ashley sat at the table with her paper to-go coffee cup.

My cheeks warmed. Awesome. Now I could fight with Ashley. She must've come here to berate me for spying.

"Everything okay?" She swirled her drink. The barista had scratched *Ainsley* in black marker on it.

She didn't look mad. Jason must not have told her yet.

"Just having a secret rendezvous with our fellow djinn fighter?" She giggled. "I hate when she freakin' calls us that."

"Me too. Scarlet wants out. No more Ifrit hunting. It's scaring her."

Ashley gauged my reaction before she commented. "People think djinn are fun until you get all up in their mix. She never understood how it worked until now, I guess."

A snarky comment about Ashley jumping for joy now that Scarlet bailed flittered across my tongue, but I bit the words back. Might as well enjoy her not hating me while I could.

"I'm sorry if that bums you out, Bax. I know how much you like her."

Ashley patted my hand. She was an incredible friend. And a good person. She and Jason deserved each other.

"Nah, I think I'm over Scarlet for good. She's nice and all, but it's time for me to move on with my life."

"Uh-oh, warn the ladies! Baxter Allen is back on the market!" She joked way too loud in her obnoxious Ashley voice, but I smiled.

"You're insane."

"Can I buy you a coffee?"

"No thanks. Not in the mood. Did Jason tell you Ifrit attacked Max on Thursday night?"

Ashley stiffened in her chair. "No! We didn't talk yesterday. He told me about your dream, though, the one with Ifrit creeping around your place. So, he's working through his list."

"Yeah. Beat Max up and ordered him to leave Mom and me alone."

"Holy freakin' shit."

"Oh, and then I found out Warren's sick. Not because of Ifrit. It's just a super awesome coincidence. He has cancer."

"And then Scarlet…" Ashley added before I did. "You're having a run of suckiness."

"That's an understatement. We need to see if Janni can pick up Ifrit's trail from Max's. Take another stab at finding Ben."

"Or Scott, now that we know Ifrit doesn't just work from what—and who—his master knows. Did you learn anything about him moving hotels?"

"Never got to it. But you think with Warren fighting for his life, he or Scott would be busy with the Djinn-verse? They have enough going on."

Ashley tapped her cup with a finger. "Look, I'm not trying to say something negative about your friend when he's sick, but what if that's their motivation? Use Ifrit to cure Warren? I mean, I'm sure everyone thinks they can manipulate djinn for good. That they can be the first person to control Ifrit. You said you've thought about that. And battling a horrible disease is a hell of a motivator to try anything. If you were Warren's son, wouldn't you?"

I couldn't argue with her. I ended up getting a nursing student fired, thinking I could use Janni's magic for something positive. "Fair point. And we still can't figure out how Ben could have jumped parole or how he knew to steal the artifact. He would have had to leave Illinois, find me, steal the box, summon Ifrit, and then have him remove his ankle tracker all before the cops arrested him."

Ashley's tapping finger sped up. "Bax, I think I need to ask Dad about Ben. He can check at the station and tell us if Ben is an escaped parolee. He might have additional information we don't."

"I think it's that time."

"But, Bax, Dad will question why I'm asking. I'll need to tell him about Ben. The whole thing with your mom, just minus the djinn parts."

Mom worked for years to keep her secret, but her secret had become a threat to her life. "If Ben is our thief, we may want your dad's help. A convict as Ifrit's master could make what we're up against a lot tougher."

"I'll ask Dad not to say anything to anyone. I don't want to embarrass your mom."

"Okay. Can you talk to him now? I need to do something before we track Ifrit. Meet you back at my place in an hour."

"Sounds good." Ashley scooted her chair back and I followed her out of West End Coffee.

I needed to patch things up with Jason.

Chapter 21

I paused outside of Jason's apartment. I had to own what I did and be honest. That was all I could do.

I knocked on the door; the sound reverberated through the hallway.

"Mom!" Michelle hollered from inside Jason's apartment before I lowered my hand from knocking. "Someone's here!" Her voice sliced through the front door.

Mrs. Franklin opened the door. "Well, hello, Baxter." She wore a pink scarf on her head and a bright green shirt. Just like the Franklins' home always seemed clean and ready for guests, Mrs. Franklin always seemed prepared to entertain. Even in the middle of a Saturday, her work-around-the-house clothes hovered two minutes away from restaurant-ready.

"Hi, Mrs. Franklin." I hung my head as if she knew what I'd done.

"Come on in. Jason didn't mention you were coming over." She welcomed me inside.

"He doesn't know."

"Is it a *surprise* visit? A *birthday* surprise?" Michelle giggled and covered her mouth with a hand. Her amber eyes twinkled under long eyelashes. Although she annoyed us—a little sister's obligation— Michelle might have been one of the cutest kids ever.

"No, not a party." I chuckled, even though her face

fell with disappointment at my clarification. "Wouldn't you remember if it was Jason's birthday today?"

She put her fists on her hips. "I would have baked a cake for it. A chocolate one. With strawberries." The jeweled beads at the ends of her braids sparkled as her head bopped.

"I'm sure your cakes are delicious."

"Girl, go finish reading or no playtime at Keesha's. Kindergarten schoolwork is just as important as college schoolwork." Mrs. Franklin swatted Michelle away, who scampered down the hallway.

"Can I get you a drink or anything? Water, iced tea, lemonade?" Mrs. Franklin didn't offer soda. The Franklins never offered soda. Mrs. Franklin crusaded against high fructose corn syrup because she said it ruined food and caused diabetes. She didn't go crazy if Jason drank it; she just didn't allow it in her house.

"I'm good. Thanks." I closed their front door.

"Jason's in his room." She wiped her hands on a towel as she returned to the kitchen.

My tennis shoes held fast to the marbled ceramic tile of the foyer. I never stalled in the foyer at Jason's, but his bedroom felt miles away, across the expanse of the living room and down the hallway. I dreaded the walk. What if he was still mad? Of course he would be. If he wanted to yell at me, then I'd take it. I deserved it. I spied on my best friends.

Mrs. Franklin turned up the music in the kitchen as pots clamored. "You're welcome to stay for dinner, Bax," she called. "I'm simmering gumbo. Never cooked it, but we had it at *Swanky's* a few months ago and I fell in love, so I took a stab at it. However, you've had my cooking, so if you stay for dinner—which I hope you do—be very aware of what you're signing up for."

Mrs. Franklin had many admirable traits—relentless activist, loving mom, impressive homemaker—but a world-class chef didn't make the list. Dr. Franklin always teased that she could screw up cereal and milk without trying. And she agreed.

"I can't. Thanks for the offer, though."

A wall separated the living area from the kitchen, but Mrs. Franklin's gaze drilled through it. After a moment, she poked her head around the corner with her eyebrows raised.

"Yeah?" I acted as if I didn't understand why she raised her eyebrows at me.

She returned to the small foyer, wiping her hands on the yellow towel again. She lowered her voice. "I'm not sure what's going on, but you seem hesitant to see Jason. I'm guessing your reason is related to Jason's atrocious mood the past few days."

Ugh. I'd really hurt him.

"Baxter, hon, friends fight. It happens. Then they make up. That happens, too. If you did something, apologize. If Jason did something, accept his apology. Unfortunately, friendships involve people, and people aren't perfect. That means friendships aren't either."

"I'm the one apologizing this time. Lately, I feel like it's me most of the time."

Her brows crinkled above her forehead. That was where Jason inherited it. "Fights need two people. But if this one is on you, march in there and make it right. Standing here won't do anything but tell me you want to help in the kitchen. And we both know you don't want to learn what I'm teaching."

She returned the smile I gave her and patted me on

my back. "Go on."

She hummed her way back to the kitchen.

With eyes on the hallway to his bedroom, I uncemented my feet from the floor and trudged to his room—the fourth door on the right.

I knocked.

"I'm busy," Jason yelled. Did he realize I knocked, or was he giving the standard answer you shouted when family interrupted your alone time?

I let myself in like on any other typical day. Jason lay on his bed on his stomach, reading. He rolled his head to see who barged in with a scowl, but he sprang to a sitting position when he saw me. He yanked the headphones out of his ears. "When did you get here?"

"I figured you heard Michelle."

He shrugged. "She's always yelling about something. Why do you think I wear headphones all the time?"

I smiled, but he didn't.

As I shut the door, I positioned myself in front of it, apprehensive about venturing deeper into the room. I'd spent as much time hanging out in Jason's room as in my own. His parents let him keep his game system in there—unlike my mom—so we'd logged millions of hours on his shaggy brown rug by his TV. My black sweatshirt with *New Orleans* printed across its front hung on his desk chair. I'd been looking for that.

"I'm sorry. I shouldn't have done it—any of it. Summoning Janni without you and then spying. I was jealous and mad you weren't telling me about Ashley. I'm not trying to make excuses." I waved my hands. "As soon as Janni returned from spying and I realized what I'd done, I swear on my life, I shut him up."

Jason set the book on his nightstand and curled his legs under him. "Have you done it before?"

"Hell no." My neck warmed. "Well, do you mean spy or summon Janni without you?"

Jason growled. "Jesus, bro. Either."

"Spy on you or Ashley, no. Never. And again, Janni only told me you were texting about meeting up before I stopped him."

"And the other thing? Breaking the No Djinn Rule?"

I focused on a dust bunny that floated between my worn tennis shoes. Time to confess. Might as well tell him everything. I hated keeping secrets from my best friend.

"A few times."

"Man, you know how risky it is to summon Janni. You were the one who said you would never do it without me or Ashley because things always ended up sideways. Or worse."

"And I stand by what I said." I tugged at the hem of my shirt. "I broke my own rule, and it backfired—like it always does."

Jason rubbed his eyes under his glasses. "What happened?"

I started pacing in a small circle. "At the hospital, after visiting Aunt Jo, I asked Janni to take money from the cafeteria register to give to a hungry, homeless guy. I thought I could use Janni for something positive for once. I mean, yeah, it was stealing, but I didn't intend to take very much and figured St. Bernard's could spare a few bucks to feed a guy."

"Hmm." Jason rubbed his chin. "Seems like a positive thing on the surface—kind of."

"Well, the manager probably fired the cashier who

got blamed for stealing the cash."

"It always goes sideways! I knew it!"

"And I also used Janni to read Mrs. Macklind's list of dates for the *Scarlet Letter* presentations."

"I thought something was up. You're a slacker, but you were *totally* unprepared. You thought you had more time."

"Macklind must've changed the dates after Janni showed me the list."

"Haven't you learned that every time a djinn does something, there's a price? I mean, that's Ancient Myths 101."

"I took the class, Mr. Morality. But I thought I'd discovered a way to use Janni for good in the world." Flipping Jason's desk chair around, I plunked down. "And regarding American Lit, in my defense, the idea of a spontaneous presentation would guarantee an episode of VS. I checked the date, but I didn't cheat for answers or grades or anything."

Jason picked up a rubber ball and tossed it against the wall, lifting the mood in his room. "I bet if you told Mrs. Macklind you were nervous about passing out, she'd have given you your presentation date. I mean, she's not plotting to set anyone up for failure. And your VS isn't a well-guarded secret."

"You're only defending her because she's hot."

"Smokin'." Jason bounced the ball. "That could be the reason I'm defending her, but I'm not wrong."

At our last session, Mrs. Bronson said we'd talk about how I could prepare for the presentation. Another reason I shouldn't have jumped right to a djinn solution.

"Stop throwing the ball in your bedroom!" Mrs. Franklin shouted from the other room. "You'll make marks all over the wall and then I'm gonna make you paint over them."

Jason dropped the ball to the floor. "Want to play a little—" He sniffed. "Do you smell that?"

"Shut up." I laughed. "I showered today—" Then I caught a whiff.

Janni.

I straightened. "Oh, no."

"Is that Janni?" Jason threw his legs over the side of the bed.

"Well, one other time I summoned Janni without you guys, I guess. But it's justified. Since we'd gone through all the clues from my Ifrit vision, I was worried Mom might be next. So before I left home this morning, I asked Janni to keep an eye on her."

Janni stumbled out of Jason's closet, his stubby legs wobbled under him like he drank too much. "IT IS TIRED. BAXTER ALLEN PROMISED HE WOULDN'T BE GONE LONG."

I squatted in front of the furry djinn. "I'm sorry. I got caught up—wait, are you here because you want to go back to the vortex, or did something happen to Mom?"

Janni's eyelids hung half over his eyes. I grabbed him by the shoulders as he swayed on his feet. "Tell me what happened."

"IFRIT TOOK BAXTER'S MOM." He closed his eyes. "IT HAS BEEN OUT OF VORTEX FOR MANY HOURS."

"I told you I'm sorry. I mean it. But who took her? Ifrit? Ben? Scott? Where did they take her?" My voice cracked.

"IT DOES NOT KNOW."

"You don't know who or where?"

Janni vanished under my grip.

"Wait! Stop!" I swiped at the emptiness Janni had occupied. "Shit! We have to get home."

I ran a frantic hand through my hair as we left Jason's bedroom. "I should have told Mom everything. Why didn't I? If it was dangerous enough to ask Janni to guard her, I should have warned her."

In the hallway, I opened the *Find It* app on my phone to track Mom's location.

Michelle snuck out of her room. "What's wrong, Jason?"

"Nothing. Everything's fine. Go away." Jason shooed her back into her bedroom.

"Her phone's at home." I rubbed my eyes to think. "So she never left for work. Ifrit kidnapped her right out of our apartment, but where'd he take her?"

I charged through Jason's living room, not sure how much time we had before Ifrit did something, and on whose behalf was he acting?

"Where are you two off to?" Mrs. Franklin poked her head out from the kitchen.

I ignored her, already out the front door. If we figured out how Ifrit kidnapped Mom, we could maybe figure out where he held her.

Jason followed me, calling over his shoulder, "Heading to Bax's!"

I stumbled down the stairs, almost wiping out. "What was I thinking, leaving her alone? Janni's no bodyguard."

Jason grabbed my arm and spun me around. "Look, we can't predict when or how Ifrit strikes. You couldn't have stayed by her side forever. Let's just check your apartment for signs of what happened. And that'll give Janni time to rest so we can summon him back and question him."

With a shake of my head, I started running. Fast.

Chapter 22

Ashley leaned against the wall, arms folded, tapping her foot outside of my apartment as she waited for us. "It took you guys freakin' long enough. Dad said they've issued a warrant for Ben's arrest. He jumped probation, and they can't locate him. His ankle bracelet mysteriously malfunctioned. But also—"

"Damn it." I dropped my apartment keys as I fumbled to unlock the door.

"It'll be okay, Bax." Jason panted from our sprint back to my place.

"What happened now?" Ashley moaned.

"In a minute. We have a problem. Another one. In an exhausting list of problems." The front door banged against the wall as I threw it open.

The setting sun cast elongated furniture shadows across my living room. I smacked on the light switch. Mom's purse sat beside her keys on the table near the front door. Down the hallway, I checked her bedroom and the bathroom. Both looked normal. No sign of a struggle, no couches knocked over, and nothing broken.

"Dude..." Jason handed me Mom's phone. "Found it on the kitchen counter."

"That's where she always keeps it. For a kidnapping, everything looks untouched and normal."

Missed calls and texts from Zia's Candles flashed on Mom's phone screen. I leaned back against the kitchen counter, staring at her phone, my legs weak. "Did she leave willingly?"

"Someone needs to fill me in," Ashley said. "But first, I have to tell you—"

"In a sec." I held my hand up to her, palm out. "Let me think. Let's ask Janni if he can sense Ifrit's energy here. We can follow the trail. He's had enough time to rest."

A knock thundered at my front door, and my already pounding heart lurched into my throat.

"Ifrit? Is he back for me?" I searched for a weapon. "My baseball bat!" I started running to my room, but Ashley grabbed my arm, yanking me to a stop with the force of twenty Ashleys.

"Stop, Bax! Freakin' listen to me!"

The knock echoed again.

I glanced at the door, waiting for the monster to break through. "God, Ashley, what?"

"I told my dad about Ben."

"We know."

"I told him about how you've been in hiding. He called your mom, but she didn't answer." She nodded to Mom's phone in my hand. "Dad's still on the mend, so he called an officer to check in on her—on you guys. That's who's at the door. You don't need a bat. In fact, I'd recommend against greeting a cop with a baseball bat."

My mind caught up with her rapid-fire word assault. Of course if Ashley told her dad an abusive ex rolled back into town, he'd send protection. I rubbed my eyes, regrouping. "Um. Okay. Well. Okay." I shut my eyes to concentrate. "Janni said Ifrit kidnapped Mom. So let's get the cop out of here as quickly as we can, then summon Janni back for more information. I think we play it cool with the police right now."

"You said he kidnapped your mom. Shouldn't we tell the police?" Ashley asked.

I shook my head. "No. Not yet. How would I explain her kidnapping unless I saw it? And if they do a missing person report, I doubt they'll let us out of their sight. We need to see what we're up against first."

"I think you're right." Jason focused on the floor as he thought. "And the police on standby isn't the worst thing. We may need help later. Let's take a beat and assure the cop everything is normal, but get his number. After he leaves, we'll summon Janni."

"Or her," Ashley said.

"Huh?"

Ashley rolled her eyes. "You said *his* number. It could be a female officer, you know. I'm saying we'll get his *or her* number."

"*Or her.*" Jason over-enunciated.

"You're doing this now?" I scowled at them both. "Work on your timing, guys."

Our visitor knocked again. A muffled voice behind the door called, "I'm Officer Malik. Please open the door, kids. I can hear your voices."

Jason puffed out his chest. "It *is* a dude."

I shot Jason a scowl. "Let's go with our plan. Be cool." They didn't need the reminder—I did.

I opened our front door. A tall police officer stood in the doorway, his super broad shoulders pressed against his wrinkleless uniform. It must've been his first call of the day.

"Hello?" I acted surprised to see him.

"Hi, son. I'm Officer Malik. Detective Bryant asked

me to stop by. Is everything okay in here? I heard elevated voices." He glanced inside our apartment. He was so tall he saw over my head with ease. Musky cologne wafted off him. Was he on duty or on a date?

"Yeah. We were joking around." I examined his eyes, searching for any glimmer of purple, but only found rich brown flecked with gold, surrounded by freakishly long eyelashes.

"Mind if I come in?"

"Sure." I stepped aside and held the door open for him.

His hand hovered near his holstered gun, and he moseyed in at a turtle's pace, scanning our kitchen and living room as if browsing at Warren's Cosmos. His shiny black shoes clicked on the floor with each slow step. "Your mom or another adult home?"

"No. Just the three of us."

He nodded, poking around the table we used as a desk in the corner, careful not to disturb anything. "Detective Bryant said your dad may be in town and have an axe to grind with your mom."

Axe to grind was one way to put it.

"We're not sure. About him being in town, I mean."

"Has he tried to contact you or your mom? Any visits, phone calls, emails, or texts?"

"No." We needed him to leave. Janni would get us answers faster than Officer Smells Good. "Maybe we overreacted to Ben possibly being in town. I'm not used to having a criminal relative." I forced a chuckle.

As he walked by, Ashley dropped her gaze and bit her bottom lip.

Seriously?

The cop nodded and returned an innocent grin.

245

Jason scowled at the exchange.

"Mind if I check out the bedrooms?"

Could he walk any slower?

"Sure. Mom's out running errands. Forgot her phone here." I held up Mom's phone even though he'd already disappeared down the hallway.

"I checked his eyes," I whispered. "They seem normal."

"There's nothing normal about those beauties." Ashley giggled under her hand.

"Do you need a cold shower, Ashley? I meant I checked for any purple. We need to be on guard."

"Does she leave her phone behind often?" the cop called from Mom's bedroom.

"Yeah. All the time." I yelled as I tapped my foot, then whispered, "We have to get him out of here. Time's ticking."

"You say something?" Officer Handsome returned to the living room.

"No," I grumbled. "Thanks for coming by."

The cop's shoes clicked on the hardwood floor as he strolled back to the foyer. He handed me a card. "Here's my number. If your mom doesn't come home soon, call me. On second thought, call me when she comes home so I know everyone is safe. Call me either way."

"Yeah, sure." I dropped the card on the kitchen table.

He rolled like molasses back out of my apartment. Jason wore a plastic smile, and Ashley's gaze dropped from Officer McHotty's broad shoulders to his ass.

I cleared my throat at Ashley as I closed the door behind him.

She smirked.

I collapsed against our front door. "Jesus, Ashley. Inappropriate much?"

She shrugged. "Whatever. You're in Mrs. Macklind's class. Welcome to my world."

Fair point.

"Why the slo-mo search of my place? Did he think Ben lurked in the shadows, forcing me to tell the police everything was normal, or that I hid him in the closet to protect him?"

Ashley sat on my couch. "You said Ben kidnapped your mom?"

Jason shook his head. "No. Janni told us Ifrit kidnapped Mrs. Allen. We still don't have confirmation who the mastermind is."

We were back to debating who stole the box? I pointed at Ashley. "She confirmed Ben jumped parole. It has to be him. Right, Ashley?"

"I mean, maybe." Ashley shrugged. "But that doesn't explain how he knew where to find you and knew enough to summon Ifrit with an otherwise junky-looking box in your backpack. The facts are that Scott was at West End Coffee that night and potentially knows about djinn. And saving Warren's life is a pretty legit motive to mess with djinn magic."

"What's up with Warren?" Jason asked.

"He has cancer."

"I'm sorry, man."

I shook it off. Had to stay focused. "I can't believe we're still having this debate." I showed them the ring. "Either way, we're wasting time."

I rubbed the jewel. It burst into bright purple, and familiar tingles rained down my back within seconds. I sucked the burnt hair odor into my lungs.

Come on, Janni, hope you've rested up. We need you.

"HOW CAN IT SERVE?" Jannie waddled out from the hallway. Thankfully, the grogginess from earlier seemed gone.

I kneeled in front of him. "Okay, now that you've powered up, you need to tell me everything you saw about Mom's kidnapping."

Janni let out a sigh as he nodded. "IT WILL SHOW YOU." Then he rested a hand on each side of my head and we closed our eyes.

****

Sara glared at her laptop screen. She dreaded paying bills. She hated shifting the pay-on date of the electric bill to match the due date, worried about overdrafting her account balance. Another job to replace the income from the Hotel St. Louis would help. Or, better yet, a single job with enough salary to replace them both. What a luxury to only work one job and build a career again.

Ben never wanted her to work, but she'd insisted on finishing her degree after they married. She loved teaching, but after a difficult pregnancy, she took a year off, which Ben interpreted as quitting. To avoid the endless fighting, she never returned, and not long after, she left Ben and Chicago.

She missed it but couldn't teach in St. Louis—too public. Her picture would be all over the school's website and visible to Ben. Instead, she worked hourly jobs where her employer wouldn't plaster her face all over the internet.

Sara stared at a crack in the wall as she daydreamed. Jo believed Ben didn't care anymore and she didn't need to worry about him. Sara wanted to believe her but couldn't risk it, not with Bax. However, since Bax knew about Ben, maybe she should rethink her strategy. If Ben had wanted to find them, he would have. They weren't in a witness protection program or anything.

She slammed her laptop closed. Time to live her life. She'd talk to Bax and they could decide together. Not just about her teaching, but maybe they'd return to Chicago to be near Jo and Anita after all these years.

No, that'd be pushing it. Too risky. They'd stay in St. Louis.

Someone knocked, causing her to jump.

She needed to call the landlord again. The building's front door only locked when it felt like it. Mr. Reynold needed to fix it. Anyone from the street could just walk inside.

"Yes?" she asked the closed door.

"Sara?"

Max?

She stepped back from the door to examine her face in her phone camera, adjusting her hair with her fingers. She brushed a hand over her pink Zia's Candles T-shirt to smooth the wrinkles.

Wait. He dumped you, and now you're worried about how you look? You're acting like a teenager.

She slapped her cheeks. She wouldn't take him back after such a flimsy and disrespectful breakup. No way. Of course, that was assuming he'd come by to apologize. But why else pay her an unannounced visit? She at least needed to hear him out. She deserved to hear his side. Then she'd make the call on forgiveness or not.

She opened the front door as casually as possible to not appear too anxious.

Max wore a crisp white shirt with a red-striped tie.

He must've come from work. She couldn't see his brown eyes with his gaze on his shiny black shoes. "Thanks for opening the door, Sara." His deep voice was soft and unassuming.

"What do you want, Max?" She tried to sound mad, but her knees melted as his gaze lifted to meet hers.

You're pathetic.

"I want to apologize."

Yes!

"What?" She brushed her hair behind her ear, feigning surprise. She needed more than an apology. He'd better have an entire explanation prepared.

Max straightened his shoulders, summoning his courage. "I got scared."

Sara sighed. She deserved something better than that. "Scared? That's such a cliché, Max." She wouldn't be some desperate woman on standby, waiting for her man to return whenever he felt ready to commit.

"Clichés aren't untrue." He shoved his hands deep into his pants pockets. "Let me come in and explain. Please."

Sara forced him to wait for a long, awkward minute before she answered. "I have to head to work in a few minutes, so I don't have much time." She opened the door all the way. No harm in hearing him out. If anything, it'd give her closure.

She stayed in the foyer, not ready to get too comfortable with him. "Go ahead."

"You said you wanted to move slowly, but my heart didn't. I fell in love with you." He scratched the salt-and-pepper stubble on his cheek.

"That's why we broke up? Makes perfect sense." She folded her arms.

"When I realized what I felt for you, I examined my life. Then I panicked. I'm not ready for a wife or a fifteen-year-old. My house doesn't have much more space than your apartment. Besides, I failed my first marriage. What if I suck at marriage? Plus, I travel for work at the last minute, which isn't fair to you or Bax. And speaking of Bax, do I jump into his life and play dad? You won't even tell me about his birth father, so I imagine there's baggage there."

He'd better not be making this her fault. "In fairness, Max, you never asked about my ex except for that once."

"And you changed the subject before I could even finish my question. Don't think I didn't notice."

She tapped her foot, but without shoes on, it didn't make the sound she wanted. "Part of dating is asking questions. It's continuous prying to figure out if the ugly, gross details of someone's life are as ugly and gross as your own." She spoke with the authority of a dating expert, not someone who'd dated one person in thirteen years.

He shrugged. "Maybe. I mean, yes. I miss you. I miss hanging out with you. I miss…"

Sara put her hand up to silence him. Her turn to speak. "You broke my heart, Max. I haven't dated since Bax's father. I'm out of practice. Plus, excess free time isn't something working single moms have an abundance of. But I gave that time to you. I let myself be vulnerable and go out with you. And yeah, I fell in love, too. Then you shit on it."

Max's deep brown eyes shimmered. "I'm sorry, Sara. Can you grant me another chance?"

"What's my guarantee you won't do it again?"

He spoke to the light switch on the wall next to them.

"There's none. Other than I promise to be honest with you. I swear if I'm second-guessing us, I'll discuss it with you. I won't end things without a conversation."

Sara rubbed her eyes, not wanting him to see her tears. "I'm not sure, Max."

He'd never been in a serious relationship since his marriage ended. She couldn't blame him for being as scared as her. She could blame him for how he dealt with it, though.

He dropped to the floor on one knee. "Please? I'm begging for forgiveness."

"Oh my God. Get up. Save it for the proposal." Her hands flew up to cover her mouth as her face burned red hot. Did those words just spill out of her mouth? "I mean for the proposal with whomever you may propose to. In the future. Somewhere. You know, whenever it might or might not happen. With anyone."

He stood, melting her with his crooked smile.

"My shift does actually start soon." She cleared her throat. "Tonight, you can buy me dinner and we can talk. No promises."

He smiled, dimples and all. "I'll take the chance. Can I walk you to work?"

She withheld a girlish giggle. "I'll get my shoes."

Desperate? Pathetic? She couldn't worry about it. She wasn't perfect either. He'd made a mistake. If their relationship continued, she'd make mistakes, too, and would expect some grace. Playing games at her age wasted time. This felt right. He felt right.

Sara leaned against the hallway wall, sliding into her tennis shoes. Max's footfalls approached from behind. She breathed in his smoky vanilla cologne. Working at Zia's gave her a heightened appreciation for scents. She stifled a smile. He wore cologne for an apology visit on a Saturday afternoon. He knew her weakness.

She inhaled, savoring it.

Something lingered under his usual scent. It seemed off, mixed with something. The familiar muskiness had another element. Something harsher. More chemically.

By the time she recognized it, a chloroform rag smothered her mouth. Max's arm snaked around her, pinning her arms to her side.

She struggled for a second before the sedative collapsed her vision and she passed out.

Chapter 23

Janni lowered his rough hands from each side of my face. I kept my eyes closed, unable to open them, waiting for him to say, *Oops, forgot the last part—she escaped*, but he didn't. Ifrit had circled Mom like a lion, waiting for her to be alone and vulnerable before he pounced. Finally, his master would have his vengeance. But did the person controlling Ifrit understand how far his new demon would go or had they fooled themselves into thinking they controlled the djinn? They would be in for a big surprise when they learned once the djinn grabbed ahold of an idea, wish, or desire, Ifrit chose the cost of making it real, leaving his master to deal with the consequences.

Ben didn't realize his anger at events that happened thirteen years ago could make him a murderer. Scott didn't understand his desire to help his dad may end up hurting others Ifrit perceived as a threat to his ability to stay in this world. It was a horrifying lesson to learn. I would know.

"What happened?" Jason extended a hand.

I grabbed his wrist as he helped me to my feet. "Ifrit posed as Max, faked an apology, and kidnapped her. Right from here."

Ashley's eyes widened. "That's why there's no sign of a struggle. At least he kidnapped her, right? He didn't...hurt her."

"Not that I saw."

Ashley bit on her thumbnail. "Measured attacks aren't Ifrit's thing. If he wanted to hurt your mom, he would have right here. She was all alone. Maybe this isn't about your mom after all. Ifrit's master could be using her to bait you if it's Ben, or using her to distract us if it's Scott."

"Janni, can you locate where Ifrit is holding Mom?" Every passing second put her in more danger.

The moist nostrils of Janni's monkey nose flared. "IT FOUND SARA ALLEN. BUT THE WAY IS DANGEROUS."

Ashley threw her hands into the air. "Is there any other way? Dangerous is how we roll."

Janni's eyes narrowed at Ashley. "GIRL IS LOUD BUT NOT WRONG. SIGN OVER DOOR SAYS ARMORY HEIGHTS BUILDING."

I grabbed my phone, but Ashley beat me to it. "Armory Heights is an abandoned factory in midtown. It'll be a hike, but we could walk there faster than taking a bus."

"Of course it's an abandoned factory." Jason sighed. "For once, I'd like these things to happen at a luxury high rise. The zoo is nice and peaceful this time of year. Or how about they hide out in the art museum?"

I didn't have the heart to carry Janni, especially if we'd be running. He'd be miserable in my backpack, flopping against my back. Plus, I needed him at full energy for our confrontation with Ifrit.

"You can return to the ring for now, Janni. We'll summon you when we're there. Hopefully, our thief didn't realize Janni watched the kidnapping, which may give us a tiny advantage if we move quickly."

"I'll take any advantage we can, no matter how minuscule," Jason muttered.

****

The Armory Heights building stood as a grim reminder of the neighborhood's long-gone industrial glory days. The three-story abandoned factory pressed against the sidewalk's edge, looming over the few pedestrians who walked the worn-down street. Broken panels spotted its large plate windows, and trash littered its base. Even the warped and cracked sidewalk in front of it seemed beat-up and exhausted. Tall, narrow houses with boarded-up windows flanked the building on both sides. Its main wooden doors, tall enough to accommodate a small truck backing into the building, were ajar, allowing a person to slide through.

We hunkered down against the front of the old building to avoid the thief seeing us if he glanced out one of the broken windows. The element of surprise and a djinn who could turn invisible were our only weapons marching into battle against an evil, shape-shifting demon. Not winning odds.

"Janni," I whispered after summoning him. "You here?"

The light bent and wavered as Janni materialized. I'd never seen him appear. Normally, he popped out from the shadows or from under something.

His ears pressed flat against his head, and he pointed up at the building. I stopped him before he could say anything. "Don't say a word. We need to be silent." I unzipped my backpack. "Hide in here in case we need you."

His brow furrowed, and he put his hands on his hips, ready to protest. I pressed a finger over my lips. "Shh.

Sorry, but we need you and might not have time to do the whole summoning thing. You're the only magic we have."

Jason kneeled next to me, putting a hand over my open backpack. "He could follow us while invisible. If he promises to stay close."

Janni's enormous eyes pleaded with me, like one of those caricatures of baby animals with massive glassy eyes.

I patted his head. "Do we have a deal? You'll stay right next to us?"

He nodded and faded away, blending into the chipped brown brick behind him. If someone examined where Janni stood, they'd be able to see a strange bend in the light about a foot tall but would assume their eyes were playing tricks on them, especially in an abandoned factory during twilight.

"Okay. Here we are. What's the plan?" Ashley bit on the same fingernail that hadn't left her mouth all afternoon. "I agree we need Janni handy, but what's he gonna do against Ifrit, if we're being honest?" Ashley spoke to the air while keeping her voice muted. "I'm sure you're scowling at me, Janni, but I'm not wrong."

I closed my eyes, hoping for a stroke of inspiration that eluded me. "I'll reason with the thief, whoever it is. They might've realized by now Ifrit doesn't follow his master's orders to the letter and wants our help to banish him. I'm open to ideas, though."

"Plans are your specialty, girl. Anything?" Jason ran a hand back and forth over his head.

"We could call Officer Malik." She held her hand up to stop Jason from commenting. "No jokes, please. I'm serious. If it's Ben, he's a wanted man, and Malik's a cop. Why not turn him in and steal the box back after he's arrested?"

"No. Not yet." I shook my head. "The cops can handle Ben, but we have a better shot of defeating Ifrit or convincing Ben to let us help him do it. Ifrit will stir up nuclear-size damage if he smells trouble for his master."

"Like when your dad questioned Bax about Nick's death." Jason shoved his hands into his sweatshirt pocket as the wind flapped his hood. "Ifrit doesn't react too well when he feels cornered."

Ashley bit her lower lip. "We don't need Ifrit going apocalyptic."

"Time's ticking. Let's see what we're up against." I squeezed through the space between the old wooden loading doors.

Inside, a stagnant, thick chill hung in the air. The holes in the floor-to-ceiling windows let in the last of the sunlight, making the floating dust shimmer. For miles before us, rusted machinery, random pieces of metal, and rubble littered the first floor. Person-sized wooden crates towered high against one wall, and a massive pile of bricks filled the far corner. A burnt-out metal barrel with punctures on its sides sat inside the entrance, a temporary furnace for homeless people escaping the biting air outside. I shivered. The place resembled a war zone straight out of *Archer Annihilation.*

"No one's here," I mouthed. "Janni?"

Jason pointed at my feet. I squinted at the shadowy distortion near my tennis shoe.

Ashley tapped me on the shoulder, then signaled to the iron stairs. For a minute, I wished we could assume no one was here and get the hell out of Armory Heights, but I summoned my courage and led the team to the stairs, watching every step to avoid stepping on a rusted nail or tripping on scrap metal.

A rat scurried by, and Ashley gasped but suppressed any sound. I patted her arm with a smile. From behind, Jason grabbed her trembling hand.

A long metal pole poked up through the grated stairs as if directing us onward and upward. I tried to shove it aside but couldn't with it wedged between two stairs. We tiptoed around it. I expected the rusted iron joints to squeal, but they held stable and solid underfoot, and the soft soles of our tennis shoes didn't clink on the metal.

Second floor.

Still no sign of Mom or Ifrit. For a minute, I thought someone had teleported us to the cellar of my building. Except for the super tall ceiling, a never-ending labyrinth of shelving extended far into the shadowy depths of the second floor. The rows and rows of shelves held a scattering of beat-up wooden crates and cardboard boxes wilted with moisture.

I listened. Nothing. From the street, I recalled three floors in the building. Not sure why he'd picked the top. In the movie *Hunt for Tiger Grant*, Tiger—the fugitive—never stayed above street level because of a longer time to escape. Maybe it provided privacy, especially with a hostage. Tiger never took hostages.

Jason tapped my shoulder and pointed up.

Keep moving.

We started up the next flight of metal stairs to the top floor, but my feet transformed to stone blocks. I struggled to lift each leg, slowing my climb to the top and final floor, where I'd meet the thief of Ifrit's artifact—the person who'd unleashed a demon we had no way of banishing until the next super blue blood moon in 150 years.

Storms and time had destroyed sections of the roof above the third floor, littering the ground with boards, shingles, and mildew from leaked rain. A chilly breeze dipped through a gaping hole in the roof before retracting into the dusk. Felt-covered half-walls lined the perimeter in perfect squares, some leaning in or out, and a small kitchenette or breakroom crowded one corner. It must've been offices at one point. The top floor provided more privacy than the street level, but also, unlike the floors below, the openness left few places potential ambushers could hide.

On the far side of the floor, straight across from the stairs, Ben sat cross-legged, typing on his phone, no doubt a gift from Ifrit. He didn't see us, and I couldn't make out much detail from the distance, but I saw enough to send chills over me. While I'd seen him in my djinn-induced visions, I was about to confront the person who forced Mom and me into hiding years ago. The guy who hated Mom for taking me from him. The guy who'd booked a train ride with a gun to pay her a visit before we tricked him into thinking we lived in Detroit.

And then the receipt at the Sunrise Hotel from Warren's Cosmos. The idea of Ben visiting my comic book store twisted my stomach into a knot. He had no right to visit that place. Did he speak to Warren? Did he buy a couple of comic books? He'd need to pass the time while hiding from the police, so why not enjoy an epic superhero story?

As I stepped forward, I saw Mom tied to a wooden chair, gagged with a dirty cloth. Next to her, a metal trash barrel glowed, sending flickering shadows against the wall behind her.

The sight of her sent a rush of anger-fueled adrenaline through me, overpowering any fear of confronting my dad. I had one shot at convincing him to banish Ifrit before the manipulative djinn showed up to defend his master.

I charged before my nerve disappeared. Jason and Ashley scampered behind me, struggling to keep up as my strides lengthened with determination.

"That must be Ben," Ashley whispered.

At the sound of my charge, Ben glanced up from his phone. His eyes widened, and he sprang to his feet, almost dropping his phone.

He waited for me as I stomped forward, crunching on grit and gravel from the roof. As I neared, his stance relaxed, and a smile swept across his face. Not the smile of a sinister villain about to succeed in his diabolical plot, but one of a proud dad seeing his child for the first time in a long time. Ben lit up with delight as he laid eyes on me, expecting a heartfelt family reunion.

"Bax? Well, hell. You look—"

"Let Mom go."

The man before me closely matched the Ben in my Ifrit-inspired dreams, except he stood taller and thinner in real life. The graying shadow on his jaw was becoming a full-on beard, and a small scar marked him under his eye that I'd never noticed in my visions. Brown smudges smeared his jeans, and his black coat looked like he'd bought it at a thrift store for the homeless.

I swallowed the pit rising from my stomach. After thirteen years, I'd finally met my dad.

My dad.

Don't lose your nerve, Bax.

Mom yelled something, her words muffled under the gag.

"Baxter, I've missed you, man. I missed watching you grow up."

I cringed at the sincerity of his tone, as if he didn't realize the backdrop to our long-awaited reunion was an abandoned factory with Mom tied to a chair. Was he that clueless, or did he think I was that stupid?

"It's your fault you missed out. Not mine. Or hers." I lowered my voice in a failed attempt to sound threatening.

"You're a brave little man. Fifteen, if I did the right math. I guess not *a little man* anymore." He grinned with a shake of his head. "And you invited friends."

Grinning? Really?

"Let her go," I repeated. "And we need to talk about the djinn." I needed to gauge if he still thought he controlled Ifrit or realized what he'd unleashed. Only then could I reason with him.

Ben inched toward me. "Look, Bax. I'm not making excuses, but shouldn't you give me a chance to make things right with you? I'd like to apologize. Your mom and I had issues, but years ago."

Remorse and an apology. My plan wavered. Was I being unfair?

A glance at my mom, his literal hostage, jolted me. Years of abandonment and anger roared back. Ifrit's visions weren't fabrications. They were windows into others' lives. And Ifrit didn't show me a sad man wallowing in Chicago waiting to make amends. He plotted to come to St. Louis—armed—to teach Mom a lesson. He didn't demonstrate one ounce of remorse until I stood in front of him, confronting him. My blood boiled.

"Seriously? You kidnapped my mom, and now you want to apologize? You could have emailed. Or called. You don't get to show up, hurt Aunt Jo, and expect me to jump into your open arms."

As if just remembering her, he glanced at Mom. "You think I did this? No, son, you're wrong."

"Don't call me son."

"It's the monster. I was mad, yeah, but I'm not a kidnapper. That wouldn't accomplish anything. In fact, I'm trying to get out of this. The monster thought I wanted to kill her, so it delivered her to me, but I-I-I don't want to kill anyone. Same with your Aunt Jo. I have no beef with her."

In my vision, Ben wanted to teach Mom a lesson. To scare her, not kill her. That didn't make him a hero, but it didn't indicate he wanted her dead. I knew how Ifrit distorted thoughts from firsthand experience. Ben found himself like I had, like everyone who's summoned Ifrit throughout history had, in the middle of a swirling nightmare of fleeting thoughts and passing wishes.

I shook my head. "I saw you pack a gun after you bought the train ticket here."

"How did you—"

"You know how. You stole the monster from me."

He dragged a hand through his dark hair with familiar wild curls. A clump stayed straight up. "Right."

"And if this isn't what you wanted, let her go."

He shook his head. "I can't. I'm in a situation here, Bax."

"He traps you. I've played the game, and it won't end until he's gone. This is what he does."

Ben squeezed his eyes shut. "She arrived here an

hour ago, drugged and tied to this chair. When she woke, she said her boyfriend kidnapped her and accused me of paying him off. I was trying to figure out what to do, but she kept screaming, so I gagged her to give me some quiet to think."

His story fit. It didn't make him innocent, but it fit. One significant piece of the story remained missing. "You found me at the coffee shop, but why steal the box? It doesn't look valuable. Did you know about Ifrit?"

"The monster has a name." Ben's shoulders dropped. "I jumped probation, yeah. I planned to confront your mom and you. Not my best moment. But it irritated me that you lived so close this entire time. Figured you'd bought a place in another country by now." Ben talked to the floor. "Some dumbass high school reunion coordinator let your street name slip, and I wanted to meet you, so…" He drew his gaze up to me, his eyes narrow. "Do you think—"

"Ifrit pretended to be the reunion coordinator to lead you here. Back when I was his master."

He shook his head and sighed. "Well, I visited the local high school near your address and waited until I found you. I recognized you, even after all these years. I followed you to West End Coffee. When you went to take a leak, I searched your backpack for your home address. Something more specific than your street, which was all I had. The rotting box…I can't explain it, but it called to me. I swear to God it called my name and the jewel on its lid started glowing. I panicked, thinking the glow would draw attention, so I tucked it under my shirt when your friend started returning to the table."

Ifrit had been manipulating Ben from the beginning. Like how he'd first tempted me as the old man.

"I checked into a hotel to plan my next move but developed a crazy itch to rub the jewel. Again, I can't explain it. The monster—Ifrit—appeared and zapped off my ankle tracker. Said he'd fix my police record, too. I thought I'd won the lottery. At one point, honest to God, I intended to approach your mom and you differently. I had a legitimate second chance. But then, the monster started doing things. I saw them in my dreams. To Josephine, to that guy, to your mom. I'm a victim, Bax, just like everyone else."

I tightened my fist, driving my nails into my palm. "You think you're a victim? Are you for real? I understand how things with djinn spiral out of control, but you're not innocent. All of this is because of you." My firm voice shook. "If the old man hadn't manipulated my desire to know you, I would have walked right by him. But I didn't. Because of curiosity about the dad who exited my life when I was a toddler, I almost died. Other people did die. Because of my wish to meet you, every night since that first visit, I've relived Ifrit's victims' pain and hurt over and over. Even after we'd banished him, the nightmares didn't stop. They replay his damage on an endless loop. All because of you."

My breathing remained heavy, even though my words lightened my insides. I'd waited years to say those things, to yell at him for everything he'd done. Tears collected in my eyes, but I refused to blink and let them escape. He wouldn't get the satisfaction.

"And when I finally learned the truth about you, thirteen years later, it actually made the story worse. You weren't a dad who abandoned us. Instead, you're an asshole who mistreated my mom and forced us into hiding. And you're gonna stand there and say you're a victim?"

Ben rubbed his chin, gathering his response. His eyes reflected the fire in the trash can.

"I'm not perfect, Bax, but this situation with your mom right now isn't my fault. If you used to control the monster, then you know. I've made mistakes, sure. Big ones. But this one isn't mine."

I tapped my phone. "I'm calling the police."

"Don't." Ben reached out.

Jason whispered, "Bax."

"We can talk this through, son, but I will not go to jail over this. I want to start over with a clean slate."

"Stop calling me son!"

An invisible force knocked the phone from my hand. It spun across the floor.

Behind me, Ashley muttered, "Holy freakin' shit."

Ifrit appeared, looming over Ben with a nasty snarl. As Ben's demon guardian angel, Ifrit protected his master. Smoke pumped in rapid bursts from his wet nostrils, forming a gray cloud above Ben's head. His eyes lit the area in purple, overpowering the yellow of the trash can fire. His chest heaved, readying himself to charge.

Mom screamed under the gag, staring at Ifrit with wide, scared eyes.

Ben pulled his gun out, pointing it at Jason and Ashley. His hand trembled. "Tell them to drop their phones, too. Bax, we can work this out. Don't make the monster go crazy on you. On all of us."

All sympathy for Ben evaporated. "You're gonna shoot us? What about being the innocent victim?"

"You're backing me into a corner, boy. I need to figure things out."

"Then let me help you get rid of Ifrit."

At the word *Ifrit*, the evil djinn slid around Ben, moving between Ben and me. The tall ceiling of the factory allowed him to stand at full height, towering over us.

Even though Ifrit growled, his words rang loud throughout the building. "Baxter Allen, you are a threat to my new master. This will be the last time we meet."

He roared, shaking the decrepit building to its foundation.

"Run!" I shouted.

Chapter 24

"Stop!" Ben yelled. Not sure if he meant us or Ifrit.

"What's the plan, Bax?" Ashley hollered from behind as we bolted for the stairs at full speed. "Oh, no! Jason!"

I skidded to a stop. Jason had wiped out but already recovered, crawling back to his feet while jogging again.

"We can't leave your mom," he called.

"I'm not sure how to save her yet." I jumped over a long piece of roofing and almost tripped myself when my feet hit the ground. Grabbing onto the iron railing, I swung around and down the stairs. "Let's draw Ifrit downstairs, lose him, then double back. There's nowhere to hide on the third floor. Too much open space."

We stumbled down the iron stairs, our feet a clanking stampede. The expanse of dusty, crumbling shelves on the second floor continued forever in all directions. The cracked windows let in gray light from the streets outside, creating an indoor twilight, perfect for hiding.

Or not. Ifrit lived in a pitch-black vortex; maybe he could see in the dark. For lack of a better idea, we'd have to take our chances.

I charged down one row, turned, and then down another. Jason and Ashley trailed behind, their footsteps clattering. Then, a loud crash follow Ashley's "Ow!"

No star athletes in our group, and the dark didn't

help.

I spun around to make sure she was okay. She sat on the floor, hugging her knee against her chest. "It's so freakin' hard to see in here!"

"Are you hurt?" I grabbed one wrist while Jason grabbed the other, helping her to a stand. "Can you keep moving?"

Even in the shadows, Ashley's eyes glistened as she fought back tears.

Shit.

Blood seeped through the tear in her jeans, midway up her shin. I separated the fabric with two fingers as she flinched. A scrape, but no exposed bone.

"Doesn't look serious." I stood.

"Spoiler alert. I tripped over some junk." She leaned on Jason, who held her wrist.

Jason used both hands to steady her. "Can you walk at all? Shallow cuts bleed and hurt the most, so it'll feel worse than it is."

"Yeah. I'll be fine." Her face scrunched as she cringed with pain.

I held up my finger to quiet them. "Hold on." Aside from our heavy breathing, silence blanketed the second floor. "Ifrit didn't follow us."

Jason scanned our surroundings, squinting. "And where's Janni? Did he come with us, or is he still up there?"

We forgot Janni.

I pressed my hands against my temples. What if Ifrit saw Janni, even while invisible, captured him, and held him hostage along with Mom? No, surely Janni jumped to the safety of the vortex where Ifrit couldn't touch him. I couldn't remember any djinn rules where Janni had to stay on Earth until I released him to jump back into the vortex.

A small hand gave a subtle tug on the leg of my jeans. Janni stared up at me with eyes glowing in the dark. "IT WOULD LIKE TO LEAVE NOW."

I swooped down and picked him up in my arms. "Thank God."

"BAXTER ALLEN—" I covered his mouth with my hand.

"We need your help, Janni. Stay invisible but head back to the stairs. Tell us when Ifrit is coming. Something's not right. He should be chasing us. Why isn't he?"

With a nod, Janni vanished.

Jason, Ashley, and I crouched behind a tall wooden crate. "We need to lure Ifrit down here so I can head back up and free Mom. Can you guys keep him busy? Yeah, I get that I'm giving you the more dangerous job, but I'm the only one who stands a chance of reasoning with Ben."

Ashley examined her shin while she talked. "I agree, but Bax, he has a gun. He may not let your mom go."

"He won't shoot his own son. Right?" Neither Jason nor Ashley met my gaze. "Right?"

"He's a desperate guy who's backed into a corner," Jason mumbled.

Janni appeared in front of us before I could respond. He didn't need to say anything with his shrill voice. His face said it all as he pointed a shaky pink finger toward the stairs.

Ifrit!

I poked my head over the wooden crate. The shadows didn't so much as quiver. Nothing.

I ducked back down. "You sure?"

Janni twitched his nose, sniffed, then nodded again.

I poked my head up again, expecting Ifrit's charcoal snout snarling at me from the crate's other side, with his teeth bared and the flame in his throat ablaze. Instead, like in a sequence ripped right from *Archer Annihilation*, I saw a fireball rolling through the air, barreling toward us. It started at the far end of the warehouse, a comet in the middle of the building, spiraling forward and filling the aisle between the high shelving. It lit up the area, igniting the old boxes it rubbed against, leaving a wake of burning wood and cardboard.

For the second time, I yelled, "Run!"

Jason and Ashley stood up in time to see the ball of flames hurling at us. We dove in opposite directions as the fireball slammed into the crate we'd been hiding behind. The heat of the explosion blew out a shock wave, propelling me even farther.

I landed, skidding face-first on the littered floor. Nails and other debris stabbed me through my clothes. I slid to a stop as wood shrapnel rained on me from the decimated crate like a hailstorm.

I shielded the back of my head with my hands, waiting for the last pieces of the crate to hit the ground, praying a splinter of wood didn't pierce my neck. After the last of the crate's pieces sprinkled on the floor, I rolled over and sat up to get my bearings. I shook the soot out of my hair. No Jason or Ashley in sight, and flaming embers burned around me, beginning to lap at the rotten wooden shelving.

As I climbed to a stand, pain in my arm jolted me. A nail stuck through my sweatshirt, sharp end first, into my forearm. It hadn't punctured too deep, but my stomach wretched at the sight of it.

I gritted my teeth, closed my eyes, and yanked.

If Ifrit didn't kill me, tetanus from a rusty nail would.

Ifrit's roar shook the warehouse, rattling my brain in my skull.

I had to make it back to Mom. Hopefully, Jason and Ashley could keep Ifrit busy and buy me time—if the explosion didn't hurt them.

Hunched over, I crept down an aisle while keeping my eyes peeled for my friends. The crackling of simmering debris fires provided noise cover, but it would do the same for Ifrit. I could be sneaking right into his clawed hands.

Ifrit used to lurk in the shadows, inflicting his damage through my dreams. Now, he'd gone full-on monster movie. And in a physical battle, I'd never beat an ancient djinn twice my height and all muscle. I had to convince Ben to at least try to banish him. I patted the incantation in my pocket.

Ashley screamed.

I stiffened, peering over a slouching cardboard box on a shelf. Just more shelves, boxes, and crates. No Ashley.

I couldn't determine the direction of the scream, disoriented in the flickering shadows and the smoke that started clouding the air, rolling through the old factory like an approaching storm cloud. The abandoned building was one massive kindling box ready to burn, and burn fast. We had to get out. I quickened my pace, worrying less about stealth. I needed to find the stairs back to the third floor. Even if the incantation didn't work permanently, it might force Ifrit to leave for a while. That'd give us time to negotiate with Ben on a plan to banish him for good.

An explosion vibrated the building with an earthquake-like force.

"Baxter Allen." Although Ifrit grumbled in his deep baritone, his words slithered across the floor and found me, drawing my attention toward the source of the sound, even though I couldn't see him.

"Bax!" Jason yelled from the opposite direction as Ashley.

Shit.

I stumbled my way down one aisle and across two as if summoned by Ifrit's call. The smoke made the darkness murky and difficult to navigate. I swallowed to relieve my throat from the chalky air.

In a small clearing, Ifrit had shoved two shelves aside and waited for me. His eyes lit up when he saw me round the corner, transforming the gray smoke around his head into a purple haze. Saliva glistened as it dripped from between his razor teeth, hissing as it hit the floor. His long black tail suspended Jason in the air by his ankle.

My friend kicked and squirmed, but aside from Ifrit's tail, he hung upside down with nothing to fight against. His glasses had fallen off, and his sweatshirt bunched up in the middle of his torso.

"What do you want?" I coughed after inhaling a lungful of smoke with my shout.

Ifrit snarled. "I despise wasting my precious freedom on you again."

I gambled Ifrit operated by some loose set of rules. "You can't hurt Jason and Ashley. Ben doesn't even know them. You're only allowed to do what he thinks.

Isn't that the rule?"

He growled. "I will do what I must to protect your father. That will preserve my time in this world."

"He's not my father." It didn't matter—not to Ifrit—but the words fell out as a knee-jerk reaction.

The demon smiled, delighted he hit a nerve. "Because you do not claim him does not make it untrue."

I hated Ifrit and hated how I always let him get to me.

"If you hurt my friends, I'll never reconcile with him. And you're obligated to fulfill that wish—his wish to reunite with me. I swear to God, if you harm Mom, Jason, or Ashley, that will never happen. Ever."

Ifrit's tail shook Jason like a rag doll. My friend's face had turned red.

"Bax!" Jason yelled, flailing his arms. He couldn't see anything in the smoky darkness without his glasses.

"Put him down!"

Ifrit stood tall, puffing his chest out. "You will be a son to Ben. Because I will continue to kill until you return to him as he wishes. I will destroy everyone in your life if necessary. And I will savor every torment I inflict upon you, Baxter Allen. You are the bane of my existence."

I shivered. He spoke the truth. I was the obstacle between Ifrit manipulating this world and his imprisonment in the vortex. "You can't threaten someone into having a relationship. You don't understand that and you never have. It doesn't work that way."

Ifrit pointed a sharp finger at me. "It will for you."

High above us, against the ceiling, a glimmer through the cloudy haze caught my attention. A long ago burnt-out fluorescent light swayed in the room's swelling heat. Behind Ifrit, the opposite wall flickered with flames, devouring the old wood. The place was going up fast.

"This will be the last time I extend the offer." Ifrit's pointed tongue lashed out. "You will return to your father as a loyal son. If you refuse, I will terrorize you and yours for the rest of your days."

I didn't need to answer. From the depths of the darkness high above, the long light fixture broke loose within the rolling clouds of smoke against the ceiling. It plummeted downward with the speed of a torpedo, whistling through the air. Janni rode the tubular light like a surfboard, clutching its chain as he attempted to maneuver and direct it as best he could.

As Ifrit raised his head to see what I stared at, Janni jumped off, letting the light crash into Ifrit's face. The djinn shrieked and stumbled backward, dropping my friend to the ground.

Jason scrambled to his feet, tugged his sweatshirt back down, and snagged his glasses off the floor. "About time!"

"You okay?"

He nodded, his red checks already fading back to their normal brown.

Ifrit roared at the ceiling, spewing a fountain of volcanic fire above us as he flexed every muscle in his arms and across his chest. The black hair on his shoulders separated and spiked.

From somewhere in the smoky shadows, Ashley materialized. With her curly hair sticking out everywhere, her eyes bloodshot from the smoke, and holding a long two-by-four with nails jutting out of one end, she'd become a crazed warrior.

After a determined nod and confident wink at me, she swung her weapon as hard as possible, slamming the nailed end of her weapon into Ifrit's thigh.

He stumbled back, grasping his leg and attempting to stop the black ooze seeping from his wound.

Without fear, Ashley wound up and swung again. This time, she landed the nails of her makeshift mace into Ifrit's gut.

He shrieked, and before Ashley could yank her weapon back, Ifrit ripped it from her hands. He threw it across the warehouse, where it slammed into a burning shelf and fell to the floor.

His pupilless eyes glowed bright, searching for his attacker, who watched him, frozen, stunned at the damage she'd inflicted.

In what had become the day's mantra, I yelled, "Run!"

I bolted down a dark aisle, waving for Jason and Ashley. I skidded behind a pile of barrels and crouched low. The smoke had me all turned around. Where were the damn stairs?

I coughed. "You guys still with me?"

"Holy shit, girl!" Jason stretched the neck of his sweatshirt over his mouth to use as a filter.

"Didn't know you had it in you, Ashley," I said.

Although out of breath and eyes still wide, Ashley beamed with pride. "You can thank me later. We still aren't free. I think the stairs are over there." She pointed.

"Let's go." I stood up and spun around, but stopped in my tracks. The smoke must have been messing with my vision. "What the hell?"

Ben crouched in front of us, hiding from Ifrit. "Do we have a plan?"

Chapter 25

Do we *have a plan?*

The balls on him to ask *me*. Like he'd been part of our crew from the beginning. Like he wasn't the reason we were in a crumbling fire hazard.

"Did you leave Mom upstairs?"

Ben coughed on smoke and ran a hand through his hair, reminding me of myself when I needed to think. "Bax, I never intended any of this to happen. You need to believe me. What can I do?"

He seemed sincere, truly sincere. A demon trying to destroy your life can change your perspective. "We need to get Mom—and the rest of us—out of here."

Behind me, Jason and Ashley watched, hesitant to interrupt but growing nervous with every passing second.

Ashley poked her head over the top of the barrel. "I don't see him."

"Baxter, I'm not perfect. Sure, I acted out of anger, but I'm not some kind of thug who'd come into town and hurt—"

"Bullshit. I told you, I saw the gun in your bag and how you glared at the picture of Mom and me in your wallet. That's thug behavior, if you ask me."

The floor rumbled as fire incinerated a rotting shelf, and it collapsed onto a pile of radiating embers.

"Bax!" The nearing blaze flickered on Jason's

glasses, hiding his eyes. "We have to get out of here! This whole place is falling apart."

"I didn't know how Sara would react to seeing me." Ben rubbed his eyes.

"And you thought a gun would reassure her?"

Ashley tapped me between my shoulder blades with the back of her hand. "Bax, now!"

Ben's eyes glistened in the flickering shadows. "I don't know what else to say. Ifrit did these things on his own, not under my orders." Ben's voice quivered. "I have so many regrets, man. I just need you to hear that in case I don't make it out of here."

I hated him for what he'd done. For how he treated Mom and forced her to leave our home and family behind. But I couldn't judge him for Ifrit's torture spree. I was no better. Because of Ifrit, I'd caused the death of a classmate and an assault on Ashley's dad. Not to mention forcing a girl to date me. Ben may have been what motivated me to unearth the djinn, but this mess wasn't his fault. It was mine. If I hadn't summoned Ifrit the first time, Ben would still be clueless in Chicago.

Another crash of a disintegrating shelf echoed nearby. The collapse blew a cloud of gray smoke over the wall of barrels we hid behind.

"Where the freakin' hell did Ifrit go?" Ashley hollered over the crackling of flames.

At the sound of his name, I instinctively turned to Ashley, but when I looked back, Ben had transformed into the monster we'd been hiding from.

Ifrit sat back on his haunches, crouched where Ben had been. His muzzle curled into a smile a few feet before me, exposing his sharklike teeth. The smoke around his head glowed purple from his emblazoned eyes.

"Poor Baxter Allen and his daddy issues." Ifrit rose to full height, extended his powerful arms, and emitted a roar that silenced the sound of fire crackling around us as if it bowed to his will.

We leaped to our feet.

"Bax!" Ashley screamed as she stumbled backward.

Before I could escape his reach, Ifrit's clawed hand lashed out and grabbed me by my throat. He lifted me off the floor, his grip cutting off all the oxygen to my lungs. I pounded his wrist with both hands, but his rock-hard forearm didn't budge. He crushed my throat as the veins on his arm popped under the coal-black hair.

Mouth agape, I tried to suck in the smoky air but couldn't. I pointed to the stairs, signaling to Jason and Ashley.

Please understand what I'm saying!

They understood but refused to listen. "We're not leaving you," Jason shouted. He searched the area for a weapon.

Ashley found another board, one without nails on the end. She swung, connecting with Ifrit's injured leg, but the djinn didn't flinch. His grip on me didn't waver.

My lungs seared in my chest. My vision narrowed. I dug my fingers between his hand and my throat but couldn't pry him off.

"We are done, Baxter Allen." Ifrit breathed his hot words into my face, forcing my eyes to shut.

My vision blurred at the edges. My muscles stiffened. I needed oxygen. I needed to breathe.

My hands tremored with the faint vibrations of Ashley, Jason, or both pounding on Ifrit's legs with makeshift weapons. The smoke stirred as Ifrit's tail swung, knocking my friends away.

I kicked him in the abdomen with the same impact as kicking a tank. Ifrit scooped a nearby shelf with his free hand, dumping boxes on my friends who relentlessly pummeled him.

The orange fuzz blackened in my peripheral vision, creeping across my eyesight. After everything I'd survived against Ifrit, I'd die in this stupid factory. Ifrit would kill me. He'd won.

My arms turned to jelly, and my muscles liquified, falling to my sides like noodles. The spreading blackness in my eyesight became a thick curtain shrouding my vision.

My brain.

Just.

Stopped.

Seconds passed. Hours? Years?

Then I gasped.

His grip had loosened.

I sucked dirty, smoky air deep into my lungs. My brain rebooted. My vision flickered back to life. I coughed but inhaled again. The charred oxygen never tasted sweeter.

In front of me, Ifrit looked upward. The tendons in his thick neck bulged.

I dropped as he let go of me. Heated air breezed past me as I saw his chest, then his stomach.

My feet weren't ready to hit the ground when they did. My legs buckled, cushioning my impact. I landed on a pile of wooden crates, their jagged corners and edges poked into my back. Something rammed into the back of my head, but I fought to stay conscious.

For a minute, my body had become immobile. The

rugged edges of the rubble beneath me sent a jolt of fear through my body. I definitely broke my back.

Sounds started filling my ears again, registering in my brain, rising in volume. Oxygen recharged my blood, which rushed to my extremities, carrying the feeling and control back to my flimsy limbs.

Ashley screamed.

Ifrit roared.

Jason's breath brushed my ear. "Hey, dude. You there?"

I turned to him and accepted his hand as he helped me sit up. The smoke no longer tinged the air. It hung around us in thick clouds, limiting my vision to less than a few feet ahead.

"You back with us?"

"I think." Thankfully, my stiff back still worked, and my senses returned. Warmth engulfed me and sweat beaded my forehead from our prison inferno.

Jason pointed, directing my focus.

Ifrit swatted and swung at the air, the dense smoke leaving tracers following his arms. He shook his head like a dog trying to shake loose a leash. My eyes watered, and I wiped them to clear my vision. What was he doing?

Janni rode Ifrit like a rodeo bull, high on his head, seated between his curled horns.

Ifrit's muscled upper body lacked the flexibility to reach between his horns, and with every swat, Janni would swing wide on one of his horns, then back to Ifrit's head. Once safely reseated, he punched Ifrit in the eye with his little fist. He might not be making much physical impact, but the crazed frustration he caused Ifrit was worth it. And while I couldn't be sure, it looked like Janni was smiling.

"BAXTER ALLEN IS SAFE!" Janni's shrill voice sliced through the chaos—and it never sounded better.

"WOO-HOO!" Janni sang, bouncing on and off Ifrit's head. A fearless spirit one-tenth the size of his opponent replaced the timid, tiny djinn I knew. I'd never seen his eyes so bright with glee.

"GO FREE BAXTER ALLEN'S MOM!"

I wiped the blood trickling from my nose with one hand, the other held Jason's arm as we cleared the pile I'd landed on, giving my legs a few more seconds to wake up.

"Let's go." I released Jason's arm and jogged past Ifrit, moving slower than I wanted but afraid I'd trip. "Wait. Where's Ashley?"

Jason squinted under his glasses. "Uh-oh."

Ashley called from somewhere in the gray smoke, "Over here!"

We followed her voice, hopping over debris. Sweat rolled into my eyes. I pulled the neckline of my shirt up and breathed through the fabric.

The smoke cleared some as we arrived at the stairs, enough for us to see Ben—the real Ben—holding Mom at gunpoint, attempting to sneak out, ready to let us die in order to save himself. I reminded myself our conversation about his remorse didn't happen—the words belonged to Ifrit.

As we approached, Ben whirled, spinning Mom with him, his back to the iron stairs leading to the first floor. One hand pointed his gun at us, and the other held Mom in the crook of his arm, secure against his chest. She smacked his forearm with both hands, but she couldn't break free.

"Baxter!" Mom hollered. "Stay back."

Ben's gaze darted around, uncertain of what to do, his eyes filled with fear, not vengeance.

"Jesus, Baxter. I never wanted any of this. None of it." The heat plastered Ben's hair to his forehead, dripping sweat into his eyes and soaking his shirt.

"Then let Mom go."

"And tell the cops a monster helped me flee the state, hurt a bunch of people, and then kidnapped my wife?" His voice cracked with genuine panic. "I'm fucked!"

Behind us, a portion of the third floor crashed onto the second, creating an explosion of sparks and a tidal wave of smoke.

"Tell them it was a misunderstanding, at least with Mom. We'll confirm your story. We just need to get out of here."

Mom's eyes remained fixed on the barrel of Ben's gun, aimed at her forehead. "I will do that. Just let us go. You're not a killer, Ben."

Ifrit roared, determined to destroy the entire building with everyone inside.

He'd somehow grabbed Janni, clutching him in one hand. Terror replaced the glee in Janni's wide purple eyes. We watched as Ifrit threw the tiny djinn. Janni's ears flapped behind him as he sailed through the air and into the flaming depths of the burning building.

"Janni!" Ashley called.

Ifrit charged us. His long hooved strides tore up the wooden floor with each pound. He stopped near us, chest and shoulders heaving, smoke and fire swirling around him.

There we stood, in a perfect triangle. Mom and Ben, Ifrit, and my crew—the djinn fighters. Flickering red and blue lights joined us, strobing from the first floor and bouncing up the stairs.

Police.

Ifrit growled. "This ends, Baxter Allen."

"Stay back!" Ben turned the gun from Mom to Ifrit. "Go away! Get back in your goddamn box."

Ben thought a timeless djinn would fear a gun. Stupid.

"Like father like son." Ifrit turned on Ben. Dried black blood streaked Ifrit's stomach and thigh where Ashley had injured him. His charcoal fur spiked with fury, ready to attack his masters—former and current.

"I said, go the fuck away!" Ben yelled.

"You are ungrateful." Ifrit's stomped his hoof on the ground taking a step toward Ben.

Mom took advantage of Ben's distraction and jabbed him in the gut with her elbow. He hunched over, allowing her enough time to peel away.

She'd just slipped under his arm as Ifrit lunged at Ben.

Ben leaped backward, but missed his footing and slipped, rolling down the iron stairs.

My breath caught in my throat, watching Ben disappear down the stairwell. He'd recover, bruised but able to escape, leaving us to deal with Ifrit, who stood between us and the stairs, our only exit. With the flashing police lights outside, maybe Ben wouldn't get far.

Next to me, Mom grabbed my hand. "I'll distract it while you kids run by. Go get help."

"No way, Mom. We know what we're doing." I dropped her hand. "I'll—"

"Wait, look!" Ashley pointed at Ifrit.

The djinn roared upward, spewing flames that

flowed into the burning ceiling. "Idiot humans!" He lowered his head and lifted his hand, watching it fade into translucence.

"What's happening?" Jason rubbed his eyes to clear his vision.

Ifrit's hands disappeared, his arms ending in cleanly severed stumps. Then, his hooved feet vanished, even though Ifrit remained at his full height, his body suspended in mid-air. We watched as his goat legs and powerful arms melted into the gray smoke swirling around him. He'd become a floating torso and head.

"You will never win, Baxter Allen. I am immortal. Wherever you go, I will be there. I am forever a part of you."

I stepped toward the disintegrating djinn. "You are a pathetic demon. Go back to hell."

Ifrit's abdomen faded to smoke. Then his chest. Then his curled horns. And finally, with one last roar, his head vanished.

Ashley, Jason, and Mom came up behind me. All of us stared at the spot Ifrit had occupied seconds earlier.

"Is he gone?" Mom grabbed my hand again.

"Why did he disappear?" Jason coughed into his sleeve.

"I wonder if—" Ashley started, carefully stepping toward the stairs. She glanced down, then spun around, covering her face. "Bax—"

I dropped Mom's hand, forcing myself forward, needing to see the cause of Ashley's reaction.

Ben had tumbled down the iron stairs and impaled himself on the long metal rod we'd jumped over when we snuck up. Its sharp tip had punctured his stomach beneath his rib cage. He lay motionless, his shirt drenched in blood, his eyes wide open with panic, staring up at me, devoid of life. Underneath him, blood flowed from his back and through the grated stairs, puddling on the first floor.

Mom gasped next to me. Either the grisly scene made her gasp, or seeing Ben dead did. I didn't know, and it didn't matter.

Jason hung back, his arm around Ashley. "Ben's death banished Ifrit."

I couldn't respond with words. The shattering sadness of meeting my dad and then witnessing his last moments created tears in my eyes. Or maybe the exhaustion of surviving Ifrit *again* caused them. Or perhaps the overwhelming relief of Mom's safety caused them. Most likely, the source of the tears was the colliding of all those emotions.

Mom yanked me toward her and squeezed. She sniffled into the top of my head, still a little taller than me, but not by much, and not for long.

"JANNI SAVED BAXTER ALLEN."

Janni?

I broke loose from Mom to greet Janni, who watched from nearby.

"You survived!" I scooped him up into my arms.

"JANNI SAVED BAXTER ALLEN!" he repeated with pride.

"Yes, you did!" I cuddled him like a puppy. Or monkey. Or furry thing. Ashley and Jason rubbed his back, causing him to emit a purr-sounding groan. "Where did all that bravery come from, little guy?"

"IFRIT HURT FRIENDS."

As I squeezed the little djinn, someone with a megaphone at the base of the stairs shouted, "Is anyone up there? This is the St. Louis Fire Department."

"I'm gonna run upstairs and get the box." Jason, always one step ahead of our situation. "We don't need to chase it down in an evidence room somewhere."

"No." I grabbed his sleeve. "It's too dangerous. Let it go. We'll deal with it if they somehow uncover it from this mess."

"And risk someone in forensics rubbing the jewel?" Jason coughed.

"IT WILL GET THE ARTIFACT. TOO DANGEROUS FOR FRIENDS."

"Wait, Janni." I wiped the sweat from my forehead. "Go get the box and hide it in my bedroom closet. Then you can go."

"IT IS HERE TO SERVE."

I rubbed his head. "You always are. And thank you. Again."

Janni jumped.

"I'm sorry for everything, Mom." I hugged her tight. The place crumbled around us, but those words couldn't wait.

"I'm glad we're finally safe." She kissed my head. "Now, let's get out of here before we can't. And then, you'll tell me everything about these ghosts. Everything."

"Djinn, Mom, get it right. And yeah, that's the least I can do."

We started down the stairs, steering clear of Ben's body. None of us could look at him. On the first floor, I relaxed after seeing the safety of the fire truck and police car lights flooding in through the open exit of the Armory Heights building.

As firefighters draped heavy blankets over our

shoulders, Ashley giggled. "Um, can I say, that was quite the movie moment. Bax was all, 'You go back to hell!' " She shook her fist in the air, mocking me.

"Shut up." I laughed at myself.

"What, too soon to joke?"

Chapter 26

Mom stared at me. She didn't blink the entire time I talked. During my story, we devoured a basket of chips and salsa, and Mom downed two margaritas. We hadn't even taken a pause long enough to order anything substantial. Not sure we could anymore. Dos Cantinas was about to close and we were the last customers.

The restaurant hosted our celebration dinners on every occasion since we'd moved into the neighborhood. The servers knew us and the cooks knew what we ordered, even though we'd never met them. The familiar smell of beans and tortillas conjured up the exact comfort Mom and I needed after the insanity of the evening.

We told the police the truth—most of it. All the parts about Ben: how we'd been hiding from him, how he showed up, kidnapped Mom, and then how we attempted to rescue her. We omitted the supernatural parts, obviously. I worried Mom wouldn't agree with our plan, but she did. She couldn't explain things to the cops she didn't understand.

After the endless questioning, I assumed Mom would want to crash at home. However, as soon as the police cruiser dropped us off and she saw the lights still on inside Dos Cantinas, she insisted I tell her the absolute truth then and there.

And I did. Everything. I told her about the ring, the box, Janni, and Ifrit. I told her about the horrible damage

Ifrit caused because of thoughts deep inside my head and how he did the same thing to Ben. She didn't ask many questions, seeing the difficulty with which I described the atrocities Ifrit inflicted on those in my life. She absorbed it all with restrained facial reactions, not wanting to discourage me from talking.

"So that's it." A strange relief washed over me, more potent than banishing Ifrit for the second time. Telling Mom felt cathartic, almost therapeutic.

Mom sipped the remaining margarita from her glass through the thin straw. "I'm speechless, Baxter. I want to say you're making it up, but I saw Janni and Afrat."

"Ifrit."

She twisted her hair into a ponytail. I could see her mind spinning and couldn't blame her. I'd dumped a hell of a lot on her.

"While I understand what you've been dealing with, I'm not happy about all the secrets you've been keeping from me—all the lies. And yes, I had my secrets about Ben, but I'm the parent."

I traced shapes in the condensation on the outside of my water glass. "I didn't know what to do."

She rubbed her eyes, still red from the smoke. "Helping you is part of my job, hon. To work with you to figure things out."

"You'd know how to banish an immortal djinn?"

She didn't smile back. "We need to get rid of the box before something else happens."

"I'll bury it tomorrow."

"Is it okay to keep it in your room overnight?"

"As long as no one rubs the jewel."

An older Latin woman in a green half-apron approached our table. She held a small notepad with her pen out and ready. "*Hola*. We're closing the kitchen soon. Get you both the a la carte tacos?"

"Please." Mom slid her margarita glass to the side. "You can put them in to-go bags. I'm sure you all want to head home."

The waitress returned Mom's smile. "To go it is. And no worries. Take your time."

Mom tapped the table with her fingertips, waiting for the waitress to leave before she asked her next question. "Do the Franklins or Bryants know? About the," she dropped her voice, "genies?"

"No. Just Jason, Ashley, Scarlet, and me. And now you. Warren, at the comic book store, kinda does."

"Kinda?" She popped a chip into her mouth. "We'll come back to him. But Baxter, your friends' parents deserve to know everything. Their kids' lives were in danger."

"No way. They can't. Mom, promise me. It wouldn't do any good. You saw him. If you hadn't seen Ifrit, you wouldn't have believed my story. Besides, you said it yourself, their lives *were* in danger. They're not anymore."

"Baxter—"

"Mom, please. I told you what Ifrit did, including Mr. Bryant's accident. It's hard enough for me to live with myself, but if he knew I caused it, I'd never be able to look him in the face again. And what would he think of me, even if he believed my story?"

"But it wasn't your fault."

"It was. Not directly or intentionally, but it was. Telling Ifrit's victims won't change anything for them, but it will for me. I want to…no, I need to put this behind me. Maybe that's selfish, but it's how I feel." I tapped my fork on the table. I understood her point, but everyone involved needed to leave Ifrit's damage in their past.

She grunted, mulling over my request. "I guess you're right. I'm not sure what telling them accomplishes. As long as it's over. But if the djinn gets out again, I'm telling them their children are in danger."

"Deal."

Mom rested her hand on mine. "I'm sure I'll think of other questions. I'm still processing all of it. But I'm glad everyone is safe again."

"Except for Ben."

She sighed, staring at her drink. "He didn't deserve to die."

I wanted to disagree with her but knew she'd never disparage him to me, even after all he'd done. Sure, Ifrit magnified his intent, and maybe Ben wouldn't have acted on his vengeful thoughts, but we'd never know.

"There's one other thing," I mumbled.

She jerked her hand away from mine. "Jesus, Baxter, I've heard enough things."

"It's not bad. But…well…part of my connection to Ifrit meant I could sometimes see from Ifrit's point of view, or…or his victim's point of view."

Her eyebrows pinched together. "Okay."

"I saw what happened when Max came over to apologize."

"Max. I need to call him." Mom nodded as if agreeing with herself. "He broke it off because he thought Ben would hurt you or me. I need to tell him Ben's dead. And oh my gosh, you said Ifrit attacked him, but he's okay?"

"Yeah. Beat up, but okay enough to break up with

you."

Mom rubbed her eyes. "I won't say anything about genies, obviously. I'll let him think Ben attacked him. They can't arrest Ben and question him, so that story is airtight. Do you think—?"

"Hold up. I mean, yes. Yes, to all of it. Call him. Blame Ben. But that's not where I was going. Right before Max arrived at our apartment, I heard your thoughts about how much you miss teaching."

"Oh." I'd thrown her another curveball in an hour of bombarding her with them. "That's disturbing, Baxter."

My face grew warm. "Yeah."

"Well, I miss it."

"So why can't you teach again?"

"If Ben…" She paused, then gasped, still assembling the pieces of our new life without her ex-husband. "Oh, Baxter."

"You couldn't teach because of Ben. But now…"

Mom bit her lower lip. Maybe this nightmare would have at least one positive outcome after all.

"Do you think I could? I mean, it's been years since I've taught. I could start as a substitute or something and build up to it. My resume is a decade out of date."

Mom had lived for so long under Ben's shadow, but Ifrit destroyed that shadow. The past day had been a whirlwind of supernatural danger, but what happened next, including the sprouting realization we were no longer hiding, formed a smile on her face brighter than any I'd ever seen. A thirteen-year-old burden dissolved off her shoulders.

"It's already November. I won't be able to start until next fall. *If* I even get a job. It's been so long."

"What grade would you teach?" I fed Mom's

excitement, loving her newfound glow.

"Hello, you two." Mr. Bryant stood next to our table, one foot in a cast but covered in a black boot so he could walk. A sling replaced one of his arm casts, keeping it tight against his midsection, and fading bruises poked out from underneath his nose bandage.

Ashley stood at his side, looking ready to catch him if he fell.

"You're up and moving! I'm so happy for you, Tom."

"Doc says I shouldn't overdo it, but I had to get out of my bedroom. Super glad to get an arm back." He shrugged his slung arm but then winced. "Almost back."

"We ordered, but you're welcome to pull up some chairs."

"No thank you, Sara. We're picking up a very late dinner after this long night."

Ashley examined Mom's every reaction. We'd texted after Armory Heights. I told Jason and her I intended to tell Mom everything. They agreed. They also agreed telling their parents anything beyond Ben's return would cause unnecessary complications.

Ashley probably didn't expect me to do it so soon. I gave her a subtle nod.

She winked.

"I'm glad you're safe again, Sara. How scary." Mr. Bryant shook his head. "Both of you. I'm sorry that happened."

"Me too, Tom. And I am so sorry my problems impacted Ashley. If anything had happened to these kids because of me—"

"Because of Ben," Mr. Bryant interrupted. "Besides, I already gave Ashley an earful about playing hero when she literally lives with a police officer." He scowled at her, and she pretended not to notice. "But at least Jason had enough sense to call Officer Malik."

"Living with a dad who's a police officer is awesome." Ashley rolled her eyes. "I got to re-answer all the freakin' questions from the scene of the crime when I got home. I told him he should read the report."

Poor Ashley.

The only loose end in our story we couldn't explain to the cops at Armory Heights was how the building started burning. While they didn't seem too concerned with it, it worried me it might come back to haunt us. "What do they think caused the fire?"

Before Mr. Bryant could answer, the waitress set a paper bag on our table. "Order for Tom."

"Thank you." Mr. Bryant smiled at the waitress, then cleared his throat. "The firefighters said those old buildings are piles of kindling. Most likely an ember from a cigarette someone tossed smoldered for a while. Not sure they'll invest too many man-hours investigating a condemned building."

And that wrapped our story up nice and tidy.

A different waitress delivered our order of tacos in a white paper bag with Dos Cantinas written across the front. Mom handed the lady her credit card.

Ashley grabbed their bag off our table. "Let's get out of here. I'm starving. And I'm kinda done rehashing our adventure over and over."

"I wouldn't call it an adventure." Mr. Bryant grunted. "Well, we should start back. I'm still slow-moving. We'll be home before morning if we head there now."

"That's what happens when you get old." Ashley

opened the bag and inhaled. "Smells incredible."

"You wait until I'm all healed. We're gonna sign up for a marathon."

"Not sure what's scarier, me running a marathon or you?"

"Good to see you guys." Mom waved as Ashley and her dad turned to leave. "Glad you're okay, Ashley."

"You too, Ms. Allen."

With Mr. Bryant's back to our table, Mom winked at Ashley, who grinned.

****

I leaped down the stairs, jumping over the broken one. Outside, the sun blazed even though winter winds swirled down my street, obliterating the last remnants of fall. Water pooling in the gutter glistened with an icy crust, and snow dusted the awning of Sally's Second Hand across the street. Thanksgiving would soon arrive, then Christmas, and then a brand-new year.

The crisp and bright Saturday morning renewed my hope from last night. No more djinn. No more hiding from Ben. Mom excited for a new career.

Perfect day to hear the latest story from Warren, assuming his treatments weren't still kicking his ass. He was a tough old guy. I could only imagine the stories he'd have about his hospital visits.

Maybe he had an idea about burying the box. If it had to be the cellar, we'd do it tonight. No more waiting around. I'd learned my lesson last time. As soon as Jason and Ashley could come over, we'd use Janni, break into the cellar, and bury Ifrit's artifact like we'd planned to do on Halloween.

A morning jogger bumped into me. "Sorry," he called over his shoulder, his hot breath puffed like a train engine.

I stopped under Warren's Cosmos' green-and-white awning. Someone had flipped the CLOSED sign. I checked the time on my phone. Even the white decals on the door with the store hours confirmed it should be open.

I pressed my nose against the freezing glass, shielding my eyes to see in, but the sun contrasted too brightly with the dark inside of Warren's Cosmos. A pit formed in my stomach. Warren never closed unexpectedly. Where was Scott?

I'd heard cancer treatments were grueling. He needed his rest. If only I had an email address for him or something. Some way to check in on him and see how he was doing. Warren's Cosmos didn't even maintain a website. If anyone searched online, they'd see the address and phone number in plain text. Not even a picture of the storefront.

As I turned to leave, the silver bell dinged as the door opened.

Thank God!

It must've been an accidental sign flip. I spun around.

"Baxter? Come on in." Scott waved me inside. He held the door open for me, his face paler than normal. Probably just cold. Something deep in my brain fired up, ordering me to turn back around and tell Scott I'd just remembered an appointment I had to get to.

You're being weird, Bax.

The inside of Warren's Cosmos appeared like it did every other day. Shelves packed with comic books, walls covered with paper covers or framed collector's issues, and even the cardboard cutout of Captain Toxic still stood seven feet tall in the corner saluting me. I inhaled the comforting and familiar mustiness. Everything was fine. I'd let momentary irrational paranoia run through me for no reason at all.

Scott's slight frame seemed ready to buckle under his thick brown sweater. He pushed his thin silver glasses higher on the bridge of his nose with one hand and scratched his head with his other. "Bax, I'm sorry, but my dad...my dad..." Tears glistened in his eyes under the fluorescent lighting.

Scott never finished his sentence. He didn't need to. I didn't want him to.

My legs thickened to stone while simultaneously turning to jelly. On a morning filled with hope of a fresh start and a new beginning, this couldn't happen. My life had started returning to normal. And normality included visiting Warren and hearing his stories. It involved asking him how he lost his fingers, whether or not I knew the actual cause.

I didn't even say goodbye. I should have said goodbye.

They were treating him, which meant he'd be back, good as new. Or as good as Warren got with his weathered skin and ravaged voice, perched on his tiny stool as he flashed me his missing fingers.

Scott wiped his nose with his sweater sleeve. He squared his shoulders. "We thought maybe he'd beat it this time, but he didn't."

My heart pounded in my ears, creating a deafening ring. How could he not tell me he'd spent his life fighting a horrible disease until only a few days ago? All the way until the end, he hid it under the guise of one of his stupid bullshit stories. Why wouldn't he say, *I'm running out of time?* He owed me that. I wasn't a rando off the street. We'd been friends for years. And Scott should have told me how bad it'd gotten. When he told me Warren started treatment, he could have recommended I visit him. He should have been direct. What was up with this family not being direct? I could handle it. I'd have visited him more often. I'd have gone to the hospital or wherever you go for cancer treatment.

I drug my feet to the empty counter with Warren's tiny stool behind it. On top of the cracked countertop sat the old-fashioned register he used to pound with his remaining fingers. Next to that was the small credit card reader he hated because it never worked. The rows and rows of comic books surrounded me, none of which could hide from Warren. You'd provide the hero's name, and he'd tell you the issue's exact location.

I leaned on the counter to steady myself. He was gone.

Scott watched me, shifting his weight from foot to foot.

Warren or Scott couldn't have told me anything more than what they did. They clung to the hope Warren would beat it. He'd been fighting cancer his entire life. It wasn't different this time. He'd beaten it for years. Kept it at bay. I couldn't expect them to admit defeat before he'd lost. We all wanted the same thing. We wanted Warren to win.

But in the end, he'd lost.

"I'm so sorry." I didn't know at first if the words came out of my mouth, but Scott nodded as he wiped his eyes under his glasses.

He and I had only recently met, so a hug seemed weird. I should shake his hand, but that felt too formal.

I opted to shove my hands deep into my jeans pockets.

Scott grieved for a dad he loved, while I grieved the loss of a dad I wanted to love. I'd spent years wondering about Ben and analyzing the discovered comic book out of desperation for a clue to his identity. When I finally met him, he shattered my fantasy. He destroyed the hope my father waited for me somewhere in the world, counting the days until he'd reunite with Mom and me. That father never existed.

Scott lost his dad. I lost Ben.

I wiped the tears from my eyes with my coat sleeve. Warren had been a fixture in my life for as long as I could remember. Warren's Cosmos served as my escape from bullies, my stability when VS made school impossible, and before everything djinn-related, the place where I'd imagined my estranged dad would return.

Scott rested his hand on my shoulder. "He always talked"—he swallowed—"so fondly about you and your visits. About the stories you swapped."

"He did most of the storytelling." I couldn't look Scott in the eye.

"He said you were writing a comic book about djinn."

My eyes flooded. He talked about me with his son. And not about how they should steal Ifrit's crusty box. He'd told him about the stupid djinn story I invented to get his advice. I sniffed back my runny nose, trying to pull myself together.

Scott handed me a small prayer card with ornate golden script: *In Loving Memory of Warren Bevin.*

I couldn't read any more of it, so shoved it into my pocket.

Scott took off his glasses and rubbed his eyes. "The service is on Tuesday. Details are on the card. He'd appreciated it if you could make it."

"Sure. I mean, yeah. I'll be there. Of course."

Scott put his glasses back on. "One other thing." He reached behind the counter and handed me a plain white envelope with my name scrawled across the front. "Before he…he asked me to contact you. He wanted me to give you this letter."

Warren wrote me a letter?

"I didn't read it, but he told me what it says."

"What does it say?" I couldn't read something he wrote. I needed Scott to tell me.

He dabbed his eyes with a tissue. "Read it. Those were his wishes. You'll understand why he told me about it after you do."

My phone vibrated in my pocket. Jason and Ashley were eager to discuss our plan to bury the box.

I turned the envelope over in my hands. No idea what he could have written to me.

"I'm so sorry." I had nothing more original to say.

Scott patted my shoulder. "See you Tuesday."

"So is Warren's Cosmos"—the name stung my lips—"closed for good?"

After saying it, I realized how selfish and self-serving I sounded to a guy whose dad just died, but it didn't seem to faze Scott. He shrugged as he looked around the store. "I'm not sure. I'm a dental hygienist, so I'd need to quit to keep this place open." He laughed. "And knowing Captain Toxic originated from the Pits of Valsar is about the extent of my comic book expertise. Too bad you aren't a few years older; I'd sell you the Cosmos."

His joke lightened the mood some. "Yeah, too bad."

I took in Warren's Cosmos, memorizing every comic book, every poster, and every stack of boxes piled in the corner. One last inhale filled my lungs with the musty scent, savoring the comfort that resonated at my core. I couldn't imagine the place closing.

"Take care of yourself, Baxter. Take your time here before you leave." Scott nodded and entered the back storage room, leaving me alone in Warren's Cosmos.

I guess he wanted to give me privacy to say goodbye in case he closed the store—which I appreciated—but as soon as the storage room door clicked shut, I left. I couldn't be in Warren's Cosmos without its owner. That wasn't the memory I wanted to keep with me.

Chapter 27

"All right, class, settle in." Mrs. Macklind rose from her desk as the bell rang and strolled her trademark stroll to the front of the room. She tapped the dry-erase marker on her palm. "We are in the homestretch of our presentations. Baxter, why don't you get us started?"

Gerald grumbled from the back, loud enough for everyone to hear. "What? He missed his due date. Can we all redo it if we don't prepare?"

Mrs. Macklind lifted a judging eyebrow as she pointed to the back of the classroom. "Mr. Grimes, if you would care to present again for half credit, I would be open to a discussion."

"It might be better than your grade the first time!" Brad snorted as the class laughed.

Gerald leaned across the aisle and punched Brad in the shoulder.

"Baxter"—Mrs. Macklind made an ushering swish with her hand like a game show host welcoming a contestant to the stage—"if you will."

I breathed slow and steady, following Mrs. Bronson's recommendation. She'd heard what happened last week and talked with Mrs. Macklind on my behalf without telling me. First thing Monday, Macklind told me I could redo the assignment on Tuesday. Thankfully, with no more djinn problems, I could focus. I spent time with Mrs. Bronson on Monday afternoon, discussing tips to reorient my brain, and then practiced with Mom. The presentation only had to be a few minutes with no required visual aids. If there ever existed a public speaking event I could nail, I'd found it.

Jason whispered from behind me, "You got this, bro."

I'd gone two years in high school unable to speak in front of people without a vasovagal syncope episode, but since I'd beaten it in the vortex, I had no more reason to worry about it. Jason texted me solid advice the night before that I reread repeatedly on the way to school:

—Dude, count the times you almost died battling djinn over the past month. And you're worried about speaking to stupid sophomores who won't even be paying attention????—

I pushed myself from my desk. Time to do my thing. My legs operated with little effort—a positive sign. I paced my breathing as I walked up the aisle, keeping it steady. One step at a time. One sneaker, then the other. Inhale, exhale.

My heart rate elevated, pumping faster with anxious anticipation. I fixed my attention on Macklind's desk—a focal point of contact.

I got this.

I banished an evil djinn. Twice. I beat VS in a timeless void where djinn hibernated. A place no human had ever seen. I'd confronted my estranged, abusive dad in an abandoned factory as it burnt to the ground. Why worry about talking to a group of kids who couldn't care less about which theme resonated with me from *The Scarlet Letter*? Half of them hadn't even read it.

Pausing at Mrs. Macklind's desk, I inhaled, then turned around.

Here we go.

Forty-five sets of eyes stared. Well, maybe twenty pairs or less. The rest focused on the papers in front of them, their hidden phones, their fingernails, or the light snow falling outside. They weren't watching me. They knew they had to do it, too and offered me polite quiet, expecting the same in return. I couldn't blame them. If Macklind had asked me to describe Lisa Renick's presentation last week, I couldn't have named her theme.

My heart rate slowed. I steadied the hand clutching my notecards.

I glanced at my scribbled notes but didn't need them. It turned out my presentation applied more to my life than any other homework assignment. How Hester Prynne and her lover Dimmesdale dealt with the fallout from their extramarital affair reflected my life, making the prep for the assignment easy after all that dramatic buildup.

I cleared my throat and began. "For my *Scarlet Letter* presentation, the theme of guilt resonated with me. It's the most obvious theme in the novel. I mean, the entire story is about an affair and how the two people dealt with it. How Hester, the main character, and Dimmesdale managed their guilt."

After talking with Mom at Dos Cantinas, after being honest, my words flowed out of my brain and over my lips.

"Hester was married. She cheated on her husband. And when the town found out she had an affair, she didn't deny it. She didn't lie or make excuses. Instead, she owned it. She knew she messed up and took responsibility for her actions, stripping the town of its power to shame her. She was like, 'Yeah, I did something wrong. I will make amends and then I'll try to be a better person because I've learned from it.'"

I'd made mistakes.

I'd hurt people.

I'd unleashed an evil on those in my life.

I didn't do it with intent, but I did it. And I corrected it. I almost died trying to make it right.

"Dimmesdale, on the other hand, did the same thing as Hester since it takes two people for an affair, but his fear the town would learn what he did became a burden he couldn't bear. He buried it deep, denying his love for Hester and living in constant terror that someday one of the townspeople would discover his secret. As a result, the guilt rotted him from the inside out. It turned him into a corpse of a miserable man, killing him in Hester's arms."

The nightmares haunting my nights since our first Ifrit battle weren't the result of lingering trauma or the unbreakable connection Ifrit had claimed. Guilt fueled those nightmares. Guilt caused my mind to relive those horrible moments because I couldn't admit my mistake, own it, and make it right. I swirled on how I didn't intend what happened. It was indirect damage from thoughts in the deep recesses of my mind that I couldn't control; therefore, I wasn't *really* at fault.

I was.

The nightmares were my mind pointing out I'd caused terrible things to happen, and I needed to own and learn from them to be a better person. I couldn't change the past, but I could change the future.

In the days since telling Mom everything, not a single nightmare plagued my sleep.

"Guilt is how we know we've done something

wrong. It's a natural, primal feeling. What we do with that guilt makes us human. If we don't take responsibility for our actions, good or bad, and learn to make better choices, we'll end up like Dimmesdale, consumed by our mistakes and unable to become better people. Better humans."

My words seemed like those of a wise teenager beyond his years, but the class paid minimal attention to me. Mrs. Macklind, however, smiled with pride at my accomplishment and nodded.

I'd finished my first presentation in front of my classmates.

And I'd survived.

"That's it."

My classmates gave the obligatory polite applause, most of whom didn't even know I'd finished talking but heard others clapping.

Suck it, VS.

Suck it, guilt.

After all the drama and anxiety leading up to my presentation, I didn't care about my grade. I'd done the best presentation I could.

Before heading back to my desk, I mouthed a thank-you to Mrs. Bronson, who watched me from the hallway. She gave me a thumbs-up through the small square window in the door, then disappeared.

I fell back into my desk, ignoring Jim Peterson's presentation but clapping when he finished.

"Nice work," Jason whispered as the class shuffled in their seats while Mrs. Macklind returned to the front of the classroom. "Maybe you'll sleep better now."

Jason and Scarlet were the only two in American Literature who knew how much the presentation hit home with me. "I already am."

I pulled Warren's envelope out of my backpack, staring at my name on the white envelope.

Baxter.

He probably didn't know my last name. I always paid with cash at Warren's Cosmos.

I'd read the letter a million times since Sunday, and as much as I dreaded Warren's service in a few hours, I'd go. He'd been such an essential part of my life that I had to say goodbye. Plus, I owed him a thank-you for solving all my Ifrit problems once and for all. I could have never done it without him.

I didn't pay attention to Mrs. Macklind's talk about characterization, and when the bell rang, everyone sprang from their seats.

"Baxter?" Mrs. Macklind summoned me to her desk before I could slip out of the classroom.

She sat in her chair, back straight. The woman never slouched. Before she could say anything, I jumped in. "Thanks for the redo."

She folded her hands on her desk, her bright lemon-colored nails popped against her dark skin. "Not to further exhaust the issue, but I wish you would have been honest about your reasons for not being prepared. I'm glad Mrs. Bronson filled me in. I'm a reasonable woman, Baxter."

"Embarrassed, I guess."

"Well, you did a marvelous job." Her smile really did light up rooms. Former runway models never lost it. "And a bit of advice: the more you put yourself out there, the more it isn't a shock to the mind. Our brains can grow used to being in safe spaces. We should always challenge ourselves."

I'd been out there quite enough in the past month. I'd never been more eager to be a nobody in a safe space again.

"Thanks again. Did I get an A?" I smirked.

She raised a perfect eyebrow. "As discussed, you've earned half credit. Hopefully, you'll use this as a learning opportunity, not unlike your presentation's message."

I only wished an American Literature assignment inspired my presentation.

Mrs. Macklind tapped her desk with her yellow nails. "You've done well enough this semester. You'll still earn a B for the class."

"That's fair."

"Next time, talk to me."

"You got it. But there won't be a next time." I turned to leave, slinging my backpack over my shoulder, another weight lifted.

Scarlet lingered in the hallway near the water fountain. She fiddled with the thin gold chain around her neck, moving a delicate charm back and forth. Over the past week, Scarlet and I exchanged distant waves but hadn't talked since the coffee shop. Things were back to normal—she had her friends, and I had mine.

"Nice presentation about guilt." She held her math book against her with both arms so the kids bustling by didn't knock it out of her hands.

"Thanks."

"I'm glad she let you redo it."

"Me too."

"Let's go, girl," Casey said from behind me.

Scarlet held up a finger. "I'll see you in THC in a few."

"Cool." Casey gave me an obligatory nod and

pranced off.

She had something on her mind, but I couldn't handle a serious conversation. Life was settling back to normal, which is what I wanted. I needed a break from all the crazy. We would not be romantic. Fine. But were we even friends? Either she wanted to be friends or she didn't, but we had to land somewhere. I couldn't keep up with the we-are-we-aren't.

"I saw Jason before class this morning and asked how things were going with *the thing*. He told me what happened to Ben. You good?"

Why wouldn't she have asked me? She talked to Jason even less than me. "With it being over? Yeah. I'm good with both being over—Ifrit and Ben."

She bit her lower lip. "The factory sounded scary."

"It was."

She shifted in place. "Bax?"

"Still here."

"I'm sorry I bailed on you. Maybe I could have helped or something at Armory Heights."

I couldn't figure her out. She wanted in, so I let her in. She wanted out, so I let her out. "You couldn't have done anything. Don't apologize. If anyone can avoid the Djinn-verse, they should. I'm hoping I'm done for good."

She patted my arm, her touch still released goose bumps on my skin. Damn, I might always harbor feelings for her.

"So is the box...safe?"

"It will be today. Our plan is in motion."

"Of course you have a plan." Scarlet smiled, but a soft solemnness laced her words as if she missed being part of our crew.

Jessica walked by us and tugged on Scarlet's sleeve without stopping. "You coming, Scar?"

Scarlet pointed at Jessica over her shoulder. "I should go."

"Yep."

"See you around, Bax."

"Yep," I repeated.

She trotted off with Jessica to meet Casey. After a few steps, she turned back and waved at me with a warm smile. We would never date, would never be best friends, would never even be good friends. But if she threw me a wave on occasion, flashed me her dimpled smile, and acknowledged I existed every once in a while, I could live with that. I knew where I stood.

I waved back like an awkward idiot and watched her return to her old life as if she knew as much about djinn as Casey or Jessica.

My phone vibrated. Jason.

—*I'm heading over in an hour. You coming?*—

I texted him back.

—*Meet you there.*—

****

Max's silver sedan rolled into the parking lot, barely stopping before I unclipped my seatbelt. It flung off with a ding against the door. "Sorry."

From the passenger seat, Mom pointed out the window. "There's Jason."

I opened the car door and grabbed the bag. "I'll see you guys inside. Thanks for the ride, Max."

"No problem." Max shot me a smile over his shoulder. His greenish-yellow bruises already started fading, the white of his left eye remained blood red, and a bandage still covered his nose, but he'd somehow avoided broken bones. Ifrit beat him up, but he'd heal in a week or two.

The day after our long talk at Dos Cantinas, Mom met up with Max and explained how Ben attacked him, which was pretty much true. She also shared her kidnapping ordeal and what happened to Ben at Armory Heights. She used the same story we told the police.

At first, Max resisted getting back together, ashamed he acted like a coward by complying with Ben's demands. Mom said she kissed him and told him he'd be a coward not to give them another chance.

A real movie moment, as Ashley would have said.

I was proud Mom fought for what she wanted. She deserved Max, and he was lucky to be part of her life. She had a fantastic son, after all.

Less than a dozen cars, including the staff's, spotted the parking lot of Karkin's Funeral Home. At first, a wave of sadness swept over me about how no one appreciated Warren, but he wouldn't have wanted an elaborate funeral service. He told larger-than-life stories but lived modestly. A small memorial fit his style.

Even the building itself reflected Warren's spirit. Its beige plaster walls, light brown roof, and dark evergreen shrubbery blended into the urban background. Its owners kept it well maintained, tidy, and straightforward. Flashy and exuberant appearances weren't Warren.

Jason and Ashley sat on the curb, in front of a leafless bush. They stood when they saw me. Jason dusted off his slacks, and Ashley straightened her maroon dress and white sweater with a brief shudder. She even had makeup on.

I almost cracked a joke about having never seen her in a dress or with eyeliner and lipstick, then decided to compliment her instead. But that felt weird, too. It was Ashley, after all. I ended up not saying anything about her lovely dress, pulled-back hair, or matching maroon eye shadow and hair ribbon. This wasn't a school dance.

Besides, Jason should be the one doling out compliments on her appearance.

"Thanks for coming, guys."

"Of course." Ashley patted my arm. "You ready for this?"

I lifted the plastic bag to show them. "I'm ready for this to be over."

"Can I see the letter?" she asked. "Do you mind?"

I shrugged and handed the white envelope to her, glancing at my name in Warren's handwriting.

She removed the letter and unfolded it. After a minute reading to herself, Ashley started to read Warren's goodbye letter aloud to Jason and me as we huddled in the parking lot outside his funeral service. I didn't know why, but I didn't ask her to stop. It felt like an appropriate eulogy.

"Dear Bax. I'm sorry to say goodbye in this manner, but your last memory of me should be behind my beloved counter. Your visits highlighted my days over the years. Your tireless search for the owner of *Shade Slayer, #276*, taught me unwavering hope exists in the world. You and I had a special relationship, even though I could not rattle off things about you that traditional friends might. I do not know your favorite movie, the girl you are smitten with at school, or what you aspire to be when you grow up. However, I had the unique privilege of watching a child full of dreams evolve into a young man who remained forever positive in the face of persistent challenge and disappointment."

Ashley stopped reading when I wiped my eyes with my white dress shirt sleeve. "Want me to stop? It seemed appropriate to read it here before we went inside, but we don't have to."

I shook my head. "No. Keep going."

"Never stop hoping, no matter what the world tells you. Faith in the positive is magical, and we both know magic exists. Speaking of, you'd said you needed an ending to your comic book about djinn. If there's anything I know a little something about, it's comic books, so I have an idea if you are still struggling with how your hero can rid himself of the cursed djinn artifact."

Ashley flipped to the second page.

"I remain steadfast in my belief the djinn's artifact must lay dormant in the ground, but maybe your hero needs assistance keeping it out of people's reach while it's there. Perhaps a friend who can watch over the box for as long as the evil djinn tries to escape it. This friend would treasure the opportunity to repay your hero for the years of levity and joy they shared. If you think this may help you complete your comic book, I already talked to Scott, who agreed to make the arrangements. Bring him the box at my service, and I will keep it safe for you forever. It would be my honor and my ultimate pleasure.

"Thank you, Baxter, for indulging my stories all these years. I hope you enjoyed hearing them as much as I cherished telling them. Your friend forever, Warren."

Ashley handed the letter to Jason and dove at me, wrapping her arms around my neck and burying her face against the side of my head. She vibrated as she cried against me. And she wasn't alone.

Sobs burst out of somewhere deep inside of me and

into Ashley's fluffy white sweater. She rubbed the back of my head as I cried along with her. Jason's arms snaked around us, drawing us together, creating a sloppy mess of sad, blubbering friends.

I'd reread the letter over and over since Scott gave it to me, poring over the words and hearing Warren's voice in my head every time I read it. I studied his letters, how he never closed his *O*s and never dotted his *I*s. He'd given me so much for so many years. Even in his final hours, he helped me more than he'd ever know.

Or maybe he knew.

After an embarrassing minute of me and my two best friends crying in the parking lot like weirdos, I broke our circle. Ashley handed me a tissue from a purse I'd never seen her carry. I blew my nose.

"Well, that was a thing." I forced a laugh, but Jason and Ashley only smiled, tears on their cheeks. "I'm disappointed neither of you are cracking any jokes."

Jason patted my shoulder. "None from me."

"Aw, man, you're letting me down."

"Inside time?" Ashley nodded to the building.

"Inside time." I led the way into Karkin's Funeral Home.

Jason held Ashley's hand as they followed. It didn't bother me. In a lot of ways, they were perfect for each other.

Mom plus Max, Jason plus Ashley, and then me. At one time, not too long ago, I'd fantasized it'd be Scarlet plus me, but I was past that. And in reality, it would have never happened, which was okay.

The swirling scent of fresh-cut flowers engulfed us in the funeral home, like walking into Zia's Candles. I couldn't identify any particular flower, but the mixture of everything created a calming and pleasant atmosphere. The light gray carpet stretched in several directions, each ending with an open door. The black letters on the old-school white marquee listed one name: Warren Bevin, Room E.

I straightened my back and found the door with Room E over it.

Folding chairs filled the room with small clusters of people sitting or standing against the flowered wallpaper. More people than I'd expected based on the cars in the parking lot. Scott stood next to the mahogany casket in the front of the room, hands clasped before him.

My stomach did a quick leap as I sauntered forward. A sense of impending death had cluttered the past month, but when I approached Warren's casket, a wave of surrealism hit me. I'd only attended one funeral for a work friend of Mom's, and I only went because I was too young to stay home alone. I didn't feel any loss over her deceased coworker. This was different.

I approached Scott with my head down, taking a cue from movies I'd seen.

"Hi, Bax."

A woman taller than Mrs. Macklind stood beside Scott, gripping his hand. She wore a dark brown dress that matched her hair.

"Bax, this is my wife, Cheryl."

"Hello."

I shook her hand, noting Scott's wife wore a female version of Scott's wire-rimmed glasses. Strange. Couples shouldn't wear matching glasses. But who was I to judge? I was single.

"I've heard a lot about you, Bax."

I'd never heard about her. Hell, I'd never heard

about Scott until a short while ago.

"Oh." I handed Scott the plastic grocery bag containing Ifrit's box. It crinkled way too loud in the muted funeral salon. "I can put it somewhere nearby if you'd like."

"That's it?" Scott peeked inside the bag.

"Uh-huh. Sorry to bring this up today, but Warren said—"

"He told me what he wrote in the letter. Dad didn't conform to silly societal rules. He marched to his own beat for sure. And whatever this box represents between the two of you meant a lot to him, and he wanted to keep it with him."

I willed my fingers to release the bag to Scott.

"Dad instructed me not to touch the box and not to let it out of my sight."

I couldn't tear my gaze from the bag, finding it hard to trust a virtual stranger by handing them a world-ending, enchanted artifact. The same guy we suspected had stolen the artifact. But we were so wrong.

"It's super important you don't leave it anywhere. I can't tell you how critical that is."

I shifted from one spot to the other as Cheryl scowled, biting the inside of her lip. Our transaction couldn't have been more disruptive to her husband who'd lost his father and wanted to grieve. Now he had to run errands for his dad and a customer from his comic book store.

My neck heated. "I know this isn't what you wanted to deal with, but—"

"It's okay, Bax. I got it." Scott gave his wife a nod, seeing her disapproval. "I loved my dad and all of his eccentricities." He smiled as he wiped his eyes. "Maybe

I'll tell you my own Warren stories sometime. In a way, I'd be disappointed if there wasn't something strange about today."

I'd give up all of my allowance for the next ten years to hear other *Eccentric Warren* stories. Maybe I could visit Scott if he continued operating Warren's Cosmos, but it wouldn't be the same. Warren and I had something no one could replace.

An older lady with a cane hovered behind me, waiting to pay her respects. She cleared her throat.

"I should get going. Thanks, Scott."

Scott rested a hand on my shoulder. "In two hours, after the service, I'll put the bag in his..." His lips pinched shut as Cheryl rubbed his back.

I nodded a thank-you to Scott and Cheryl, then stepped to the side, closer to Warren's casket, allowing the lady with the cane to express her condolences. I wondered how Warren knew her, but I'd never know.

Oversized bouquets and arrangements of white and yellow flowers haloed Warren's casket. His body lay under the open lid of the top half.

His broad frame filled the entire space. Makeup smoothed his leathery skin, lipstick shined his cracked lips, and his cheeks had a haunting rosiness. He didn't resemble himself anymore. I'd seen people die in my dreams or right in front of me, in Ben's case. And they looked like themselves. Warren looked off. Like a ghost replica.

Anxious to leave the shell of my former friend, I joined Mom and Max in the back of the salon. Mom drew me close. "You hanging in there?"

I leaned into her and rested my head on her shoulder. No matter how old or tall I got, Mom's shoulder always radiated a comfort like nothing else on the planet.

Next to Ashley in a back row, Jason answered his phone as he rushed out of the room.

From her seat, Ashley watched him leave, then gave me a shrug.

That didn't look good.

Instinctively, I patted my pants pocket with the ring. It'd become my safety net, the new Mr. Cuddles from my childhood, and I couldn't bury it. I'd learned my lesson, though, and confessed to Jason and Ashley I wanted to keep it. Ashley giggled with excitement, but Jason couldn't hide his disappointment, even though he said he understood. We shook hands, making a renewed pact I'd only summon Janni when at least one of them was with me.

I vowed to never break the No Djinn Rule again.

Jason returned but stayed in the salon doorway, staring at me. The crease across his forehead had returned with all its fury.

Uh-oh.

"I'll be right back." I left Mom and Max to meet Jason and Ashley.

Jason's skin had faded to the lightest shade of brown I'd ever seen. His lips parted, but no words came out.

"What's wrong? You're freaking me out."

He closed his eyes and rubbed them under his glasses. "Come outside."

We followed him as Ashley groaned.

Jason spun on us in the chilly November day, with the afternoon fading into evening. He stammered, his words pouring out of his mouth as fast as he could spit them out. "Remember how I said that Dr. Bashir, who helped us translate the incantation, called Dad asking where we found the artifact?"

Crap.

With everything else swirling, I'd forgotten. "Yeah. We told him we found it online at a museum in Mexico."

Jason rubbed his head as if inflicted by a sudden migraine. "Well, Bashir still had a copy of the incantation from when we asked him to translate it. He talked to the museum, who said they have no record of a wooden box with that inscription. No record!"

"Because we lied. Maybe he thinks they lost it. Relax."

"Relax?" Jason slapped his forehead.

Ashley held up her hands. "Wait, wait, wait. Why is everyone so worried about where we got the incantation?"

I turned to Ashley. "Some friend of Bashir's called him because he found an object at an archeological dig in Minnesota with the same type of inscription."

"Neither of you could spare thirty seconds to tell me about this before now?"

"Sorry. There's been more important stuff going down. Okay, Jason, put the panic attack on pause. So Bashir can't track Ifrit's artifact in Mexico. What does that have to do with the discovery in Minnesota?"

"I told you, Bashir still has a copy of Ifrit's incantation."

"And?"

Jason exhaled. "So he compared the two inscriptions, and the new one's inscription matches Ifrit's. Seven lines. Same structure. But more importantly, Bashir's contact said strange things have been happening at the site since they discovered it."

"Strange?" Ashley's voice quaked. "Holy freakin'

shit. Like djinn strange?"

Jason stopped talking, watching me, then Ashley, then me again.

My heart skipped. No way. It couldn't be happening. We'd banished Ifrit *again*. "Jason, are you saying that there's, there's, there's—"

"Possibly another djinn? Yeah. That's exactly what I'm saying."

Acknowledgments

Thanks to The Wild Rose Press for giving me a platform to build out my Djinn-verse and introducing me to so many talented authors. While we've only met through our books and exchanged emails, you've inspired a heartfelt sense of solidarity, comradery, and community. I've learned so much from each of you.

Thanks to Melanie Billings and Misha Verity for leading me through the editing process and refining my story into an actual novel. Diana Carlile, your amazing cover art perfectly captures the essence and mood of my book.

I share this novel with my trusted circle of avid readers and writers who've read drafts, provided feedback, and acted as sounding boards. Michael Penrod, you've been with me on this journey from the beginning and I couldn't ask for a better writing co-pilot. Robin McMinn, your eye for detail improves my writing with every draft you review. Maggie Simms, I so much appreciate your timely comments on my millions of iterations of the exact same sentence. And Stacey Przygoda, your unfiltered opinions are always appreciated, almost as much as your dance moves.

From Ash & Darkness would have been impossible without the support of my family and friends who've always indulged my make-believe worlds. You make it seem almost normal.

Most importantly, thanks to my loudest cheerleader, my idea keeper, and my partner on life's unbelievable journey, Kara. We're raising two amazing daughters who challenge me every day to be a better parent and keep me grounded in reality. The four of us can do anything.

A word about the author...

J. L. Sullivan writes young adult novels inspired by fantastical tales that percolate in abandoned buildings and desolate alleys. He began his writing journey in high school with a local newspaper before venturing into creating writing in college where he found himself lost in contemporary stories with magic simmering just underneath the surface. The first novel in his djinn series, From Brick & Darkness, won multiple awards following its spring 2022 release.

He currently lives in St. Louis with his wife, two daughters, and a dog named Princess Penelope Picklesworth, but you can also find him at www.jlsullivan.net.

Thank you for purchasing
this publication of The Wild Rose Press, Inc.

For questions or more information
contact us at
info@thewildrosepress.com.

The Wild Rose Press, Inc.
www.thewildrosepress.com

www.ingramcontent.com/pod-product-compliance
Lightning Source LLC
Chambersburg PA
CBHW051522050726
47503CB00014B/736